Martha Rogers takes us to the heart of Texas with an inspirational plot, warmhearted romance, and characters so real you almost expect them to show up on your doorstep.

—Margaret Brownley
Author of Rocky Creek Series

Autumn Song is a charming story of following God's call and reaping unexpected blessings. It's a feast of family and friends, with a feisty, unconventional heroine.

—Vickie McDonough
Author of the *Texas Boardinghouse Brides*, *Texas Trails*, and Whispers on the Prairie Series

Autumn Song

Autumn Song

MARTHA ROGERS

Most Charisma House Book Group products are available at special quantity discounts for bulk purchase for sales promotions, premiums, fund-raising, and educational needs. For details, write Charisma House Book Group, 600 Rinehart Road, Lake Mary, Florida 32746, or telephone (407) 333-0600.

Autumn Song by Martha Rogers
Published by Realms
Charisma Media/Charisma House Book Group
600 Rinehart Road
Lake Mary, Florida 32746
www.charismahouse.com

All Scripture quotations are from the King James Version of the Bible.

The characters in this book are fictitious unless they are historical figures explicitly named. Otherwise, any resemblance to actual people, whether living or dead, is coincidental.

Cover design by Gearbox Studio
Design Director: Bill Johnson

Visit the author's website at www.marthawrogers.com.

Library of Congress Cataloging-in-Publication Data:
Rogers, Martha, 1936-
Autumn song / Martha Rogers. -- 1st ed.
p. cm.
ISBN 978-1-61638-457-9 (trade paper) -- ISBN 978-1-61638-579-8 (e-book) 1. Young women--Fiction. 2. Texas--History--1846-1950--Fiction. I. Title.
PS3618.O4655A96 2011
813'.6--dc23
2011026001

First edition

11 12 13 14 15 — 987654321
Printed in the United States of America

O sing unto the Lord *a new song:*
sing unto the Lord, *all the earth.*

—Psalm 96:1

CHAPTER ONE

August 1889

"KATE MULDOON, I simply can't understand why you haven't found yourself a husband among all the eligible men in this town." Sarah picked up a book from the bedside table in Kate's room. "You're twenty-three now, and hiding yourself away to read and study all the time will not help you find the right man."

Kate grabbed the book from her sister-in-law, who had wandered into her room for a chat. As usual, the talk had turned to men. "I don't need a man," Kate declared.

"How can you say that?" Sarah gasped.

Kate shook her head. Marriage and family ranked last in the things she wanted out of life right now. Kate fought against the swelling tide of anger that had landed her in trouble on more than one occasion. Why did everyone think a woman's only role was that of a wife and mother? Sarah meant well, but then she loved living on a ranch and taking care of her husband Donavan Muldoon. Sarah believed everyone should be in love, as did her other sisters-in-law.

Once again Kate tried to explain. "Sarah, I do not intend to marry a rancher or anyone connected with cattle. I was born on a ranch, grew up on a ranch, and have lived around cattle and horses all my life so far, and I don't plan on spending the rest of it on one." Despite her love of horses and riding, the ranch held no pull or fascination for her as it once did when she was younger. Kate hugged her textbook to her chest. "Why do you think I've studied everything about Florence Nightingale and nursing and moved into town to help Aunt Mae?"

Sarah waved her hand airily, dismissing Kate's plans. "I don't know about that, but I do know Auntie Mae's boardinghouse is full of men who are not ranchers. Why, there's my cousin Seth who just moved out here to pastor our church, and then there's Doc Jensen's nephew who came to town to assist his uncle with the infirmary. They're both unattached. Sometimes I think you're just too picky."

Picky wasn't exactly the word Kate would choose, but preachers and doctors held no interest for her other than as people she could work with. She did enjoy working with Doc Jensen and his nephew, Elliot Jensen, but they were teaching her to be a nurse. Besides, Elliot wasn't really a friendly sort even if he did have an excellent bedside manner with his patients.

Kate sighed. Her sister-in-law was raised in an upper-class family in Boston, where the entire focus of her life in the last few years had been on her whirlwind romance, marriage to Donavan, then moving to Texas and having Jeremy. How could she possibly understand Kate's dreams? "I'm learning all I can about nursing and treatments so I can work more with Doctor Jensen," she explained with as much patience as she could muster. "He lets me help with some of the lighter cases and says I'm getting good at recognizing symptoms. Besides, I was thinking that the preacher would make a wonderful match for Erin."

Sarah brightened at the thought. "That might not be a bad idea now that she is of marrying age. Erin would be a good wife for Seth and a good mother for their little ones. She loves little Jeremy and has been a big help to me in taking care of him." She turned to leave. "I'll look for you Sunday at church and then afterward for dinner out at the ranch. Now I need to rescue Auntie Mae from Jeremy."

As if Aunt Mae needed rescuing. Kate waved her hand in the air to say good-bye. Dinner with the Muldoon clan meant much food and lots of laughter, but it also meant another boring afternoon listening to talk of cattle drives and auctions and horses by the men, and talk of babies and mothering by the women—none of which held any interest whatsoever for Kate.

Three older brothers—Brody, Donavan, and Ian—had ranches of their own, and that's all they talked about. The fourth older brother, Cory, had his sights set on being a lawman and had moved into town to be a deputy for Marshal Slade. Erin, the baby of the family, still lived on the ranch. She'd just turned nineteen and was by far the prettiest of the Muldoon clan.

Kate welcomed Cory's company and his presence at the boardinghouse. At least he wasn't interested in finding a bride, and he didn't pester her about finding a mate. He had his sights set on being a marshal himself one day and figured that job too dangerous to take a wife. Kate snorted. So it was OK for a man to be unmarried and pursue his dreams, but not a woman.

She laid aside her book and sauntered down to the hallway to find the mail from Aunt Mae's boarders. One of her jobs at Aunt Mae's included taking care of the mail. With a start, she realized she'd have to hurry to get there before the afternoon train arrived.

One afternoon train from the west would be picking up mail headed for the East Coast. An earlier train had dropped off its delivery, and that mail waited for her now at the post office.

Ever since the railroads had been completed, Kate had seen more men coming to town to work the ranches around the area as well as find their own land and start farming or ranching. All the land around Porterfield belonged to ranchers and farmers, but in a state as big as Texas, there seemed to be plenty of land to go around.

She donned her wide-brimmed straw hat to ward off the sun's rays and hurried out to complete her task. The Grayson General Store and Post Office beckoned her to hurry. The train would be here any minute. Her feet kicked up puffs of dust as she walked. Her shoes would need a good cleaning later, but she didn't mind as she enjoyed the four-block walk to the general store that housed the post office.

When Kate stepped into the store, the balding proprietor

grinned and tilted his head. "Is that mail from the boarders at your aunt's house?"

Kate plopped the letters on the counter along with coins for stamps. "Yes, it is."

Mr. Grayson affixed a two-penny stamp to each envelope. "How many boarders are there now?"

Kate closed her eyes to vision the count. "Counting Cory and me, there's eight. All but one of the rooms is filled, and Aunt Mae is happy as a lark. For some reason, men come to this town, like it, and stay."

Mrs. Grayson joined her husband. Her blue eyes sparkled as she gazed at Kate. "And when are you going to choose one of these men here for your own?"

Heat rose in Kate's cheeks. Everyone thought they had to ask that question. "I don't plan on marrying anytime soon. I'm studying to be a nurse, and besides, who'd help Aunt Mae take care of the house and all the meals if I wasn't around?"

The plump, rosy-cheeked Mrs. Grayson laughed. "She'd do fine without you, and I've seen how Mr. Fuller over at the bank looks at her. Wouldn't surprise me if she takes a husband one of these days."

"That's hard for me to imagine." The very idea of her aunt with another man after the love she shared with Uncle Patrick caused Kate's insides to quiver like the branches of a just-felled tree. Aunt Mae did have a few of the men, including Mr. Fuller, looking her way, but she paid them no mind. If Aunt Mae did decide to marry, Kate wouldn't interfere, but she'd have no part in bringing about that possibility.

As soon as Mr. Grayson dropped the envelopes into the

outgoing mail bag, he headed outside and toward the depot. Mrs. Grayson handed her mail from the boardinghouse box.

"Thank you." Kate slid the envelopes into her pocket and wiggled her fingers at Mrs. Grayson. "Bye, now. It's time to get things started for dinner at Aunt Mae's."

On her way back to the boardinghouse, the idea of Aunt Mae marrying danced through her head. Would Aunt Mae give up running the boardinghouse if she married? Kate knew how much her aunt loved visiting with the boarders and preparing their meals. It was impossible to think of her ever leaving the place. Certainly she had found her calling, and for once in this town it didn't focus only on being a wife and keeping house! Still, when Uncle Patrick was alive, Aunt Mae had combined being a wife and managing all those boarders without much trouble. Perhaps Kate could do the same sometime in the far-distant future.

Daniel Monroe finished his letter and sealed it in an envelope. In a few days he'd leave for the greatest adventure of his life, and he wanted Seth to know when to expect him. He reread the post from his friend telling him that the mayor was more than willing for Daniel to come to Porterfield, Texas, and practice law as they had no lawyers in the town. If lawyers were needed in Porterfield, then that's where he'd head.

Seth Winston had gone to Texas last year to pastor the church where his cousin Sarah and her family were members. The idea of going to Porterfield had grown more appealing as Seth had described it when he'd returned to Briar Ridge for his sister Rachel's wedding this past spring. True, Texas was a long way from Connecticut, but images of the untamed West and all the adventures Daniel could have outweighed the distance.

He envisioned cowboys, gunfights, saloon brawls, and train robberies. The tales he'd heard about Texas rolled through his mind in an endless stream of pictures. All the action and excitement sounded much better than the quiet town of Briar Ridge where he spent most of his time writing wills and taking care of legal documents for land sales or contracts for service.

He'd already reassigned all his clients to other lawyers in Briar Ridge, and none had truly complained, which only served to emphasize the fact that he wasn't really needed here. Daniel cleaned out his desk and put it all in a box to carry home. He planned to have the desk, a gift from his parents, shipped to Texas with him. Now all he had to do was purchase his train ticket and say good-bye to family and friends. Since his parents, especially his mother, didn't approve the move, he didn't expect a going-away party.

Father seemed on the verge of understanding Daniel's desire to travel to new frontiers and make a life for himself. Mother, on the other hand, wouldn't and couldn't accept the fact that her only son wanted to leave home and move thousands of miles away. His sister, Abigail, would hardly speak to him, but that did not keep Daniel from making arrangements to leave. After his twenty-fifth birthday last month, the desire for a change came over him, and Texas seemed the best place to do just that.

On the way home he stopped at the depot and purchased a ticket that would begin his trip. He'd have stops in

Philadelphia, St. Louis, Oklahoma City, and Dallas before the last leg of the journey to Porterfield.

The ticket agent handed Daniel his passage. "That's a mighty long trip. I take it you're heading out West to join Seth Winston. I can see the need for a preacher out west, but what's a fancy lawyer like yourself going to do there?"

Daniel laughed. His mother had asked the same question. "Not sure, but I hope to help tame some outlaws." How he'd do that he had no idea, but it sounded good when he said it.

"Well, now, just don't go and get yourself shot by one of 'em."

"I don't plan to, Mr. Colley." He tipped his hat and walked back out to his rig. At least he knew how to ride a horse well. With all his many long trips to Hartford by horseback, he figured he'd have no trouble riding in Texas. The rig today was simply a convenience for carting home his personal belongings from his office. Tomorrow the desk would be crated and shipped westward.

He entered the foyer of the comfortable, two-story home he still shared with his family. At his age, many other men had places of their own, but Ellie's cooking and the free lodging had tempted him to stay.

After handing over his hat to Stevens the butler, Daniel turned toward the voices he heard in the drawing room on his left. He knocked then pushed open the doors. "Good evening, Mother, Father."

His mother stood and hurried to him. She wrapped her arms around him. "Oh, Daniel, please tell me you've changed your mind and are staying in Briar Ridge. I can't bear for you to leave us."

He patted her back and glanced at his father, who simply lifted his gray bushy eyebrows and shrugged. He turned back to his mother. "I'm sorry you feel this way, Mother, but I purchased my train ticket on the way home this evening and will leave the beginning of next week."

She pushed away from him and held a handkerchief to her nose. "I simply can't believe it. I don't understand why you have to go all the way to Texas to practice law. New Haven and Hartford are much closer. Why, even Boston would be better than way out West."

"We have a multitude of fine barristers in the cities here in the East. As I've said many times, this will give me the opportunity to travel and see what is happening in the rest of our great country." No matter how many times he explained, his mother would never truly understand his desire to move on. She had grown up in this town, as had his father, and she would never leave it or her beautiful home.

Stevens appeared in the doorway. "Mr. and Mrs. Monroe, dinner is served."

Mother hooked her hand into Daniel's arm. "Thank you, Stevens. Tell Ellie we'll be right in." She patted Daniel's hand now resting on hers. Although she held her head high, he noted the slight tremor in her voice as she spoke. "I had Ellie prepare your favorite meal tonight. She'll be serving all your favorites until your departure." She swallowed hard as she walked beside Daniel into the dining room.

Daniel's younger sister, Abigail, bounded down the stairs but stopped short when she saw her parents and Daniel. Her next steps were much more sedate. "Good evening, Daniel. I didn't know you were home."

Father waited to escort her into dinner. "And what is your great hurry, my dear girl? Is Ellie's food that tempting?"

"No, Father, I'm just happy about my trip to see Rachel and Nathan in Hartford next week. I haven't seen her since the wedding, and I'm anxious to visit and talk with her."

Daniel assisted his mother in her chair at the table. "I'm sure you two will have much to talk about. What's it been? Two, three months since the wedding?"

She turned to glare at him. A month ago she wouldn't have minded the teasing, but since his decision to leave, she had been less than sisterly. "Three, if you must count, but it may as well be three years." Abigail dismissed him and turned to her mother. "I truly miss having Rachel here in Briar Ridge."

Father held her chair while she seated herself. He bent and brushed his lips across her hair. "Then I'm glad you will have this chance to visit Rachel in Hartford."

After his father said grace, Ellie brought in a platter emanating the most delicious aroma. His favorite roast beef as Mother had promised. Along with it came perfectly creamed potatoes, buttered asparagus, carrots, fresh baked bread, and his favorite sweet pickles. "What, no soup tonight?"

Mother pressed her lips together. "You said you didn't care for soup at every meal, and since this is your meal, we skipped it."

"Thank you, I prefer to fill up on the main course and not the first one." He glanced over at Abigail, who scrunched up her nose as the asparagus was passed to her. "Not to worry, dear sister, after I'm on my way to Texas, you won't have to worry about asparagus. Ellie only cooks it because she knows how much I like it."

"Humph, that *will* be one good aspect of your leaving." She placed two stalks on her plate and handed the bowl to their father.

As his parents began discussing their day, he noted the total lack of reference to his leaving the coming Monday. His mother believed if she ignored it, that perhaps it wouldn't really happen. Father cast a wistful eye Daniel's way a few times, as though he wanted to talk with his son. Perhaps after dinner he and Father could have a conversation.

Daniel gazed around at the opulent surroundings. Sparkling crystal, fine china, silver cutlery, and damask table cloth and napkins reminded him of his parent's wealth. He would find nothing like this in Texas.

Then he glanced again at his mother and swallowed a lump in his throat along with a bite of potato. He didn't want to hurt her, but he could see in her face and the way she only moved the food around her plate without actually eating it that he had done just that.

How could he make her understand his desire to move away and seek a new life? Somehow between now and Monday he must convince her that God had called him to the frontier. He had spent many hours in prayer over this move, and now he gladly embraced the future and all it held in the grand state of Texas.

Chapter Two

THE CONDUCTOR WALKED through the car with a watch in his hands. "Porterfield next stop in half an hour."

Daniel nodded to the man and turned his gaze again to the scenery outside his window. The wide open spaces, hills, desert, and scrub brush he'd expected to see had not appeared as yet. Instead they had traveled through forests of great pine trees growing tall straight up to heaven. From Seth's letters, Daniel knew cattle ranches existed in this area, but he'd seen only a few groups of cattle so far.

Then the stately pines gave way to open land and fields dotted with cattle. Trees still graced the landscape, but in the distance with slopes of grassland rolling toward him. Very few fences could be seen, and those were mainly to keep the cattle away from the tracks.

The train pulled into a station somewhat larger than Daniel had imagined. His adventure now was truly about to begin. As excitement filled his breast, remorse filled his soul.

No one would be here to meet him except maybe Seth, but Daniel had given no set time for arrival, so even the appearance of his friend seemed unlikely.

Just like back home when no one came to see him off except his father. Mother and Abigail refused to acknowledge his leaving. Mother had not come from her room, and Abigail had glared at him then flounced past him and out the front door. Only Ellie had embraced him and wished him Godspeed on his journey, and she had even wiped a tear from her eye.

Daniel shook the image from his mind. At least his father had not completely ignored the departure. He hated to leave Briar Ridge without his mother's blessing, but he'd made the decision, and to back down then would most likely result in his being mired in Connecticut forever.

The sharp blast of the whistle as the train braked to a stop caused Daniel's heart to thump. He stepped down to the platform amid a bevy of people greeting those arriving, mostly men. Just then someone called his name.

Daniel turned to find his friend headed toward him. "Seth Winston. You *are* a welcome sight. I had no idea whether you would be here or not." He grasped Seth's hand and shook it.

Seth clapped a hand on Daniel's shoulder. "I've been meeting every train for the past two days hoping you'd arrive soon. It's good to see you."

He turned toward the station, and Daniel followed. A lanky young man near his own age and wearing a badge strode toward them. He wore cowboy boots and a wide-brimmed hat. Seth waved. "Cory, my friend Daniel Monroe finally arrived."

The lawman stopped and offered his hand in welcome to Daniel. "I was about to think Reverend Winston had made you up. He's been that anxious about your arrival. I'm Deputy Cory Muldoon, and I understand you're a lawyer. It'll be nice to have our own lawyer instead of waiting for one to come with the circuit judge."

Daniel grinned. "Pleased to meet you, Deputy. I'm hoping that having a lawyer in town will be a good thing for Porterfield."

"Call me Cory, and you'll find quite a few of us Muldoons around these parts. In fact, the reverend here arranged a room for you at my Aunt Mae's boardinghouse." He glanced around the platform. "Let's get your bags, and we can head on over there."

"You must have better things to do than tote my luggage around. If you have a livery, I'll hire a wagon. I do have more boxes than usual because I brought my desk and chair and many of my law books. The rest of the books and other things for my office are being shipped and will arrive later."

Seth stopped by the stack of baggage loaded onto the platform. "I don't know how much of this is yours, but this is twice as much as I've ever seen at one time." He shoved his hat back from his forehead. "I think a wagon is the best solution. We can head down to Frank's place now and get you set up."

"Good, and I'll want to see about boarding my horse there too. He's in a separate car. Maybe I should get him first."

Cory laughed out loud. "So you brought a horse all the way out here. We do have plenty of them, you know."

Daniel grinned and walked toward the car where his horse had made the journey. "I figured as much, but Black Legend and I have a good relationship, and I didn't want to leave him behind."

The sound of Daniel's voice roused the horse. He whinnied and raised his head and shook it. "That's my boy. Our trip is over and our adventure begins." He led the horse down the ramp then waited while the baggage handler lifted down a saddle to Daniel.

Cory whistled low. "That's some fancy saddle you have there. From the looks of it, you know horses."

"That I do. I traveled to Hartford frequently from my hometown, and Black Legend never let me down. I figured he deserved a change of scenery as much as I did." He hefted the saddle onto the horse and swiftly buckled it. "Now, if you'll lead the way to the livery, I can get him groomed and settled."

Daniel grabbed Black Legend's reins and followed behind Seth and Cory. Except for many of the buildings being wood instead of brick and stone, this town didn't differ much from Briar Ridge. He spotted the telegraph station next to the depot, a very nice-looking hotel, the bank, a barber shop, a dressmaker's, a bakery, a land office, and a general store. Just as he'd expected, a saloon with swinging doors stood down the street. Several other smaller businesses filled the spaces between. It wasn't exactly as primitive as he had imagined, but he was pleased with what he saw.

They arrived at the livery, and a man with bulging muscles and wearing a blacksmith's apron greeted them. "Afternoon, Preacher, Deputy. What you fellers need?"

Cory nodded toward Daniel. "Our friend Daniel just arrived in town and would like to stable his horse here. He's the lawyer the mayor's been talking about the past few months."

"Welcome to Porterfield. Name's Frank Cahoon, and I'm the smithy, so I'll take care of you. I also live at the boarding house and heard tell you were coming." He eyed the black horse. "Mighty fine-lookin' animal you have there. Just so happens we have an empty stall where I can board him for you." He stepped over to the horse. "Looks like you take good care of him. He don't look any worse for the journey." He took the reins from Seth and headed into the building.

After settling on a weekly boarding fee, Cory said, "Hold off on renting that wagon. I thought I saw my Aunt Mae's by the store." Back out to the street, Cory pointed across the way. "I was right. That's her wagon over there. Kate must be in town picking up supplies. We can see if she'll be willing to let us load up your bags in the wagon and take you to Aunt Mae's."

"I don't want to put anyone to any trouble on my account. It'll be just as easy for me to rent a wagon of my own and take it down."

"Won't be any problem. Kate's my sister, and she can handle a horse and wagon just about as good as any man around these parts. She grew up on the ranch."

Seth grinned and shook his head. "Besides being one of the prettiest women around, she's about the most independent woman I've ever met. Reminds some of my aunt Mabel back in Boston."

Daniel hadn't met Seth's aunt, but he'd heard plenty about her from his sister who had visited Aunt Mabel in Boston with Rachel. He looked forward to meeting Kate Muldoon.

∞

The train blared out of the station as Kate made her way around the general store. Supposed to be a new boarder on that train one of these days. The mayor had told everyone a young lawyer man from Connecticut was coming to live in Porterfield, but he hadn't shown up yet. Aunt Mae was prepared for her new boarder, but Kate wasn't sure the rest of the town would be.

The mingling of peppermint, coal oil, fabric dyes, and dill pickles tickled Kate's nose as she collected items from Aunt Mae's list. The dyes from the many bolts of fabric on the back shelves usually caused her eyes to water, so she stayed away from that area.

Mrs. Grayson hurried from the back of the store. "Your aunt told me she'd be needing a good bit this time. We just got a shipment of canned goods in yesterday, so let's see what's on your list."

She glanced at the paper Kate showed her and headed for the canned goods. With Mrs. Grayson's help, Kate soon had her list complete. Flour, sugar, cornmeal, and jars of molasses and syrup joined the other items on the counter near the front of the store.

While Mr. Grayson totaled up the order, Kate meandered her way through the aisles. Neatly organized shelves lined the walls, and tables holding other merchandise filled the empty space between. Since its expansion into a vacant building next door, the store held a much wider variety of goods. Catalogs stood on one table where customers could page through, place an order, and have items delivered to town. That might be OK for some people, but Kate preferred to have a look at whatever she happened to be buying. When she returned to the front, Mr. Grayson had bundled her merchandise and had the receipt ready for her.

"Thank you. Aunt Mae hopes the new boarder comes in

today. She's fixing a special meal for him. I think she wants to impress him so he'll stay on."

Mr. Grayson laughed. "As if she needed to cook a special meal to get him to stay! Her cooking is about the best around these parts."

"I agree." Kate surveyed the stack of supplies. "Looks like I'll need to make at least two, if not three trips out to the wagon." Aunt Mae was really going all-out in her efforts for the next few days. She picked up the two smallest parcels. "At least all the boarders get the benefit when she cooks special."

"Let me help you with that, Kate. It'll save some time." Mr. Grayson headed around the counter.

Kate held up one hand. "No, I have plenty of time, and you have new customers. I'll get it." She turned and walked out to the wagon. As she lifted her load onto the bed, she glanced across the street and saw Reverend Winston and Cory talking to a strange man in a fancy suit. When he turned to glance at Kate, the box in her hands dropped with a thud into the wagon. Even with a hat on, he was about the most handsome man she'd seen lately. He must be that lawyer feller from Connecticut, because he sure didn't look like he belonged in Texas.

Cory called her name and waved. He strode across the street with Reverend Winston and the stranger close behind. "Hi, Kate, got someone here for you to meet."

Reverend Winston stepped up onto the boardwalk. "Kate, this is my friend from back East, Daniel Monroe. He just came in on the train. Daniel, this is Kathleen Muldoon. She's Aunt Mae's niece and Cory's sister."

Daniel removed his hat. "Pleased to meet you, Miss Muldoon. I'm going to be living at the boardinghouse."

Kate narrowed her eyes. Handsome and polite. Now that was a new combination. "Oh, so you're the new lawyer." Of course he was. No one else in town dressed like this man except maybe the banker and the mayor.

Cory draped an arm around her shoulders. That could mean only one thing. He wanted something from her. He didn't disappoint.

"Since you have the wagon, you can help Mr. Monroe here get his belongings down to the boardinghouse. There's too much for us to carry, especially since he has boxes of books and stuff for his office."

Kate didn't answer at once but studied the man beside the reverend. He hadn't said much, but what he did say had been pleasant. The wagon had plenty of room, and she was going back to Aunt Mae's anyway. She shrugged and headed back to the store. "OK. You boys get his things, and I'll finish getting my supplies."

Daniel stepped forward and removed his hat. "Could I help you load your boxes, Miss Muldoon? It's the least I can do to say thank you."

Kate stopped, hands on her hips. "Thank you, but I can take care of it. You go on back with Cory and the reverend and get your bags ready. I'll come on down to the depot soon as I'm loaded up."

He settled his hat back on his head. "All right. We'll wait for you there."

Kate grinned at his departing back. At least he didn't

insist. Besides, despite his broad shoulders, he didn't look like he had the muscles it took to load anything very heavy.

Five minutes later she arrived to find a mound of trunks and crates on the platform. Daniel had removed his hat and coat and rolled up his sleeves. Kate swallowed a chuckle. Seemed Fancy Pants didn't mind getting himself sweaty. "I'm here, boys. Ya'll ready to load 'em up?"

The three men began lugging the largest of the crates to the wagon. It took all three of them to hoist it up into the back. August in Texas was hot, and perspiration had soaked their shirts by the time they finished loading the wagon.

Mayor Tate hailed them from down the street and hurried their direction, huffing and puffing all the way. He removed his hat and swiped at his perspiring bald head with a large handkerchief. "Sorry I wasn't at the train to meet you." He stuck out his hand. "Mayor Tate, and I take it you're Daniel Monroe, our new lawyer."

Daniel shook the mayor's hand. "Yes, I am. It's good to finally meet you, Mayor Tate."

"The pleasure's mine. Once you're settled in, drop by my office and I'll give you a rundown on Porterfield and what to expect."

"I'd like that, sir. Maybe tomorrow morning?"

"That'll do just fine. Now I'll get on back to my office and let you fellows finish up here." He glanced up at Kate. "Good afternoon, Miss Muldoon. I'm sure you and your aunt will take good care of Mr. Monroe." With that he popped his bowler back on his head and scurried away.

Heat bore down on Kate's shoulders, and she was thankful for the wide brim of the straw hat she wore. Despite that, her hands had itched to get down and help the men, and curiosity filled her like the creek bed after a heavy rain. Where would he put all that stuff? His room at the boardinghouse sure wouldn't hold it all. Of course, some of it would go to his office above the dress shop.

The three men said a few words before Cory headed off to patrol the town. Daniel wiped his brow with a large white handkerchief. "Whew, it never gets this hot in Connecticut. I never felt such heat from the sun."

Reverend Winston laughed and slapped Daniel's shoulder. "Oh, you'll get used to it. Besides, it sure makes a glass of cold lemonade taste better, and I know Aunt Mae will have some available." He climbed into the back of the wagon. "I'll ride with you to help you unload. You ride up there with Miss Kate."

Daniel seemed to weigh his options before moving. Humph, she didn't care if he rode beside her or sitting on top of a crate, but he'd better hurry and make up his mind, or she'd go off and leave him.

After a moment he grabbed his coat and hat from a bench on the platform and joined Kate on the seat upfront. "I do appreciate your willingness to haul my belongings to the boardinghouse. Perhaps I can return the favor at some later date."

For answer Kate clucked at the horses to move on. She'd had to bite down on her tongue to keep from laughing at his accent. He certainly talked faster than others around here, and a mite fancier too. His sleeves were still rolled up and his muscled arms glistened with sweat, dispelling any thoughts about his being a weakling. Fancy pants and fancy speech aside, Daniel Monroe had a fine physique, and that made him all the more intriguing. She looked forward to seeing how he adapted to life in Texas.

Chapter Three

Daniel rolled down his sleeves. His arm grazed Kate's at one point, and it sent a shock wave through her elbow to her shoulder. Her first impulse had been to move over out of his way, but that might give him the wrong idea as though she didn't want him there. Well, actually she didn't. Porterfield had no real need for a lawyer, especially a fancy dressed one from the North.

"Mayor Tate seems like a nice enough fellow." Daniel folded his jacket across one knee.

Kate nodded. "He's a good mayor, but a little pompous if you ask me. Always thinking everything is his idea and taking the credit for lot that isn't his doing." Although he had done a number of good things for the town, he did some things that caused her to shake her head in wonder—like seeking out a lawyer and bringing him into town.

"Politicians are apt to take credit for the good and shift blame if something doesn't go the way they'd planned."

Kate had to laugh at that. "Exactly. And that's why they can't always be trusted. Anyway, he's a nice enough person." He and his family attended her church, but she'd never seen any real indication that he took his faith seriously.

Daniel glanced back at the wagonload. "That's quite a haul for a woman. Was there no one at the boardinghouse to help you get all those supplies?"

"I don't need any help." Kate pressed her lips together. If he thought she was some helpless female, he'd better think again. She pulled her own weight at Aunt Mae's just as she had back on the ranch, and she was probably the best horsewoman in these parts.

"I'm sure you're quite capable, but it would seem that with all the men who are supposed to live in this town, that one of them would handle hauling supplies."

Thankfully they reached the boardinghouse side yard or else she might say something to tell off this fancy young man from the city. She bit her tongue and decided his new name would be Fancy Pants, but only in her thoughts. Aunt Mae would never put up with insults to a guest.

"Well, I see the boardinghouse is much larger than I expected. It's a rather pleasant-looking place." He glanced around with admiration in his eyes.

What had he thought he'd find? Some ramshackle old house needing repairs? When the wagon stopped, he jumped down then hurried to assist Kate, but she ignored his polite gesture and scampered down on her own and retreated to the back of the wagon. Her distaste for Daniel grew deeper by the minute. She tried to remind herself that he was only being polite, but something about Mr. Monroe didn't sit right with her. Best to just avoid him as much as possible.

By the time she reached the back of the wagon, Reverend Winston and Daniel had set two crates on the ground. She reached up for one of the bags to move it out of the way.

Aunt Mae appeared on the back stoop and waved to Kate. "It's about time you got back. What took you so long?" Then she noticed Mr. Monroe and swiped her hands down her apron before scurrying to meet him. She held out her hand and beamed like the man was the president himself.

Kate shook her head and climbed up on the back of the wagon. Reverend Winston and Daniel had let the back down, so she was able to hoist herself up. Daniel's things took up most of the room, but she managed to skirt around them and get to what she needed to unload. Mr. Monroe would have to take care of his own baggage. Aunt Mae's voice drifted up to Kate. "We're so glad you've finally arrived. Your room is all ready for you." Then she must have seen the wagonload. "Gracious me. Is all that yours? I don't know where we can put it all. Your room isn't that big."

Kate snickered and slid down from the back, a box of groceries in hand. That had been the same question in her mind. Without a glance in their direction she hurried inside and left Aunt Mae discussing bags and trunks with Mr. Monroe and the reverend.

After setting her burden on the table, she sauntered back to the door and leaned over just enough to catch their conversation.

"Mrs. Sullivan, I appreciate your concern, but most of this

will be placed in my office tomorrow. If I can leave it in the wagon, I can haul it down there tomorrow morning."

"Well, I suppose that'll be all right. And call me Aunt Mae. Everyone else does in this town. Kate! Come out here and help Mr. Monroe get his things unloaded and the wagon into the barn."

Daniel's eyes widened. "Oh, no, Mrs.—Aunt Mae, I couldn't let her handle these heavy bags. Seth and I will take care of it."

Kate's temper flared. She could carry as much weight as he could. She marched off the porch and out to the wagon. "Let's get what you need upstairs so I can get Danny Boy here brushed and fed." She reached up for one handle on a trunk.

His hand covered hers, and the warmth flowed through the rest of her body. She couldn't take her gaze away from his hand over hers.

"No, I can't let you carry that heavy thing. Seth and I'll get a few of the men to help us. Go ahead and get the rest of your aunt's things inside."

That snapped her to attention. "I'll carry what I want to carry, thank you." Even as she pulled the trunk toward her, she realized it was much heavier than she imagined. Her stubborn pride took root. There wasn't a chance now that she'd admit she couldn't handle it. Fancy Pants reached up for another trunk and pulled it toward him easily. Kate clamped her mouth shut and managed to get the one she pulled onto the ground.

Daniel stood there with a frown of concern on his face, watching her. With a great heave she managed to get the trunk up and took a few steps. This was going to be much harder than she imagined. Every muscle in her body screamed in pain, but she refused to set it down until she reached the stoop. She let it go with a thud and dusted her hands together. "There. It's on the stoop. I didn't say I'd help get it to your room."

Again that frown crossed his face, and the reverend laughed out loud. Kate flounced her skirt and ignored them, heading back to the wagon to retrieve the rest of the groceries. One of these days that stubborn streak would really get her into trouble and not just give her sore muscles.

∞

Daniel couldn't help but join in Seth's laugh when Kate disappeared through the door with the last of the groceries. If she hadn't been so adamant about helping him, he would have told her the trunk she picked up should stay in the wagon. It held most of his law books as well as some from his personal library.

If he hadn't feared a slap to his face, he would have told her, but that determined fierceness in her eyes had caused him to back off. One thing for sure, women in Texas were far different from the women in Connecticut. He couldn't imagine Rachel or Abigail doing such a chore as Kathleen Muldoon had assumed. Abigail may be stubborn about many things, but his sister knew when to let a man take over for her.

Mae grabbed Daniel's arm. "Come on inside, and I'll take you up to your room. We can get all these things later when it's a bit cooler. I have some lemonade that'll help. You can come too, Reverend Winston."

"Thank you, but no, ma'am. I have to get on over to the church and tend to business there." Seth waved at Daniel. "I'll come back and see you after I finish if I have time." Then he sauntered off in the direction of the steeple down the street.

"Suit yourself, young 'un." Aunt Mae guided Daniel through the kitchen, still talking. "Dinner is served at half past six, and them that's late might not get any at all. Breakfast starts at six a.m. for the ones who have to be at work early. We have eight boarders in all, if you include Kate and my nephew Cory. Kate and I live in the two bedrooms downstairs, and our two lady boarders also have their rooms on the first floor. We take care of all the bed linens, but you're responsible for your own personal laundry."

That was fine with Daniel. He didn't like the idea of a female living in the same house taking care of his personal items. He followed right behind Mae, about to ask a question, but she continued to talk so fast and changed the subject so often that he could barely keep up. If she talked like this all the time, how did anybody get anything said?

At the top of the stairs she turned to her right and opened a door on the left. Daniel walked in to find a single bed, washstand, an upholstered chair, a three-drawer chest with a mirror above, a small table with a lamp by the bed, and several hooks on the wall behind the door.

"You have a front room, so if you look out your window, you can see much of the town. I trust it's suitable." She crossed her arms at her waist and tilted her head.

Of course it would be suitable. He didn't dare say otherwise. The two women he'd just met were not ones he wanted to upset. "It's fine, Mrs. Sullivan...I mean Aunt Mae. I can put a few of my personal books on the shelf over there, and the bed looks quite comfortable."

"Finest feather bed you'll find in these parts. Had them special made for my guests. The quilts were all made for the beds, and each room has a different one. Yours is the Log Cabin pattern." She turned toward the door. "Now I'll leave you to freshen up some or bring up more of your belongings, whatever you choose. And here's your key if you decide you want to keep the door locked. I have an extra key for all the rooms, so we can get in to clean and change linens. There's a room downstairs where you may take a bath, but you'll have to haul the hot water for yourself and empty it out when you're done. Two bath towels a week are furnished. If you want more, you can get them at the store in town. You'll share the space with the other boarders, so you'll need to clean up after yourself." As soon as she finished the last sentence, she disappeared into the hallway and left Daniel to his own devices.

One thing about Mae Sullivan, she didn't lack for words to say. He hadn't heard that much coming from one woman since his teacher from school days in Briar Ridge. He sat down on the edge of the bed and ran his hand over the handmade quilt. In shades of red, green, and brown, the quilt added just the right touch to the room, and the bed was quite comfortable. Although much smaller than his bedroom at home, this one would do quite nicely.

Daniel spent the next hour bringing up the rest of his belongings and arranging then in the room. He placed a few of his favorite books on the shelf and hung his shirts and jackets on the hooks. The rest of his clothes were stored in drawers in the chest.

All the while he worked, the image of a certain red-haired young woman played in his mind. Her thick, lustrous hair was a shade of red he'd heard called auburn. Whatever, it was most appealing, as were her hazel eyes. She roused his curiosity as no woman had ever done before, but then he'd never met a woman quite like her.

By the time he'd finished, delightful aromas wafted up the stairs and reminded him he hadn't eaten since a meager lunch on the train. His nose savored the scent of roasting meat and what he thought might be apple pie. He pulled his watch from its pocket and noted the time to be almost half past six. After washing and drying his hands, he hurried down the stairway behind two other gentlemen.

Daniel grabbed the only vacant chair left, and it happened to be beside the young deputy. Two women besides the men sat at the main table. He noted two other tables held groups of men and several couples. He estimated about fifteen others also dined at the boardinghouse.

Aunt Mae pushed through the kitchen door. She spotted Daniel and grinned. "Good. You're right on time." She set a platter of sliced roast beef on the table then carried another one to the other table seating eight.

Kate followed her aunt carrying bowls of steaming vegetables. A large basket of bread already sat on the tables along with a bowl of pickles and a plate with a ball of butter. This would be a hearty meal and one Daniel planned to enjoy.

Then he noted all the chairs were filled. Where did Aunt Mae and Kate plan to sit? The two women stood behind Cory.

Cory glanced around the table. "Let us pray." He bowed his head and said, "Lord, thank you for this bountiful feast and the hands that prepared it. Amen."

Accustomed to his father's lengthy prayers at mealtime,

Daniel started at the short one uttered by Cory. As soon as Cory said "amen," Kate and Aunt Mae disappeared back to the kitchen then returned with more platters and bowls for the other tables.

Daniel noticed the men let the women serve themselves first. So the men of the West did have a few manners after all.

He leaned toward Cory. "Where are your aunt and Kate eating dinner?"

The young deputy forked several slices of beef and transferred them to his plate. "Oh, they take supper in the kitchen after we're done. Saves them having to get up and down during the meal to take care of refills and such."

"I see. I didn't realize there would be this many to eat. Your aunt said only eight people boarded here, so who are the others?"

"Aunt Mae opens the noon and evening meals to anybody who wants to come. Most of them make reservations. She says it's as easy to cook for twenty as it is for ten."

This was something else different, but then Daniel had never been in a boardinghouse before and didn't know the routine. He spooned out a big helping of mashed potatoes then drowned them in brown gravy. The first bite told him he wouldn't be missing Ellie's cooking all that much. Aunt Mae was just as good if not better.

After everyone had filled their plates, Cory spoke to those at their table. "This is Daniel Monroe. He's just moved to Porterfield, and he's the lawyer Mayor Tate asked to come. So if you have any legal needs, Daniel here is the one to see."

A man across from him nodded. "That's good. I have a few

things I may want to discuss with you. My name's Wilder, and I work for the newspaper."

One of the women smiled. Her blue eyes sparkled as she spoke to Daniel. "I'm Eloise Perth, and I'm one of the schoolmarms here. I teach the younger students. It's nice to have you, Mr. Monroe."

To Daniel she looked more like someone's grandmother than a teacher. "Thank you, Miss Perth. I think I'm going to like your town."

The remaining guests introduced themselves. The other woman, Mrs. Bennett, was a widow and the dressmaker in town. The other men included Mr. Fuller from the bank and Frank Cahoon from the livery. He put his lawyer's mind to work and made note of all their names and something about them to remember them by. He'd found that to be the best way to make friends and influence clients in his business. A person hearing his own name spoken was more likely to be trusting than not.

The kitchen door swung open again, and Kate entered. "Everything all right in here?" She reached across for a bowl. "I see the potatoes are gone." She swooped up the bowl. "I'll refill it."

Daniel grinned up at her. "This is a very tasty meal. Did you help prepare it?"

Kate laughed. "Afraid not. Aunt Mae is the cook. I just do the serving. Burned biscuits are more my type of cooking."

Cory sopped a piece of bread in his gravy. "She's got that right. If she was doing the cooking, I'd be finding me somewhere else to live."

Kate's cheeks bloomed pink. "Cory Muldoon, you don't

have to agree with everything I say." She flounced back to the kitchen.

Cory turned back to Daniel. "Kate's not good for much around the house. She's a great horsewoman though and knows a lot about medicine and treating sick people and animals. Can't understand why she didn't stay out at the ranch and help Ma and Pa. Too blamed independent if you ask me."

Daniel raised his brow but said nothing. He had already seen that independence. Miss Kate Muldoon would be interesting to get to know if he could figure how to talk to her without insulting her.

CHAPTER FOUR

AT BREAKFAST THE next morning, only the actual boarders joined together for the hearty meal of scrambled eggs, sausage, biscuits, applesauce, peach jam, and good, strong coffee. If he ate like this every day, Daniel feared being able to fit into his clothes. Perhaps a brisk walk into town each morning would work some of it off.

Aunt Mae bustled in and out of the kitchen with refills, but Kate did not make an appearance. When Aunt Mae refilled his coffee, Daniel asked, "Where is Miss Kate this morning? I expected her to be helping you."

Cory laughed at that. "Kate doesn't help at breakfast. She spends mornings at the infirmary helping out the doctor. She goes over early to open up and see to all the supplies. She'd rather bandage wounds and nurse sick people than serve us. If she's not over there, she usually has her nose stuck in a medical book."

Aunt Mae swished her hand across Cory's shoulder. "Don't

go laughing at your sister. Her being able to help out the doc and study in the morning was part of the arrangement when she came here." She leaned toward Daniel. "Kate has a love for helping people and has always been interested in medical things. Doc Jensen says she's a big help to him."

"I'm sure she must be." However, Daniel didn't understand why any woman would want to be around sick or injured people. Most found taking care of their own families enough nursing for anyone. He remembered how Rachel Winston had nursed her mother back to health last year and admired the young woman for it, but then caring for family was part of a woman's lot in life.

Miss Perth broke open a biscuit and slathered it with fresh butter. "Mr. Monroe, when do you plan to have your law office open?"

"Seeing how this is Friday, I figure I'll need a few days to get everything settled and hang out my shingle. I should be ready for clients by Tuesday." That is if everything went according to plan and all the furniture he needed was available.

"Good. I'd like to make an appointment with you for Tuesday afternoon after school." She bit into the biscuit oozing with peach jam.

Daniel grasped his coffee cup. "That will be fine, Miss Perth. I'll look for you then." What an elderly spinster woman would need with a lawyer escaped him, but he'd be of service in any way he could.

Talk then turned to other interests. Daniel again noted how Mr. Fuller seemed fascinated by every move Aunt Mae made, and his face lit up with a smile whenever she came back into the room. A positive response shone from Aunt Mae several times as her gaze met with Mr. Fuller's.

Daniel swallowed a chuckle. The thought of the older man and woman being romantically inclined amused him. Still, they had as much right to love and happiness as anyone else. It would be interesting to watch the relationship develop.

Cory pushed back from the table. "Daniel, if you're about ready, we can walk into town together. The exercise is good after one of Aunt Mae's hearty breakfasts."

"I thought the same thing myself." Daniel stood and laid his napkin on the table. "Give me a moment and I'll be right with you."

A few minutes later the two men ambled down toward the main part of town. Cory pulled his hat tighter on his head against the slight breeze. "Things are changing fast around these parts. We're the new county seat and just elected a new sheriff, name of Rutherford. We also have a federal marshal named Slade who goes from town to town to handle any federal cases such as bank robberies, murders, and such as that. I think he plans to make Porterfield his home."

"Having both a sheriff and a marshal will go a long way toward keeping the town a safe place to live. But what about your job? Will you still be a federal deputy?"

Cory shook his head. "I'll be working with both men to keep law and order in town. Not sure what my official title will be." He pointed toward the saloon. "Our main problem is going to be keeping things quiet at the Branding Iron when it opens next week. Most of the problems come when men mix gambling and drinking."

"Is it always this warm so early in the day?" Daniel removed his handkerchief and swiped it across his brow. It never got this hot in Connecticut even at midday in summer. Sweat trickled down his neck. He'd have to do something about the heavy clothing in his wardrobe.

"Yep. Texas summers are hot and usually dry. We've had a few prairie fires, but not the dust storms of the western half of the state. I think you'll like our winters. Not nearly as cold as up north."

Now that he could look forward to. No more months on end with piles of snow and freezing temperatures. However, he had to learn to live in the heat first.

Daniel stopped in front of a building and gazed upward. Mayor Tate had already managed to have one window painted with bold, black letters:

DANIEL MONROE
ATTORNEY-AT-LAW

Well, it did look good and matched the sign at the bottom of the stairway leading up to his new offices. He waved Cory on his way and ascended the steps. Delightful aromas from the bakery next door wafted their way upstairs. Directly under his office was Henrietta Bennett's dressmaking shop, opening at nine, or so said the sign.

He selected the key from those on a ring and unlocked his door. The space was divided into two rooms. One would be a reception area and the other his actual office. He stepped through the door and immediately envisioned the walls lined with his books. He wished now that he'd let Mother send that rug she thought he might need, but he had vetoed the idea.

The desk would fit in front of the window where he could watch the everyday activities of the town.

Daniel sauntered to the window overlooking Main Street and gazed out. A movement to his right caught his attention, and he turned just in time to catch sight of Kate Muldoon rushing from the infirmary back toward the boardinghouse. A real mystery, that Kate. As pretty as the rising sun, but as unreadable as a book in a foreign language. Maybe after a while he would learn to translate her, but it would take more than a few months, of that he was sure.

∞

Kate hurried back to the boardinghouse. All the guests would be gone, and Aunt Mae would need her to help clean up before she could settle down with her lessons. Doc Jensen treated her just like she was in nursing school and gave her quizzes over what she had read each week. The more she learned, the more she wanted to learn. Taking care of injuries and sickness filled her with a sense of pride and accomplishment. God had been good to allow her this opportunity and to have Doc Jensen so willing to teach her.

She dropped her books on the table in the front hall and headed for the kitchen, where the aroma of beef stew for the noon meal already filled the air.

"Good morning, Aunt Mae." She hugged her aunt and kissed her cheek.

"Things must have gone well with your lessons this morning."

Kate tied an apron around her waist. "It really did, and I

so appreciate your letting me leave early every morning. Now I'm ready to tackle those dishes."

After priming the pump, she filled the sink part way with water then reached for the pot of hot water her aunt kept on the back burner. Steam from the hot water rose to dampen her face as she poured it into the cooler water. She tested it with her hand. "Just right. At least I know how to do some things around the house." She rolled up her sleeves and placed the already scraped dishes into the water.

"How did things go at breakfast? Everybody on time?" She rubbed the bar of soap over a dish cloth to work up a few suds.

Aunt Mae laughed. "Yes, they were. And Mr. Monroe can match that brother of yours bite for bite."

Heat rose in Kate's cheeks. She had hoped to catch a glimpse of Daniel before she left, but he had come down late. The man intrigued her with his fancy clothes and talk. She couldn't believe he and Cory had become friends so quickly.

"I suppose he plans to move some of those trunks and things to his office today." Kate finished the last dish and set the plate on the counter to dry. As soon as she completed her chores upstairs, she'd try to get some studying done, but maybe she'd see him.

"Yes, Cory offered to help him, and I'm sure Reverend Winston will do the same." Aunt Mae set out ingredients for cornbread. "Soon as we finish upstairs, I can get on with lunch and you can get on with your studying."

Kate followed her aunt up the stairs with a broom and dusting cloth. When she opened the door to Daniel Monroe's room she gasped. Everything was neat and tidy with not even a sock or shoe out of place. At least he was organized, but how long would that last if he got busy with his practice?

"Well, now, looks like our new boarder is going to be a nice one to have around. I'll take the ewer down, empty the bowl, and refill it. You can dust, but I don't see that it really needs it this morning." Aunt Mae picked up the pitcher and bowl from the stand and headed downstairs. She did this for each room so the boarders would have fresh water when they returned for the noonday meal.

After her aunt left, Kate gazed around at the room. Several pairs of shoes were lined up in a neat row. Shouldn't be long before a pair of cowboy boots joined the ones there. Shirts and trousers hung on hooks on the wall in way that had colors matched up.

Kate ran a cloth across the top of the chest where Daniel had placed a brush on a small tray that looked like it might hold keys and coins. One thing to be said for the young attorney, he liked things neat and in order.

Less than an hour later, Kate had completed the other rooms, and they all stood ready for their occupants to return at noon. Down in her own room, she opened her books and began to read. She hadn't read more than a page when laughter and noises outside distracted her. A glance out the window revealed Cory hitching Danny Boy to the wagon as Reverend Winston and Fancy Pants rearranged the load. Indecision filled her. She needed to study, but concentration would be impossible with all the noise.

A moment later Kate stepped out onto the porch. "How can you expect me to get any studying done with all this commotion going on right outside my window?"

Daniel set a box on the bed of the wagon. "I'm sorry. We didn't mean to disturb you. We'll be quieter, won't we?" He glanced from Reverend Winston to Cory.

A grin as broad as the backside of Angus steer split Cory's face. "Yes, we'll try to be quieter, but wouldn't you rather come join us?"

Daniel stepped forward. "No, there's no need. She should be studying, not hauling boxes."

Kate narrowed her eyes. Daniel smiled, and his brown eyes sparkled, but teasing her would get him nowhere. "As a matter of fact, it's time for a break." She strode toward the wagon.

"If you really want to help, I have a few boxes to take upstairs. They contain my diplomas and some pictures from back home. They might be easier for you to handle."

Anger began a slow burn in the pit of her stomach. There he went again, treating her like some weak girl. She opened her mouth to retort, but he shoved a small box into her hands.

His hands touched hers for a moment, and she almost dropped the box. She gulped and held tight to the container. He gazed into her eyes for a moment, and something passed between them that sent warning signals racing up her spine.

"It would be nice to have you come by later and give me some advice on arranging things and picking out some furnishings for the office."

Again warning bells sounded in her mind. She didn't know if she wanted to get that involved with him. "I'll consider that, Mr. Monroe." She stepped around him. "Now if you'll excuse me, I'll put this in your room."

He moved back to let her pass, but she sensed his gaze on

her back as she headed into the house. Cory followed, carrying another box.

"Now there's a good match for you, Kate," Cory teased as they carried the boxes upstairs and set them in Daniel's room. "Smart, polite, and I think he's smitten with you."

Heat rose in Kate's cheeks, and she slapped at Cory's arm. "Don't you go getting any ideas about trying to match me up with anybody. I thought you were better than that."

"Nope, just hadn't seen anyone who might be man enough to put up with your independence. Looks like he'd be a match for that."

Kate's face flamed even hotter. No matter what her first impressions had been of Daniel Monroe, no one, not even her brother, would have a hand in how she treated the lawyer. She stole a glance out the window as Daniel picked up a small trunk to move it closer to the front of the wagon. With his sleeves rolled up, she once again noticed the ripple of muscles as he balanced the trunk in his arms and set it down.

What had started out as very dull, hot summer was ending with an interesting turn of events that just might be fun to explore. On her own terms, of course.

CHAPTER FIVE

ADA MULDOON RUSHED her husband from the church and out to the buggy waiting for them. "We're having a houseful of guests today, and I want to be sure to get home before any of them do." If the signs told the truth, young Reverend Seth Winston would be asking to court Erin any day, and Ada was curious to learn more about his friend, Daniel Monroe. Reverend Winston had been a guest before, but she'd only met the young lawyer this morning.

Callum helped his wife up into the carriage. "I don't see any cause for such hurry. By the time those young folks finish their visiting and catching up on news from town, you'll have the food ready to put on the table." His blue eyes twinkled as he climbed up beside her.

"With twenty of us eating today, I have to make sure we have room and plenty of food." The food didn't really concern her, but finding a place for everyone did. Of course, with the two little ones they could use high chairs, but that still left eighteen for the big table. Since they'd both come from large families, Callum had made sure to include plenty of dining space when he'd built the big, new house fifteen years ago.

She mentally calculated where everyone would be seated, especially making sure Reverend Winston would be next to Erin, and of course Daniel would sit between Kate and Cory. A sigh escaped Ada's lips. "Kate worries me. She hasn't shown the least bit of interest in any of the men in town. By now you'd think she'd have found someone to suit her."

"Now, Ada Muldoon, just set your mind at ease. Kate is a grown woman living on her own. When the right man comes along, she'll be willing to give up some of that independence and settle down." Callum reached over and covered her hand with his. "Mark my words; when she finally decides on a man, she'll love him with all she has."

Ada twisted her mouth into a frown. Callum might be certain of their daughter, but that girl had a stubborn streak a mile wide. Ada and Callum both came from strong Irish stock, and it seemed Kate had inherited the strongest traits of both sides of the family. Only Brody had married an Irish lass, Megan. Their other two sons had met their wives on trips to the cattle market, although she'd never understood completely how Sarah, a young woman from back East, had ended up at the Cattleman's Association meeting in Kansas City. Jenny was the daughter of a rancher, so she had been a natural choice for Ian.

As soon as the buggy rode into the yard, Callum stopped so Ada could hop down and start getting things ready inside. She hurried into the house, pulled off her hat and gloves, and tossed them onto the bed. Then she bustled to the kitchen to tie on her apron. Most of the cooking had been done the night before, but the huge roast sat simmering on the back of the stove.

She lifted the lid and sniffed deeply as the aroma of carrots, potatoes, and onions mingled with that of the beef. Satisfied it was done, she removed it from the stove and placed it on towels on the table. Next she lifted the cloth to peek at the rolls. Ready to pop in the oven. They'd be done by the time everyone arrived.

Callum entered the back door. "Anything you want me to do?"

"Yes, make sure we have enough milk for the children." She hadn't seen how much had been brought in this morning and placed in the icebox. "We'll need at least six glasses, and seven if little Elizabeth drinks from a cup." Sarah had quit nursing Jeremy, but he still took a bottle, and Sarah usually carried it with her.

By the time all her family arrived, Ada had everything on the table ready to go. Erin entered with Reverend Winston, and her eyes, as blue as her father's, glowed with happiness. It wouldn't be long now before the young preacher would seek permission to court their daughter, maybe this afternoon. Even though the custom of asking permission to call upon a young lady was going out of style, Ada admired the young man for not being forward with Erin.

As they settled around the table and held hands for Callum's prayer, Ada's love and pride for her family filled her to the brim. The good Lord had filled her cup to overflowing. Then she couldn't help but notice the sour expression on Kate's face as Daniel reached for her hand. Something was amiss here. The two could have barely met, but Kate acted as if she dreaded being near him. Ada bowed her head in prayer. That situation would require a little investigation on Ada's part, and most likely a lot of prayer.

∞

Kate's mind wandered during the prayer. Because her sisters-in-law kept harping on courtship and marriage, she had come to dislike these visits to the ranch on Sundays for family dinners, but Ma and Pa expected it, and she hadn't been able to come up with any plausible excuses as yet. Today Daniel joined them, and Ma had made sure Kate sat between him and Cory. Surely Ma wasn't up to matchmaking, although from all the signs, that's what she was doing with Reverend Winston and Erin.

When Pa ended the prayer, conversation began and food passed around faster than a carousel in the park. Daniel joined right in with her brothers and asked questions about ranching that delighted them to answer. Jenny and Sarah were busy with their babies, and Megan had her hands full with her three young ones. That left Kate to sit back and observe her family from Daniel's viewpoint.

She had learned from Cory that Daniel had only the one sister, Abigail, and she had been Reverend Winston's sister Rachel's best friend back in Connecticut. Even so, all the lively talk and confusion didn't seem to faze Daniel. He laughed at Donavan's corny jokes and talked about their meeting at Rachel's wedding last spring.

When she turned her head from talking to Cory, Daniel was watching her.

The heat rose in her cheeks. "I hope you don't find our family too rowdy for your tastes."

Daniel laughed. "Not at all. I really enjoy being with your family. Seth has two brothers and two sisters, so it was always lively around their house, and I enjoyed many splendid times there. I think that's why Abigail and Rachel were so close. They were almost like sisters." He leaned closer. "If I'm not mistaken, I think Seth is quite taken with your sister and she with him."

Splendid times, taken with each other...there was that fancy talk again. She had to listen close to understand him as sometimes he spoke faster than she could listen. "I think so too, and Reverend Winston couldn't find a sweeter girl to be a minister's wife. She's got all the talents: cooking, sewing, and taking care of a family."

"Really? I would think that you would be talented in those areas yourself, although I do remember what Cory said about your cooking." A smile curved the corner of his mouth.

Every time he looked at her like that, something happened to her insides that heated her temperature faster than the ninety degrees outside. "Don't believe everything Cory tells you, Mr. Monroe."

Before he had time to answer Ma said, "I understand you're getting all moved into your offices in town. When will you be open for business, Mr. Monroe?"

Daniel laid his napkin neatly on the table. "I had hoped it would be this week, but a few things still need to be done. I asked Kate if she could help out, but it seems her studies are taking up her spare time."

Kate's face flushed again as all eyes turned toward her. "I–I just don't think I'd be of much help with fixing up your office."

Erin's eyes lit up. "Oh, Mr. Monroe, I'd love to help you. I'm quite good at arranging furniture."

Kate almost choked and grabbed her glass of water. Erin help Daniel? She should have told him yes. What did Erin know about offices and such? Of course, coming in to town to help him would give her more opportunity to see Reverend Winston, but Ma would never allow it.

But then her ma surprised her, saying, "Why, I think that's a fine idea, Erin. You have a good eye for colors and styles. Maybe you can bring a woman's touch to the place that will make it more inviting to Mr. Monroe's clients."

Kate's mouth gaped open. Ma was actually approving of Erin doing this? A little seed of jealousy planted itself, but Kate refused to acknowledge it. Let her sister do whatever she wanted to help Mr. Monroe. Kate Muldoon had more important things to do.

∞

Daniel ducked his head to hide his grin at the look on Kate's face, even though she quickly composed herself. Erin was not exactly the sister he'd wanted for help, but maybe he could learn more about Kate while working with Erin.

Although completely different in coloring and a few years younger, Erin did remind him of his own sister and her enthusiasm for projects. A bit of homesickness crept in as the image of Abigail's chestnut hair and sparkling brown eyes filled his mind. "I think that will be fine. I look forward to hearing your ideas."

Erin fairly bounced on her seat. "Oh, Ma, can you take me into town tomorrow? We can look through the catalogs at the store and see what's available."

Mrs. Muldoon chuckled and shook her head. "I suppose that can be arranged. The sooner you can get started, the sooner he can open for business."

Kate said nothing but twisted her fork in a swirl through her food. Erin babbled on about a rug and lamps and furniture for the reception area. Whatever she suggested would be all right with him. He glanced around the table at the family and missed his own more than he'd like to admit. All six of the Muldoon offspring had some red in their hair, ranging from the deep auburn of Kate's to the carrot red of Ian's. Erin's was more golden than red, but when the sun hit it, he couldn't help but notice the bright streaks of red. This was a fine-looking family and one he truly desired as friends.

He smiled and leaned toward Sarah. "I must say Jeremy has grown quite a bit since you were in Briar Ridge last spring for Rachel and Nathan's wedding."

She bounced the boy on her knee. "I know. Mama would hardly recognize him now that he's started walking." At that moment the toddler stiffened his back and pushed his feet toward the floor. Sarah laughed. "OK, you can go play with your cousins." She set him on the floor, and he toddled away with his finger in his mouth.

Mrs. Muldoon rose from her chair and picked up a few dishes. "Time for us to get these things cleaned up and let you men go talk business."

All the women began helping, but he noticed Erin draw close to her mother and whisper a few words. Mrs. Muldoon grinned and shooed her away. A huge smile filled the girl's face as she moved to Seth's side.

Seth grinned and nodded then tapped Mr. Muldoon on the shoulder. "Sir, if you don't mind, Erin would like to show me around the ranch."

Mr. Muldoon glanced from one to the other then waved his hand. "Go on and have a little fun. You might keep an eye on your nieces and nephews while you're out there."

"Thank you, Pa. We'll look out for them."

Daniel watched the young couple walk side by side, not really touching, but in definite contact with each other. Seth had come West to serve God, and God had blessed him with the company of a pretty girl to boot. No such relationship had been on Daniel's mind, but it would be nice to find a girl and settle down.

Perhaps a trip West would be good for Abigail too. She'd see that the place wasn't all heathens, and some very nice people lived here in Porterfield. Of course, his parents would be dead set against such an idea, but he could see Abigail's spirit of adventure and desire to learn new things giving her an enjoyable time in Texas.

He turned toward the parlor where the men had retreated and came face-to-face with Kate. Heat rose in his cheeks, and his tongue glued to the roof his mouth.

"My brothers and Pa will be talking cattle all afternoon. You should join them. It will help you know more about the people who live around here."

What he'd rather do was stroll with her outdoors as Seth and Erin were doing. "I thought you'd be helping your ma."

She shook her head, and the auburn curls trembled on her

neck. "She's got plenty of help with Megan, Jenny, and Sarah. All they talk about is babies and food. I have no interest in either one."

"I see. So what would you rather be doing?"

"Nothing out here, but I'm headed to check on the children. Sarah and Jenny say it's time for Jeremy and Elizabeth to have a nap, so I'm going to corral them and bring them inside."

This should be interesting. Those two little ones could be a handful. "Could you use my help?"

She narrowed her eyes and pursed her lips. "I can handle them. Neither one of them knows you, so they might start screaming." Kate turned with a flounce of her tan skirt. A bit of ruffled petticoat peeked from beneath the hem.

That he hadn't expected to see. Kate seemed to be more of the no-frills type with her plain dress. He admired the way the brown belt encircled her waist and made it appear even smaller than it was. When she picked up each child and tucked them under her arms, he also realized she had strength that blouses and skirts hid. He laughed at the sight of her marching toward the house, a toddler kicking and squirming under each arm.

No matter if Kate said she had no interest in babies or other things of the household, she'd make a fine mother some day, and it would be nice to have her as mother to his own. His breath caught in his throat, and he gulped. Where had that thought come from? He'd known her less than a week, but already her hazel eyes and deep red curls captivated him more than he liked to admit.

Chapter Six

Kate stifled a yawn. How she would like to go into the back room and lie down with her sleeping niece and nephew. The afternoon heat bore down, making outdoor play for the children unbearable, so they were now in the kitchen enjoying cookies and lemonade.

By the time she had returned from delivering Elizabeth and Jeremy to their mothers, Daniel had joined the men in Pa's office. Reverend Winston and Erin were still out wandering around, although how they could stand the heat, she'd never know.

Another week and September would be upon them. Even the arrival of September in Texas didn't mean cooler temperatures. Sometimes the fall days were worse than midsummer.

She sat in the shade of the front porch and pushed the swing back and forth with her toe. If she could talk Cory into leaving early, maybe she'd still have time to read before the evening was over. Of course she'd have to help Aunt Mae get ready for the boarders the next morning, but there should be time to do a little reading.

Reverend Winston and Erin sauntered around from the stables. Erin had her hands hooked through the preacher's elbow and seemed oblivious to anything else around her. Her bonnet had slipped from her head, and her golden-red hair gleamed in the sunshine. Once again Kate pushed down a tide of jealousy. Why couldn't her hair be as pretty as Erin's instead of the dark red that was neither brown nor red? The sun didn't seem to bother Erin's complexion either. It fairly glowed.

Kate stood and waved. "Hey, you two, how can you stand the heat? Come on up to the porch out of the sun. Ma made lemonade."

Erin's hands dropped from the preacher's arm, and her cheeks flamed. "Oh, it hasn't been that bad, but lemonade does sound tasty right now." She hurried past Kate and went inside.

Reverend Winston sat in a chair across from Kate. His sandy hair clung about his forehead in damp curls. He held his hat between his knees and twirled it in his hands. "A lemonade sounds good about now."

"I'm sure it does." Kate leaned back and gave the swing a gentle push. "Tell me how a young man like you wound up way out here in Texas. I know your cousin had something to do with it, but there has to be more."

He nodded and swiped at his face with his neckerchief. "I saw all the wonderful things my father did as a minister and decided that's what I wanted to do with my life too. My cousin Sarah and I kept up with each other through letters, and she told me about the church here needing a pastor, and the next thing I knew, I had an offer to come out here and pastor this church. I can't believe it's been over a year."

Kate blinked. It had been that long, and she hadn't really bothered to get to know this young man. Now he was interested in her sister.

"Well, I for one am most happy that you did." Erin stepped through the door bearing a pitcher of lemonade and several glasses. "And look who I found to join us for a little cooling refreshment." She grinned and set the tray on the table by the chair.

Daniel nodded and sat on the swing next to Kate. Suddenly the afternoon became even warmer than it was, and she straightened up so as not to be so close to him. Her palms grew moist with perspiration, and she rubbed them on her skirt. Erin chattered on about Daniel's office and what she'd like to do. At least it kept Kate from having to say anything.

When Erin finally stopped for breath, Kate said, "I thought you had joined the men in Pa's office."

"I did, but when your mother came and said she had lemonade and cookies, it sounded too good to pass up, and then I spotted Erin headed out here where you and Reverend Winston were talking and decided to join you. I hope you don't mind."

His lopsided grin threatened to undo her again. She didn't really mind, but being around him gave her the most uncomfortable feelings she'd ever experienced around a man. "Not at all. Reverend Winston was just telling me about his coming to Porterfield."

"I'm so glad Reverend Blackman decided to stay in town.

His mentoring me through this first year has been a great help."

"And I'm glad you considered me when talking with Mayor Tate. He certainly has big plans for this town." Daniel sipped his lemonade and glanced at Kate.

She turned her head and grabbed a glass. Why did he have to look at her like that? She swallowed some lemonade then said, "Yes, he gets involved in everything. He even instigated an end-of-summer celebration for next Saturday."

Erin laughed and brushed cookie crumbs from her skirt. "He's also sent invitations to other towns around here to tell them more womenfolk are wanted to attend. It's difficult to have a big country dance if you don't have enough females."

Daniel placed his elbow on the back of the swing. "It seems that the men do quite well for themselves. I haven't heard any complaining at the boardinghouse."

"Which only goes to prove that a man doesn't need a woman to run a household for him. He's quite capable of doing it himself. We women who live in Porterfield aren't that desperate to have a man looking out for us either. I'd much rather be helping at the infirmary than cooking meals and taking care of a houseful of kids." Kate crossed her arms over her chest. Just let Daniel say one word, and she'd jump up and go in the house quicker than a field mouse running from a barn cat.

Erin's mouth gaped open. "Kate Muldoon. How can you say such a thing? The Bible says that women are to take care of and honor their men. God put us on Earth to grow and multiply and serve each other."

Heat rose in Kate's cheeks. "Well, the Muldoons have certainly done a good job of that. I'm just saying that women should be allowed to pursue their own interests and not be expected to get married and settle down so soon." She stole a glance at Daniel, who sat beside her with a bemused smirk on his face. Anger began with a tiny flame. She stood and clenched her hands into fists on her hips. "I don't know why you think that's so funny, Mr. Monroe. If you came to Porterfield expecting to find a wife to take care of you and host your grand social life, you're due for disappointment." She grabbed the folds of skirt at her hips and swirled around to head indoors. She refused to stay on the porch and get into an argument with a perfect stranger.

The door slammed behind Kate, and she leaned against the wall. Daniel wasn't really a stranger, and he had done nothing to provoke an argument except to smirk at her statement. Ever since that man had arrived in town, her life had turned topsy-turvy. Only one thing to do. Avoid him like the plague.

∞

Daniel set his glass down on the tray. What had set Kate off like that? He hadn't said anything to create that anger.

"I'm sorry, Mr. Monroe," Erin apologized. "Ma and my brothers' wives have been after Kate to find a husband. She has her mind made up for a nursing career, and she gets riled up when people think she should marry instead."

Daniel stroked his chin. "I would say that Kate Muldoon has whatever it takes to be whatever she wants to be." From what he'd seen, Kate was intelligent as well as strong. She just didn't always keep her temper in check.

Cory sauntered out to the porch. "What happened out here? Kate came tearing into the kitchen saying she wanted to leave now and get back to town. Said she had some reading to do."

Erin sighed. "Oh, you know, Kate. One little mention of families and wives and husbands and she gets her dander up."

"Well, Ma says she can't go back to town alone, so it looks like we're going to have to go back with her."

Daniel jumped to his feet. "No, you two stay here. I'll go back with her."

Cory shook his head. "You don't know what you're getting yourself into, but if that's what you want and Kate is agreeable, it's OK with me. Reverend Winston and I have our horses, so we'll come later. Thanks."

Daniel nodded and stepped through the door. The women's voices raised in conversation reached his ears. The other Muldoon brothers and Mr. Muldoon continued to talk as though nothing unusual was going on.

At the kitchen door he stopped. Kate stood with her back to him, hands on her hips in that stubborn stance he'd come to recognize. Mrs. Muldoon sat at the table gazing up at her daughter with just as determined a look as Kate's stand.

"I don't care how much you want to get back to town. I am not letting you take the wagon back alone." She held up her hand at Kate's protest.

"No buts. March yourself back out there and be the hostess you should be." At that moment she spotted Daniel in the doorway. "Hello, Mr. Monroe. How can I help you?"

Kate's shoulders stiffened, and her hands clutched the folds of fabric in her skirt.

Daniel said, "I've come to say that I will be glad to escort

Miss Kate back to town. I confess to being a bit tired from my travels, so I don't mind leaving now."

Kate spun around, all color drained from her face. "I don't need an escort. I can handle the wagon and team on my own."

Daniel dipped his chin in agreement. "By all means, I'll let you do just that, but it seems to me that you're not going to be able to leave without someone with you, and I certainly don't mind being that someone."

Mrs. Muldoon clapped her hands and grinned broadly. "That's the perfect solution. I'll just fix up a little parcel for you take back with you, Mr. Monroe. You might want some of that berry pie when you get back to Porterfield."

The other women all turned to tasks that took them out of the kitchen while Mrs. Muldoon cut several slices of pie and put them on a tin plate then covered them with a cloth. During this entire time Kate didn't say a word, but Daniel noted the flash in her eyes. There was plenty she wanted to say, but she refrained in front of her mother.

Mrs. Muldoon handed Daniel the plate. "Now go if you're so fired up about getting back to town. It was nice meeting you, Mr. Monroe, and I hope you can stay longer next time." Her gaze cut to Kate as though daring her to say otherwise.

"I'll get my things and meet you outside. I'm sure you'll want to say good-bye to everyone." Her red hair, tied back with a dark blue bow, bounced on her shoulders as Kate strode through the door and across the dining area.

This might prove to be one of the most interesting rides he'd ever taken in his life. Daniel followed after her, stopping to greet the other family members and thank them for their hospitality.

Cory leaned against the porch rail, watching as Kate hitched up the horses to the wagon. He pushed his hat back on his head and turned to Daniel. "I sure hope you know what you're getting yourself into," he cautioned. "She's either going to talk your ear off about whatever riled her, or she's going to give you the cold shoulder and say nothing all the way back to town. Either way, I'm glad it's you and not me."

Daniel planted his hat on his head. "See you back at the boardinghouse." He was glad now that he'd accepted a ride out to the ranch with Sarah and Donavan. Otherwise he'd have no reason to ride with Kate.

Her back straight and head held high, Kate sat in the driver's seat and held the reins. No way he'd be able to wrangle the reins from her. He placed the cloth-covered plate on the floor and climbed up beside her. "I'm ready when you are, Miss Muldoon."

She clicked her tongue and flipped the reins but didn't say a word. So maybe he was to get the silent treatment. He'd rather listen to her voice whether it rose in anger or not.

An apology would seem in order, but he didn't know exactly what to apologize for. Still, it was worth a try. "Miss Muldoon, I am truly sorry if I said something amiss earlier. One minute we were having a pleasant conversation, and the next you were angry and ran into the house."

She didn't turn her head, but he noticed her take a deep breath. "The apology should come from me. I jumped to the conclusion from your reaction to Erin's statement that you are like my brothers and most of the other men I know and think women should confine themselves to the home."

"Oh, I think your brothers just love you and want you to be happy like they are."

"But I don't need what they have to be happy. I have my own life, and I like it the way it is."

"Yes, and I want to say that I admire you for wanting to be a nurse. Taking care of sick and injured people is a noble endeavor, and I'm sure Doctor Jensen appreciates your help."

This time her mouth dropped open but closed tight again right away. Her eyebrows remained raised as she stared straight ahead. Even though he had meant what he said about admiring her desire to a be nurse, he still couldn't figure out why any woman would want to be around sick people not of their own family or face the blood and stench of wounds inflicted by guns or accidents.

He reached down for the plate Mrs. Muldoon had given him. "This will be very tasty with a glass of tea when we get back to town. Your mother is a fine cook. Does she serve a meal like that every Sunday?"

"No, my sisters-in-law take turns with her. It's a nice time to get together and see all the family."

At least she was talking now. That was a step in the right direction. He swiped at the back of his neck with a handkerchief. "I'm glad I didn't wear my jacket. I still can't get over the heat."

This time Kate laughed, and it was music to his ears. "I know it must have been close to one hundred degrees today. Too bad you came in August and have to experience our worst months, but it'll make you appreciate the cooler weather even more. We don't have much of a fall around here. Cold weather comes so late that our trees don't turn color until it's winter in most places."

Her voice had such a lilting quality to it that he could listen to it all day. If something happened and he became ill or was hurt, Miss Kate Muldoon would certainly be his choice for a caregiver. If he could learn to stay away from topics that brought on that Irish temper, he could foresee a delightful relationship developing.

Chapter Seven

Mae stood at Kate's door early Monday morning. Last evening, when Kate and Daniel returned from the ranch, a tension filled the air that troubled Mae. After eating only a few bites of the pie Ada had sent, Kate had jumped up and disappeared into her room. Daniel had said Kate wanted to read and that was why they had come back early.

Maybe so, but Mae sensed much more to it than simply wanting to read. She knocked. "Kate, may I come in?"

Muffled sounds on the other side reached her ears. Then the doorknob turned and Kate opened the door. "I was just getting ready to leave to go over to the infirmary."

"I figured you were, but I'd like to talk a moment if we may."

Kate opened the door wider and gestured for Mae to enter. The bed had been made hastily, and last night's garments lay in a heap at the end of the bed. Kate hung her head and grabbed at the clothes. "Sorry, I'll clean up later." She deposited her bundle on the bed and moved some books from a chair for Mae to sit down. "What do you need to talk about?"

"You seemed upset last night when Mr. Monroe brought you home. Didn't you have a good visit with the family?"

Kate shoved her things aside and flopped onto the bed. "Yes, I did, but then talk turned to the role of women. Erin is just like everyone else, find a man, settle down, and have a family. There's just so much more to life than cooking, babies, and family."

Mae smiled. Beautiful, talented Kate, the little black sheep who wanted to go her own way in life and not follow the others. No matter how hard Ada tried, she couldn't tame the spirit of her eldest daughter. Of course with four brothers, Kate always thought she had to be doing everything they did and even sometimes do it better. Kate reminded Mae of herself before Patrick Sullivan came into her life. "I see. And how did that conversation get started?"

Kate flung her arms over her head and clasped her hands together. "I don't even remember. With so many choices and opportunities available to women these days, why does it always come down to a woman serving a man?" She sat up straight and held out one hand. "And I know what the Bible says about wives submitting to husbands, so don't start that on me."

Mae would have to choose her words carefully to keep in Kate's good graces. She didn't want her niece deciding Mae wouldn't or couldn't understand. "Honey, God gave us a free will to make choices in life. Women make choices to live the life they want by marrying and raising a family or by choosing to remain single and pursuing service to God."

Kate let that soak in a minute then tilted her head. "Aunt Mae, do you think the girls who work in saloons made the choice to live like they do?"

Mae sucked in her breath. What had prompted a question like that? "I'm not sure. Their choice may have been from necessity to make a living or to escape their past. Why do you ask?"

Kate shrugged. "I don't know. I've heard so many tales about what goes on in a saloon that I wonder why any woman would want to live at a man's beck and call."

"Like I said, it may be out of necessity. Maybe they can't get out once they get started." Gilford, the next town over, had a saloon that was the site of many a gun battle and gambling woes. No telling what would happen here when that new place, the Branding Iron, opened up on Saturday.

Mae shook off those thoughts. No sense in letting her mind ramble when Kate was her concern. "Honey, did Mr. Monroe say anything to make you upset? You sure were in a hurry to get away from his company."

Kate gathered up her books and stood. "Oh, his fancy clothes and speaking and manners get on my nerves. He's well educated, but from the looks of things, he still has old-fashioned ideas of a woman's place in society."

She hurried out the door. "I'll be back to help after my lessons."

Yes, she would. No matter how much time she spent with the doctors, Kate never forgot her duties at the boardinghouse. Mae sighed and headed to the kitchen to finish breakfast preparations for her boarders. He'd only been in town a few days, but already she could see that Daniel Monroe had stirred up more than a little interest in Kate.

Kate hurried down Main Street to the infirmary. Doc Jensen wouldn't complain if she was late, but she didn't want him to think she'd begun to shirk her responsibilities. When she arrived, Elliot Jensen was already there sorting the instruments and checking a strange new contraption.

"Sorry I'm late, but I was talking with Aunt Mae, and time got away." She stashed her books in a corner of the reception room and hung her straw hat on a hook by the door.

Elliot didn't acknowledge her presence for a moment. In fact, at times it seemed he resented her even being here, but he still did what his uncle asked and helped her learn her duties. He turned around and studied her with his deep blue eyes. She had considered him to be a handsome young man when his uncle first brought him to Porterfield, but Elliot's personality left much to be desired, in her estimation.

Finally he spoke through thin lips. "Uncle Nehemiah isn't here yet." He stood by a container that looked like a large steel cook pot with a lid that had strange contraptions on the sides. "Come look at this autoclave. It uses high-pressure saturated steam to sterilize medical instruments. This is a great step toward having more sanitary conditions for our patients."

"Oh, that's what your uncle bought from that medical supply catalog. Has he used it yet?" The only thing she knew about the pot was that it was supposed to make the instruments they used cleaner and safer than just pouring alcohol over them. Doc Jensen was very particular when it came to the safety of his patients.

"Of course not. We just unpacked it yesterday."

He didn't have to be so rude. Kate leaned over to examine it more closely. "Let's get all the surgical instruments together so we can try this thing out."

"Good idea, Kate," Doc Jensen said.

Kate turned to see the doctor hanging his hat and jacket on the hooks. With his thick white hair, mustache, and rosy cheeks, he looked more like someone's grandfather than a doctor. Too bad he and Mrs. Jensen never had children of their own. He rolled up his sleeves and strode toward them. He nodded to Kate, and she gathered up the scalpels, scissors, and other instruments they used. She placed them on the table by the pot.

"Now while I take care of this, Elliot, you take Kate and drill her on anatomy. I'm going to test her on the terms later." His light blue eyes twinkled as he shooed them out of the room.

Much as she wanted to stay and see what he did with the autoclave, Kate gathered up her books and headed to the examination room. Despite Elliot's patient tutoring, Kate's mind wandered away from medicine to law.

Today Erin would be in town to help Daniel with decorating his office. Envy crept into Kate's heart. Why did her sister inherit all the talent in the family? Erin could cook anything a person wanted, and just like Ma, she rarely if ever used a recipe. She made her own clothes, helped Ma make the curtains and quilts for the boardinghouse, and she could knit and crochet beautiful pieces. Kate had been too busy chasing after her brothers and riding horses to worry about such things, and Ma had let her be after several attempts to teach her household skills had failed.

Surely her ability to take care of sick and wounded people with great care and without flinching should count for something. Daniel did say he admired her for that, but it wasn't what a man would want in a wife. Kate flinched at the thought. She had no intentions of marrying, she reminded herself, least of all one Daniel Monroe.

Elliot interrupted his tutoring to clear his throat. "Kate, your mind is elsewhere this morning. Perhaps we should save this for another time when you're not so distracted and more willing to learn."

"I'm sorry, Elliot. I know you're trying to help me, but I've had a lot on my mind this weekend. If we're not busy this afternoon, I can come back then." If she hurried back to the boardinghouse and finished her chores, maybe she'd have time to catch up with Erin and Daniel and see what they were doing.

He scowled at her. "Whatever you want." Then he began gathering up the books and papers scattered around him.

Kate shuddered. He didn't have to be so rude. It was such a contrast to the kindness he showed his patients. She'd never quite understood him.

He glanced up at her just then as though wondering why she was still there. The sadness in his eyes leapt at her and clutched her heart. Maybe she should be nicer to this young man and find the reasons behind his behavior. But then again, it was none of her business, and it would be rude to ask. Besides, he was such a private man he would never confide in her anyway.

She gathered up her belongings and explained to Doc Jensen why she had to leave. She glanced behind her just in time to see Daniel enter the building and go up the stairs to his office. Now her feet fairly flew the rest of the way. Chores this morning would be done in record time.

ꝏ

Daniel unlocked his office and stepped inside. With the desk and two bookshelves now in place, the room didn't look quite as bare and lonely. He still had to decide what to do about the outer room. It was designed to be a reception area, but without someone to receive clients, it was of little use now.

He strolled to the window to again survey the town. A flash of color down the street caught his attention just as Kate rounded the corner to head for the boardinghouse. Kathleen Muldoon was one mysterious young woman. He had watched her in church yesterday, and the expression he saw in her face could have only come from having peace with God. It sure made a stark contrast to the looks of anger and frustration he'd witnessed later in the day.

Kate could sing too. He'd heard her clear soprano voice over the others. All the Muldoon family had good singing voices. With their number, they could be their own choir, but Kate's voice still stood out. She could sing, handle a team of horses, serve meals to fifteen or more people at a time, and take care of sick people. A very talented young woman, Kate aroused feelings in Daniel that he hadn't experienced before. Even Rachel had never made him feel this way. But then he'd known Rachel all her life.

A wagon with Mrs. Muldoon and Erin stopped at the

general store. Maybe he could learn more about her from Erin today. He returned to the street to greet the ladies just as they alighted from the wagon.

"Good morning, Mrs. Muldoon, Miss Muldoon. I take it you're ready to see what can be done with those two rooms I have for an office." He doffed his hat and grinned.

Erin's cheeks turned pink. "We are, Mr. Monroe. If you could show me the space, I can get some idea of what we need."

"Certainly." He grasped her elbow to assist her across the hard-packed dirt.

Mrs. Muldoon smiled at Daniel. "Nice to see you again, Mr. Monroe. I'll be in the store when you're finished." She turned and headed over to Grayson's store.

When they reached the office space, Erin walked completely around both rooms. "What a lovely piece," she said, stopping before a large cherry desk whose surface shone with many years of use and polishing. She ran her hand across the surface. "It's beautiful, and the carved drawer pulls are extraordinary."

"Thank you, it is special. It belonged to my grandfather who was a judge in Hartford. I inherited it when he died several years ago." Not only did the desk remind him of his grandfather's integrity, but it also brought a piece of home closer to him. "I also had the bookshelves from my old office shipped. Father had them made especially for me, so I wanted to keep them. As you can see, they're already filled with my books. Aside from my leather desk chair, that's all the furnishings I have." It did look rather bleak now that he observed it from a layperson's point of view. He stood silent as Erin continued to walk and stroke her chin.

"I saw a wool rug at Grayson's that would look quite nice on the floor, and a few tables and chairs for your clients can be ordered from the catalog he has. He also has some cane-bottomed ladderback chairs. I remember seeing several lamps in his store that will do nicely as well. They are solid colors and will blend with the rug."

"Yes, I can see that will be perfect. In Hartford we had electricity, but here I suppose I'll have to go back to oil lamps." As far as he could tell, no signs of gas for lighting had been visible either. This was about as primitive as he had imagined, but the town was larger than he had anticipated.

Erin took one last look around. "Let's head on over to Grayson's now and see what we can find."

An hour later they were back in the office rolling out the rug Mr. Grayson had helped bring over. After getting it situated, he could see the space beginning to come alive already. They'd also bought one of the cane chairs and ordered a side chair upholstered in a dark green fabric and a small table and lamp to sit beside it.

Erin stepped back and surveyed the room. "With the furniture we ordered, you'll have a nice work space. I see you have your diploma and credentials or whatever they're called on the wall, but I think a few paintings would be nice too." She turned with her finger on her chin. "Are you interested in going with a Western theme, or do you prefer something more traditional?"

He hadn't even considered a theme for the office, but anything to do with Western culture should be appropriate for Texas. "Let's go Western."

"Perfect. We can go to Dallas and find some good ones

there." She turned to leave. "I think that's about all I can do for now."

Daniel held out his hand. "Would you stay another minute or so? I–I have a few questions." If he didn't ask now, he may not have the chance again soon.

She cocked her head, surveying him. A long silence fell as he struggled with what to say. Finally a grin spread across Erin's face. "Does this by chance have anything to do with my sister?"

Heat rose in Daniel's face. Of course she would think of that first. "Yes, it does. I'm afraid everything I do seems to irritate her, and I'm at a loss as to how to approach her."

Erin laughed. "Kate is one unique person. I've lived with her almost nineteen years, but we couldn't be more different. She's independent and speaks her mind, that's for sure."

Daniel had seen that much in her already, but it still didn't explain why she didn't like him. Before he could respond to Erin, Kate burst through the door.

She stopped short just inside his office. "Oh, I see you've been busy, Erin. It looks nice."

Erin cut a glance toward Daniel and grinned. "Yes, we've been busy. What brings you up here? I figured you'd be studying or at the infirmary."

"I was this morning, but when I finished helping Aunt Mae, I decided to come see how things were going with the decorating."

"I see. Well, my part for the day is done, so I'll leave you two to make any further decisions." With a wave of her hand Erin was gone.

Daniel gulped. What to do now? He gestured toward the

leather desk chair. "Have a seat and tell me what you think of my office."

Kate eased into the chair as though not sure whether she should sit in it or not. Then she ran her hand over the satin-smooth top of his desk. "This is beautiful. No wonder you wanted to bring it with you. I guess it helps to have something from home when you're this far away."

"Yes, it does." An idea popped into his head, and he spoke before he could get cold feet. "Miss Muldoon, would you be so kind as allow me to escort you to the end-of-summer celebration this Saturday?"

Her mouth dropped open, but she quickly closed it and stared at him. Perspiration trickled down his neck. Why hadn't he waited until they knew each other longer? She probably still considered him a stranger.

A moment later, she grinned. "I think that would be quite nice. Thank you, Mr. Monroe." She stood. "Now if you'll excuse me, I have some things I need to do. I'll see you back at the boardinghouse at noon."

Daniel stood speechless in the center of the room as she glided across the floor and out the door. When he heard the door downstairs close, he plopped into his chair and let his breath out in whoosh. She said yes. Maybe this would be the first step toward a friendship that could blossom into something more. At least he hoped that to be true.

Chapter Eight

When Saturday dawned, Kate chose her coolest blouse and skirt for the end-of-summer celebration, although no matter what she chose, it'd be damp by midmorning. A party on the last day of August had been the mayor's idea. Of course it didn't mean the actual end of summer, but school did start the next week.

On Monday Daniel had asked to escort her for the day. Despite her pledge to avoid him, she couldn't help but delight at the complete look of surprise on his face when she had accepted. Kate chuckled. Keep a man guessing was her motto. As long as he didn't figure her out completely, she could have a little fun confusing him.

When she exited her room, Daniel waited in the front hallway by the stairs. He had chosen denim trousers and a cotton shirt like her brothers wore. He also wore boots and carried a beige-colored wide-brim hat in his hands. Her heart did a double take. Daniel didn't look the least bit like the fancy lawyer he'd been all week. In fact, he looked even handsomer than he had that first day in town.

He bowed at the waist and swept his hat across the way. "You look lovely this morning, Miss Muldoon. I'm sure I'll be the envy of every young man in town."

There he went again with his fancy talk, but it was rather nice to hear. She smiled and positioned a wide-brim straw hat over her hair. She secured it with two long pins then picked up her purse. "I'm ready whenever you are."

Aunt Mae followed them to the front door and waved as they made their way down the walk to the street. "Y'all have a good time, and you can come back here for lunch."

Kate returned the wave. They probably would be back to eat, but it would be interesting to see what kind of things might be available in the booths lining Main Street. "It looks like they've gone all out for decorations. You'd think it was the Fourth of July or something. But then Mayor Tate isn't one to do things halfway."

"I've talked with him at great length this week. He says plans are underway to build a courthouse in the middle of town and turn it into a town square. Some of the stores may have to move, but it could be quite an asset for Porterfield."

Kate imagined the objections from the businesses that would have to move, but if it meant progress for the town, they'd eventually concede. She glanced about the street and took in the bank, the mortuary, the infirmary, and other establishments. Suddenly she stopped short.

"Is Jim Darnell opening his saloon today?" She narrowed her eyes at the flashy new sign above the Branding Iron Saloon, the latest addition to Main Street. This establishment shouted trouble ahead.

"Yes, I'm afraid so. I just hope he will abide by the rules set up by the town council. It'll be up to Cory to see that they're followed, and the new sheriff isn't one to put up with a lot of trouble either. He likes his town peaceful and quiet."

That's what Kate figured. "I hope you're right. Drinking and gambling are the last things this town needs." She pointed across the street. "Let's go see what the schedule is for today."

They sauntered over to the town hall building housing the mayor's office and the town meeting room. Stopping in front of a flyer listing the day's activities, Daniel grinned and put his finger on one of the entries. "Now that's what I thought I'd find in Texas: a sharp-shooting contest."

"Look there, some cowboy competitions are planned. I think Pa and some of the other ranchers are bringing in bulls and untamed horses for the cowboys to ride, and the calf-roping is sure to bring out lots of men." That was another thing about men that puzzled Kate, their need for competition and winning at all costs.

She gazed up at Daniel. He didn't appear to be the competing type, but then his skills probably didn't fit in with those necessary in competitions like the ones planned. Even in his more casual clothes he didn't look like other men. His broad shoulders showed he did have strength, but the way he walked and carried himself spoke of the true gentleman inside.

Daniel pointed toward the station. "That must be what's going up down by the railroad depot. I see some type of arena being erected."

"That's where the cattle are brought after round-up.

Pa and the others don't take the cattle on long trail rides to Kansas City anymore. Trains are far easier for transporting and don't take near as long. Pa still takes a good many of his men with him to make sure the cattle are handled properly and are loaded in the right places for auction."

"You do seem to know a lot about cattle and horses."

Kate laughed. "I've been riding ever since I could straddle a horse, and I roped my first calf when I was six. Ranching is all I knew growing up. I loved the animals and helped Pa and the men take care of them. Horses are an important part of ranching, and we take good care of ours."

"Is that when you developed your love of medicine?"

They turned and began walking toward one of the game booths. "Yes, whenever one of our animals was sick or injured, I always helped take care of it. The hardest part was putting one down because of a broken leg or other injury we couldn't treat." She'd never forget the first time she watched Pa shoot one of his horses. It hurt her to the core, but she also recognized the grief in her father's eyes as he took care of the burying.

"I think having to kill those animals we couldn't treat is what made me decide treating people might be easier. I loved the animals, but saving lives was more what I wanted to do."

"Sometimes you can't save human lives either. One of my good friends in college fell from his horse while playing polo and broke his neck. There was nothing the doctors could do to save him."

Kate glanced at him quickly. "That must have been difficult for you. I've only seen three people die, and it was even harder than watching a horse go down."

"Yes, it was difficult to see a life cut short in its prime.

Those are things we have to learn to deal with as we grow older. My faith in God has helped me through some trying situations."

Kate understood that. If she didn't have faith that God was the ultimate healer, she'd never be able to face some of the injuries and illnesses that came into Doc Jensen's office.

They stopped at a game booth, but before Daniel could speak to the gamer, Mayor Tate and Cory called out to him. As her brother and the mayor approached them, Mayor Tate removed his bowler. "Sorry to call you to work during the festivities, Mr. Monroe, but we need you to come with us to visit Jim Darnell. Since he's opening his saloon today, we want to make sure he understands the rules we've set up. He's been given a copy of the bylaws, but we need to make sure he plans to keep them."

Daniel turned to Kate. "Looks like I need to go with them. Where can I find you when I return?"

Kate waved her hand. "I'll be at the church where the children's games are."

He joined the mayor and Cory to head up the street toward the Branding Iron. Kate stood with her hands on her hips and shook her head. What a sight they made. Daniel and Cory both were well over six feet tall and towered over the shorter, pudgy mayor. No doubt he believed he needed their presence to get his point across to Darnell. Kate wished she could follow and be a witness to the meeting, but Cory would never let her set foot inside a saloon, and Daniel would probably protest as well. Men. Always trying to protect women from what they thought women shouldn't see or know.

With a sigh she turned and headed to the church yard.

She'd have to be satisfied with waiting until later and getting an account from Cory, if he'd even tell her then.

∞

Daniel glanced over Mayor Tate's head and grinned at Cory. They were along to reinforce the mayor and give him confidence. The mayor may bluster his way through many situations, but this wasn't one of them.

They entered the saloon, and it looked just like what Daniel had imagined it would. A burly bartender sporting a handlebar mustache and slicked-back hair wiped glasses at the bar. Round tables were scattered about the room, a few of them with felt tops with holders for chips and cards. Several tables were already filled with men and a few of Jim's ladies.

Daniel noted right off that these were older women with just a few younger ones. Their costume necklines and hemlines left little to the imagination. Heat rose in Daniel's cheeks. This was one establishment he didn't intend to visit unless absolutely necessary.

When the clientele realized who had entered, they stopped talking and stared. Even the piano player stopped and turned to observe.

The mayor straightened his shoulders and stood as tall as his stature would allow. "We're here to see Jim Darnell."

"I'm Darnell." Daniel turned to see a tall, well-dressed gentleman with a trim mustache and a cigar between his teeth approaching them.

The mayor removed his hat, as did Daniel. Cory merely flicked his to the back of his head. The mayor gestured toward an empty table. "May we sit and discuss some business with you? This is Deputy Cory Muldoon and our town attorney, Daniel Monroe."

Darnell nodded, and the four of them seated themselves at the table. "May I order you something to drink?"

Daniel and Cory both declined at the same moment. The mayor hesitated then shook his head. He placed his hands on the table. "We're here to make sure you understand our rules and laws concerning establishments such as yours."

A smirk crossed Darnell's face. "I've read them. Fairly primitive for a town of this size."

Mayor Tate turned red, and his cheeks puffed out. "Just so you understand. The saloon must close at midnight on Saturday and remain closed until Monday. You will handle your clientele and make sure there are no brawls that will cause our sheriff and deputy to get involved. You are not to serve liquor to anyone under the age of eighteen. We have a law against firearms in saloons, so your customers will have to check theirs at the door. Deputy Muldoon or the sheriff will be around periodically to check to make sure you're in compliance with the law."

All during the discourse, Darnell's bland expression revealed nothing as to his opinion regarding the mayor's statements. Daniel could sense this was a man not to be tangled with. He knew his business and his rights. He would abide by the laws but at the same time stretch them to the limits.

Darnell removed his cigar and grinned. "Like I said, very primitive for a town with as many cowboys as there are and the lumber camp just down the road. Don't you think those boys deserve entertainment?"

The mayor sputtered as he looked to Cory for support. "Of course…of course…but the law must be followed."

"We'll do our best. Now, if that's all you need to tell me, I have a business to run. With this holiday, we'll soon be mighty busy." He stood in dismissal of them and headed toward the back.

Mayor Tate's face splotched with red. "Well, of all the…Cory, be sure and keep an eye on this place today. Check for guns before you leave."

Cory shrugged and shook his head in Daniel's direction. "Whatever you say."

As for Daniel, he couldn't get out of the place fast enough. This was a day he'd planned to spend with Kate having a good time, not worrying about some saloon keeper. He pushed through the swinging doors to the bright sunshine and peered down the street. Kate said she'd be at the church, so he strode off in that direction.

When he arrived at the church yard, children ran from game to game shouting and laughing. Several waved prize toys in the air as they rushed to their parents. Kate leaned against a tree in the shade watching the children. She was turned away from him and didn't notice his approach. Even with the broad brim of her hat, he could see her hair spread in a wave of curls across her shoulders. While the other women all seemed to wear their hair fashioned on top of their head, Kate let hers flow free, another sign of her independence.

As pretty as she was, Daniel saw beyond the beauty to the strength within. His old friend Rachel and his sister, Abigail, had strength, but theirs was in their ability to face any situation that might arise and handle it with grace and dignity.

Kate's strength was more. It was a physical strength and a faith that led her to believe she could be in control in whatever circumstances she found herself. She believed in herself, and she wasn't afraid to stand up for those beliefs.

Everything he'd seen in just over a week reaffirmed his opinion that she'd make a fine nurse. He'd never met anyone quite like her before.

At that moment she turned and saw him. She waved, and he headed toward her. Kate's face shone with happiness, and she grabbed his arm. "I've got a surprise for you. Aunt Mae fixed us a picnic basket, and if you'll get your horse from the livery, I'll get mine and we can ride down by the creek for lunch. We can be back in town in time for some of the cowboy competitions."

The competitions he could skip if it meant more time with Kate. "Now that sounds like a grand idea. I'll head down there now and get Black Legend and come back to the boardinghouse to meet you."

They strolled down the few blocks to the boardinghouse. Kate stopped near the back door. "It would be more convenient for you if Black Legend were here in our barn. We have an extra stall. You might ask Aunt Mae about it." She waved and ran toward the house. "I'm going up to change into my riding clothes, but I'll be ready when you return."

"Good. I look forward to our ride." He tipped his hat and headed for the livery. He controlled his gait until he rounded the corner toward the livery. Then he ran, not wanting to waste one minute more than necessary of an afternoon with Kate Muldoon.

Chapter Nine

When Daniel returned, Kate waited with her horse, Red Dawn. She had exchanged her dress for a split riding skirt and cotton blouse to be more comfortable in the saddle. She shaded her eyes and peered up at him. He did look good in the saddle of his black mount. Maybe he did know how to ride like he said. "Beautiful horse you have there, Daniel."

"His name is Black Legend, and we made many trips together between Briar Ridge and Hartford." He patted his horse's neck and nodded toward hers. "She's a beauty too."

Although smaller, the red horse was strong and like the ones they used on the ranch for cutting and roping. Kate swung her leg up over the mare's back. "I've had her a few years. Pa gave her to me because he said her coloring matched mine and we'd be good riding companions. He was right about that." She flicked the reins and turned to the west.

"There are quite a few trees down along the creek, so we should have plenty of shade and be somewhat cooler." She patted the basket attached to her saddle. "Aunt Mae fixed fried chicken and gave us part of her famous chocolate cake."

"Now that sounds like a feast. Your aunt is a good cook. All of the meals she's served have been delicious. I can see why so many in town like to eat there."

Kate considered her own skills. Maybe she should let Aunt Mae teach her a few more things about cooking. She might be living on her own one day, and knowing how to cook would come in handy. She shook her head. Why was she thinking about food? She could think of many more interesting topics of conversation than cooking, especially when she wanted to know more about this man from the North.

"Tell me about Connecticut. From what I've heard so far, it's a lot different from Texas."

"It certainly is. Connecticut is a small state and would tuck nicely into the northeast corner of Texas. Doesn't take long to get anywhere in our state. Briar Ridge is a typical small town although much older than Porterfield. We have all the seasons with beautiful springs and fragrant flowers to warm summers, fall with colors that rival any I've seen anywhere, and winters that bring several feet and more of snow and ice."

Kate laughed and pulled up her horse beside the creek. "Here we have summer with a few weeks of spring and maybe a few weeks of fall and very mild winters. The heat does get almost unbearable in the summer, but I wouldn't live anywhere else." She dismounted and untied the basket.

Daniel stepped down from Black Legend and tethered him to a bush along with Kate's horse. She spread the quilt Aunt Mae had included as well as the yellow checkered tablecloth.

"Looks like your aunt thought of everything." Daniel helped with the quilt and set the basket on the cloth.

"Aunt Mae's experienced at picnic lunches. My brothers and their wives were the recipients of many of them when they were courting." Kate gulped. Why had she said that? She couldn't let Daniel get the wrong impression. "Of course, she's planned a few for her boarders too, so she knows what to do." She knelt on the quilt then tucked her feet beneath her.

Daniel joined her and waited while she opened the basket. Along with the fried chicken, Aunt Mae had included fresh baked bread, fresh tomatoes from her garden, home-canned pickles, canned peaches, a container of sweet tea, and two slabs of chocolate cake.

"This looks better than anything we could have bought in town, and the scenery is more delightful as well as quieter." Daniel spread a large cloth napkin across his lap then peered at Kate. "Do you mind if I say grace?"

"That would be fine."

He reached for her hand and held it as he asked a blessing for the food. Although she heard the words, they were only words. Her mind rested on the feel of Daniel's hand holding hers—smooth and firm with a softness that wasn't in the calloused hands of most men she knew. Warmth filled her arm that didn't come from the heat of the day. When he finished the prayer, Daniel squeezed her hand then released it.

Kate sat still for a moment, the touch of his hand still imprinted on hers. She blinked then picked up a piece of chicken. Nothing like this had ever happened to her before. She must get her feelings back under control and not let anything or anyone deter her from her goal in life.

Daniel would have liked to keep holding Kate's hand, but then it would have been awkward for both of them, especially since they were simply friends. With Kate so bent on her desire to be a nurse, he would have to tread softly and take his time to win her favor. Today he planned to avoid all talk that might bring up that anger he'd seen more than once.

He finished a piece of chicken and followed it with a bit of the fresh bread. Holding up another chicken leg, he said, "It tastes as good as it looks. I'll have to give Aunt Mae a hug when we get back."

Kate nodded then tilted her head to the right. "You've met all the Muldoon clan, so tell me about your family and friends."

Now that would be a safe topic. "I have only the one sister, Abigail, and I think she's still angry with me for coming to Texas. I've had a letter from Mother, but not a word from Abigail."

"She must miss you since there are only the two of you. I can't imagine that. I was number five in our family then Erin came along. I've never known anything but a full house. When one brother wasn't around, there was always at least one or two others to give me grief."

Daniel shook his head and suppressed a chuckle. "I probably gave Abigail a hard time when we were growing up. But she had a good friend, Rachel, and they were always underfoot. Rachel is the one who married my best friend, Nathan Reed, last spring."

"Oh yes, I heard you speak of them. He's a lawyer, and you two went to school together."

"That's right, and a most unlikely pair to become such good friends. He was from North Carolina, but we hit it off at the very beginning." Someday he may tell her about that friendship and Nathan's story, but not now. He didn't want anything to spoil this afternoon.

"It's always good to find someone like that. I don't have any real friends because there are so few women my age in town." She placed a piece of the chocolate cake on his plate. "Tell me about your parents. Is your father a lawyer? I remember you said your grandfather was a judge."

"My father is a banker and investment broker. He made a good bit of money, and so our family lived very comfortably. My mother loves to entertain and is considered the best hostess in Briar Ridge. The mayor's wife even consulted with her about party arrangements." He stopped when he realized it might sound like bragging to mention his father's wealth. Of course, Mr. Muldoon had made money with cattle, but Daniel didn't want Kate to think he was making his family sound better than hers.

She didn't say anything but devoured her piece of cake. Daniel could sit and watch her all afternoon and evening. Her hair had been pulled back and tied at the neck with a piece of brown ribbon. Her hat hung from its strings down her back, and a few curls escaped the ribbon to float around her face. Miss Muldoon had no idea what an attractive picture she made sitting across from him.

A few minutes later she hopped up. "We'd better gather everything up and pack it. I want to get back in time to see my brothers compete in the rodeo events. I think Donavan entered the sharpshooter contest too."

She wrapped the chicken bones in a napkin and stowed it in the basket. Daniel folded the cloth and the quilt and handed them to her. When their hands met, a shock once again raced up his arm, but she jerked away.

"Let's get this basket back on Red Dawn and head back to town." She kept her face turned away from his as she tied on the basket then swung up onto her horse.

There was nothing Daniel could do but to follow suit. He'd much rather stay here, but he sensed Kate's agitation. Had he angered her again, or did she just want to get back to the celebration?

∞

As they rode back to town, Kate rode ahead of Daniel as much as she could to avoid further conversation. He'd already upset her twice today when their hands had met. The picnic had been a bad idea. Best to put as much distance between her and Daniel as she could without appearing rude. She'd vowed no man would ever deter her from nursing, but Daniel was getting too close.

Aunt Mae came running to meet them when they neared the boardinghouse. "Oh, am I glad to see you're back. There's a big ruckus in town. Some cowboys and lumberjacks got into a fight. Doc Jensen said to send you soon as you got back."

"I'm on my way." Kate handed Aunt Mae the picnic basket and kicked Red Dawn into high gear. In moments she pulled up to the infirmary. Men milled about talking to each other, and Kate pushed her way through the crowd and into the infirmary.

"I'm here, Doctor Jensen. What do I need to do?" He was

taking care of one of the lumberjacks who appeared to have a broken arm.

"Wash up good and help Elliot with sutures. Got two cowboys with pretty bad cuts on their heads."

Kate washed her hands with the strong soap by the basin and dried them on a clean towel. When she found Elliot, her mouth dropped open. Two men from her pa's ranch lay on the cots. Elliot had the suture tray out and had begun work on the first one.

"Jeb and Zeke, what in the world are you two doing here?" At least the men had the grace to turn red. Jeb winced as Elliot placed the first suture.

"Hold still, or it'll hurt more." Elliot glanced up Kate. "Seems to have been an altercation with some of the cowboys and the lumbermen. Haven't figured out exactly what the fight was about yet."

Kate donned her apron and picked up a needle to work on Zeke. Before she touched him, he yelled a string of words that burned Kate's ears. In essence, he wasn't about to let her get anywhere near him.

Elliot never looked up. "She'll do a good job on you, so you better shut up and let her stitch you up now."

"No way is a woman gonna touch me with that needle. It ain't fittin' for a woman to be doctorin' a man."

Kate planted her hands on her hips. She'd known Zeke for over ten years, and his attitude had always been negative toward her. "If you don't let me stitch you up now, you can just sit there in pain and bleed and get infected and whatever else."

He glared at her. "You're not going to touch me, Missy."

"Fine. Have it your way. I'm going to help Doc." She whirled around and marched back to the other examining room.

Doc Jensen grinned. "I heard that all the way in here. Zeke's a stubborn fellow, but if he wants to wait, he'll have to suffer whatever consequences there are. Here, give me a hand with this cast."

As the doctor finished the cast, she glanced at the man on the other cot. His face was bloody, and he held a cloth to his nose. "I suppose you don't want me to touch you either."

The young man grinned. "No, ma'am. You can do whatever you need to do."

Kate shook her head and blew out her breath. This one was about the same age as Erin. How did he wind up in a lumber camp? At least he didn't mind her treating him. She washed his face, and he grimaced.

"Ow, that does hurt." A wary look entered his eyes.

"Your nose is broken, but you'll be OK. Just don't get into any more fights anytime soon." She dressed his cuts and bandaged his nose. "There, one of the doctors will have a look at you, and then you'll be released."

Pa stomped through the door. "Where are those cowboys of mine?"

Kate pointed to the other room, and Pa strode in there to confront his men. A few minutes later Pa aired his lungs. He may be a Christian, but sometimes he spouted words that blistered the air.

Kate turned to the doctor. "Do you need me for anything else?"

Doc shook his head. "No need for you to stay around and

listen to that kind of talk. Thanks for your help. I'll see you in the morning."

She stripped off her apron, washed her hands, and fled out the door. A solid chest met her nose, and she yelped. The hands that steadied her belonged to Daniel. She pulled from his grip, pushed past him, and headed for her horse.

His steps were right behind hers. "Miss Muldoon, you shouldn't have been in there with all that mess. Women don't need to hear that kind of language from any man, whether it's your pa or not."

Kate whirled around with fire in her eyes. She looked him up and down, taking in his clean cowboy shirt and jeans, his expression of shock and outrage, and the determined jut of his jaw. She stiffened. "I don't like it either, but when a man's hurt, he's going to say things he might not say otherwise. It's my job to treat them and see that they don't injure themselves more."

He put his hands on his hips. "I still think it's wrong for you to have to listen to it and be around men like that. It's not fitting for a woman to be dressing a man's wounds anyway."

Kate narrowed her eyes. "I thought you said you admired me for my nursing. Must be you were lying." Now his true attitude came to light. All those fancy words were only to woo her, but apparently he assumed that she'd be just like every other woman and do his bidding once he captured her heart.

She continued to glare at him. He turned red and swallowed hard. "Got you there, didn't I, Mr. Monroe." She swung around and climbed up on Red Dawn.

Daniel grabbed the reins. "Wait a minute. I did say that, but it's still not right. I wouldn't want my sister or mother or any woman taking care of sick men who can't watch their mouths. No telling what else they might try."

"So you're saying I should forget nursing?" She clenched her teeth and glared at him.

"Not exactly, but it seems you could confine it to nursing women and children."

That did it. "Mr. Monroe, I will do with my life exactly what I want to do with it, and no man is going to tell me otherwise." She jerked the reins from his hands and kicked her horse into a gallop. Now she knew the true colors of one Daniel Monroe. With all his fancy speaking and fancy clothes, he was still like all the other men around her.

Settling down and taking care of a husband and family were at the bottom of the list of things she planned to do in life. Soon as Mr. Monroe and all the other stubborn mules like him realized it and left her alone, the happier she would be.

Chapter Ten

Mae heard Kate storm into the boardinghouse and into the kitchen. Something must have riled her up. Should she go in and calm the girl down or wait until Kate came to find her? A few minutes later, the door to Kate's room slammed, and Mae decided it was time for action.

She knocked on Kate's door. "I heard you come in, and you sounded upset. May I come in?"

No sound came forth for a few seconds then Kate opened the door. Her red splotched face meant she'd either been crying or her anger was in high gear. "How did the picnic go this afternoon?"

Kate flounced around then plopped on her bed. "The picnic went fine. It's what happened after that fired me up."

"Oh, you mean that ruckus in town? Heard tell that a few cowboys and lumberjacks got into a fight." Mr. Fuller had wasted no time in coming to tell Mae about what happened, but he hadn't known the cause for the melee.

"Yes, and Jeb and Zeke were the two cowboys. All four of those men got hurt, but Zeke wanted no part of me stitching him up and tending to his wounds. I wanted to crown him. He had no business fighting anyway." She crossed her arms over her chest and frowned.

"Oh, that Zeke. Pay him no mind. He's an ornery old cuss and has funny ideas about women. I imagine that's one reason he's never found one willing to marry him." Mae had never really cared for the cowhand, but he did a good job at the ranch, and that's what counted with her brother, who could be just as stubborn.

"That makes no difference. He had no right to talk like he did. I helped Doc Jensen put on a cast and then tended to the broken nose of one of the lumberjacks. He's just a kid, but he didn't mind my taking care of him. Then Pa came in, and he started a tirade that made my ears burn."

Callum usually controlled his temper and his tongue, so whatever set those men off had to have been something to get her brother that angry. Still, that didn't fully explain her niece's mood. Suspecting it was romance troubles, she changed the subject with a direct question. "So what do you think of Daniel Monroe after your time together?"

Kate set her mouth and said nothing.

Mae pressed her gently, careful to keep her voice noncommittal. "I thought you said the picnic went well."

Kate folded her arms. "It did at first, but then he made me so mad, I wanted to slap him. I don't want to be anywhere near him this evening."

"Land sakes, child. What did he do to upset you so?"

"I don't want to talk about it, Aunt Mae. I have some

reading to do." Kate grabbed a book and opened it. Her shoulders hunched down, and she lowered her head.

Nothing more from this young'un right now, but something got her temper up, and Mae aimed to find out what before the night was over. Daniel Monroe was a fine young man, and she'd seen his interest in Kate. Those two would make a good match if they ever could agree on things.

Mae sighed and shook her head as she entered the kitchen. There she settled into her familiar routine of peeling and chopping vegetables in preparation for dinner.

A voice floated in from the hallway. "Mae, are you here?"

"Ada? I'm here in the kitchen." She hurried to greet her sister-in-law and saw immediately that something was bothering her. "Come on in and have some cold sweet tea. It's blistering out there."

Ada followed her into the kitchen, settled at the table, and watched as she poured the tea.

"Here you are, dear," Mae said, handing her the glass. "Now what's on your mind?" Maybe Ada knew more than what Mr. Fuller and Kate had told her. Mae took the seat across from her sister-in-law.

Ada, brows pursed in a perplexed frown, retold the story of the fight, then described how she was on her way to the infirmary to check on Callum when she witnessed Daniel and Kate arguing and saw Kate storm off. "I approached Daniel Monroe and asked what was going on, and he told me I should take better care as to what my daughter was exposed to. Then he marched off before I could ask anything more." She lowered her voice. "I know Kate isn't likely to tell me anything, so I came here to see if you knew."

Mae shook her head. "I don't know much, but apparently Callum was swearing a blue streak—"

"What?" Ada exclaimed.

Mae put up her hand. "My brother doesn't use language like that often, so he must have had a reason for it. Anyway, putting two and two together, I'm betting Daniel heard that language and saw the roughness of those cowboys and told Kate that no self-respecting woman should be in such a place. That would get Kate's dander up."

"Oh, dear," Ada sighed. "I'm so ashamed Daniel should hear Callum swearing like that. He's a good Christian man, and I don't know what happened to make him so ready to bust his gut."

"I can tell you, Ma." Cory strode into the room. He held his hat in his hands, gripping the brim. "Seems those lumberjack fellows were accusing Pa and the other ranchers of depriving them of a livelihood by not letting them cut timber on their property. That didn't sit well with Zeke or Jeb, so they started arguing. Before you know it, they had a brawl going. Pa just called a meeting of the Cattlemen's Association to discuss it."

Ada sighed. "I guess that means I won't be going home for a while." She drank the rest of her tea and shook her head.

Cory turned to leave. "I just came to tell you that I won't be here for dinner, Aunt Mae. I have to ride over to the lumber camp with the sheriff and see what started the idea the ranchers wouldn't sell their timber. I'll probably be back late."

"Don't worry about it." Mae waved Cory away. "Just go and do your job." One less at the table wouldn't hurt any. Besides, Ada might end up staying for dinner anyway.

Cory left, and Ada rested her head on her hand. "Well,

at least one good thing came of this day. Erin and Reverend Winston are officially seeing each other now. That's a matchup I really like. They're perfect together."

Mae nodded. "I wish we could find someone for Kate, but she has her mind so set on being a nurse, she can't see a good man when he's in front of her face."

"You mean Daniel Monroe? I like him too. But I can't say either my husband or my daughter made a good impression on him today."

Mae met Ada's resigned gaze, and they both shook their heads. That was the problem, or rather part of the problem. Kate was just as stubborn as her pa, and if Daniel and she got crossways, it'd take a heap of fixing to set things straight again.

∞

Daniel waited with Callum Muldoon in the back of the town hall for everyone to arrive for the Cattlemen's Association meeting. Mr. Muldoon had sought Daniel out in his office and asked for his help with the association business. They had walked over to the town hall together to attend the meeting, which had been called for five o'clock.

Mr. Muldoon removed his hat, revealing his thick head of fiery red hair, and leaned over to speak. "I'm truly sorry you and my daughter heard me use the words I did. I had no need to spout off like I did. I just let my anger get the best of me."

"I understand, sir. That was a pretty harsh accusation by the lumberjacks." Daniel didn't know the reasoning behind the claims, but then he hadn't been in town long enough to know about any friction between the two groups. "Exactly why is it that you need me to be at this meeting?"

"I want you to hear all the details and help with negotiations with the lumber camp. We need to straighten out this mess and find out what's really going on."

As the ranchers filed into the town hall, Daniel noticed a few other landowners who weren't ranchers. They had timber on their land and had an interest in anything that might come from a contract for the timber rights.

Daniel chose a seat over in the corner and sat down. He couldn't get over the picture of Kate bolting out of the infirmary. He didn't care what she wanted to do with her life. Like he told her, no woman should be hearing the words that blistered the air from Zeke and then her pa. If she wanted to be a nurse, she could find plenty of it in taking care of family and the occasional neighbor.

He remembered Rachel and how she had nursed her mother back to health and taken over the household responsibilities. That's what Kate needed to be doing, not fixing a broken nose or stitching up cuts on men who had no more manners than a polecat.

Some apologizing would be in order, but at the moment he wasn't in the mood to apologize to anybody for anything, especially when he believed he was right.

Callum Muldoon called the meeting to order. "The first thing I want to know is if any of you have been approached by the lumber camp about timber rights on your land."

The men mumbled and conversed for a few minutes, then they all indicated that none of them had.

"I haven't either, so I don't know where they got this idea we didn't want to sell any timber. It'd be profitable all around. We ranchers can fence off the area at the timberline to keep the cattle away, and they can cut what they need. It will all hinge on what they plan to do to restore the trees cut down and how much they plan to pay for those timber rights."

Daniel listened for a few minutes. From the sound of the talk, he'd be riding with Callum Muldoon and other ranchers to discuss business with the lumber camp. He remembered how Maine and other New England states had sold timber rights. Those companies had made sure new saplings went in wherever trees were cut. They had not stripped an area bare each time but had left enough trees to prevent erosion and mudslides on mountain and hills.

Then his thoughts meandered back to Kate. With the mood she was in when she rode away, he had no hopes of escorting her to the dance tonight even if he did apologize. With her attitude, he may as well forget about her as any more than a friend, if she'd even be that.

∞

Daniel owed her a big apology, but with Kate's mood at the moment, she was in no frame of mind to accept it. Kate read the same page three times and still didn't absorb one word of it. She tossed it aside in disgust with herself. Daniel's face when he yelled at her for being around those men kept getting in the way.

No man but her father had ever scolded her the way Daniel had. He had no right to either. Even if they were good friends, he had no right to tell her what to do.

She let her anger seethe until the aroma of baking chicken and apple pie wafted into her room. Her stomach grumbled even though she should still be full from the picnic lunch she and Daniel shared.

Why couldn't the rest of the afternoon have gone as smoothly as their time together by the creek? Daniel had been polite and most certainly a gentleman then. She had found herself thinking of him in more than friendly terms, but how wrong that had been.

Finally Kate could no longer deny the hunger in her stomach. She checked her image in the mirror. Satisfied with her appearance, she sauntered out to the dining area. If Daniel was there, she'd retreat immediately, but his chair sat empty. She recognized Mrs. Bennett and Miss Perth. Then her mouth dropped open. Ma sat in Cory's place. What was going on? She should be with Pa.

"Ma, I didn't expect to see you for supper."

"Your pa's busy with an association meeting, and Cory's gone to the lumber camp with the sheriff to find out the cause of the ruckus this afternoon."

Aunt Mae pushed through the swinging door from the kitchen. "Ah, there you are. Go ahead and sit down. There'll just be us ladies tonight." She set a platter filled with slices of baked chicken on the table.

Miss Perth peered across the table at Kate. "I hear you were in the infirmary treating those hooligans this afternoon."

"Yes, I was. One man had a broken nose, and I took care of it for him. Old Zeke wouldn't let me touch him to stitch up his cuts." Everyone in town must know about what happened at the infirmary.

Miss Perth pursed her lips. "From what I've seen of that

man, he's one stubborn mule. I'm glad you could help the other one."

Before Kate could thank her, Aunt Mae clapped her hands then said grace for the meal. When she finished, her aunt sat back with a smile as broad as all outdoors. "Well, it's nice to sit down to a meal with just you ladies."

It was also nice to be at the table with guests rather than in the kitchen. Kate helped herself to the potatoes. "Ma, what did you mean about Pa being at an association meeting? Did it have anything to do with the brawl?"

"Yes. Those two lumberjacks were claiming the ranchers were stealing their livelihood by not selling their timber rights to the lumber company. Pa had never heard that before, so he's meeting with the ranchers to discuss the possibility of selling timber rights."

Selling timber rights? Surely Pa wouldn't let them cut down the beautiful trees on their land. They'd come in and ruin the beauty of the woods. "What's Pa going to do?"

"I'm not sure, but he had Daniel stay at the meeting with him to discuss the legal part of selling the timber. Cory and the sheriff went over to see why the men from the camp had said what they did in the first place."

Mrs. Bennett shook her head. "Well, if you ask me, they should all have been put in jail. Fighting in the streets like that is barbarian. It's bad enough that new saloon opened today, and then to have fisticuffs in the middle of Main Street…" Mrs. Bennett sniffed and buttered a piece of bread.

If Kate wasn't so mad at Daniel, she could go find him and see what had happened at the meeting. She would have to wait until Pa came and see if he would tell her anything.

Aunt Mae pushed back from the table. "I don't know about you ladies, but I promised Mr. Fuller I'd give him a dance or two tonight. Ada, if you'll clean up for me, I'll go and get ready."

The dance. Kate had completely forgotten about it. It would be starting soon, and she'd promised to go with Daniel. Forget that idea. He probably didn't want to be around her any more than she wanted to be around him right about now. There'd just be one fewer female there tonight.

Ma waved her hand at Aunt Mae. "Go on and have some fun. Kate and I will take care of the dishes. That is, unless you plan to go to the dance too." She stared at Kate, waiting for an answer.

Kate grabbed up her plate and the bowl of potatoes. "No, I don't plan to go down there. Let's get this kitchen cleaned up."

The less she saw of Daniel, the better off she'd be. She'd have to come up with a plan to avoid him at mealtime in the days ahead.

Chapter Eleven

KATE HAD MANAGED to avoid Daniel all week by being out of the house before breakfast and staying in the kitchen during the noon and evening meals. Once he'd come into the kitchen, but she had fled out the back door and down to the barn, and he hadn't tried to follow her. So much for his apologizing. If he really wanted to do it, he would have made more of an effort to seek her out.

Because she wasn't speaking to Daniel, and her pa wouldn't tell her what was going on, Kate fumed about the selling of timber on the Muldoon land. From news about town, she had learned the ranchers were willing to grant timber rights if conditions were right. What those conditions were, she didn't know, but Pa was smart and would make sure things were done to the ranchers' advantage, but she'd rather it wouldn't happen at all.

Kate headed out the back door of the boardinghouse. The list in her hand contained a number of staple items Aunt Mae needed from the store. She'd have to take the wagon in again. Hitching up the team wasn't a problem since she'd done it enough times at home, but she much preferred to walk when the weather fell into balmy Indian summer like today.

She made her way around to the barn structure where Aunt Mae's horse and cow were stalled. The chicken coop ran along the southeast side, and the hens there paced back and forth scratching for whatever they could find.

In the barn, she grabbed the bridle and harness from a peg by the door and sauntered over to the stall housing Danny Boy. The brown horse was in the prime of his years. All the while she worked, Kate talked with the animal. Danny Boy's ears twitched, and he snickered a few times as if in answer to her words.

"You know I'm bragging on you, don't you? Sorry to be hitching you up, but Auntie Mae has too much for me to tote alone. You don't mind though, do you, Danny Boy?"

The horse's head bobbed up and down as if to agree with Kate. From the next stall, another horse nickered and bobbed her head. Kate laughed and leaned around to speak to her own horse. "Don't you worry, Red Dawn. I'll be back to take care of you later. Danny Boy here will do the work."

"You always had a way with horses. They take to you like you're one of them."

Kate jumped and swirled around. "Cory Muldoon, you scared me half to death. What are you doing here this time of day anyway?"

He leaned against the barn door, his arms crossed over his chest. "Nothing much going on in town, so I thought I'd drop back by here and get another piece of Aunt Mae's buttermilk pie."

"You and your stomach. I think I saw a piece or two in the pie safe, but you'd better check with Auntie first. She'll skin your hide if you take it without asking." Aunt Mae didn't mind their coming in for a little extra in the afternoons, but they'd both learned to get permission first before diving into any leftovers. One never knew what the lady had planned for the extras.

A train whistle sounded in the distance. Cory straightened up and waved to Kate. "That's the two o'clock train from Dallas, so I'll get my pie and get on back to town. No telling who might be arriving today."

Kate finished her chore and led Danny Boy and the wagon out to the yard and climbed aboard. Seemed like every train these days brought someone new to Porterfield. Sometimes they were strangers, and sometimes they were relatives to families already in town. The mayor was constantly recruiting ranchers and other businessmen to move here and set up shop.

The wagon wheels creaked as she rolled down the main street. Once only a few blocks long, the hard-packed street now stretched out over ten blocks with side streets leading to houses or out of town to one of the many ranches surrounding the area.

As far as Kate was concerned, the town had grown enough already. Not only had the town and land around her changed, but cattle ranching had also. Some of the changes she didn't like, but Pa said they were necessary to keep up with progress.

Changes had certainly come to the ranching business. Instead of once- or twice-yearly roundups with cattle headed out for the Chisholm Trail, the cattle now boarded trains and headed up through Fort Worth and then up to Kansas. Ever since the blizzard of 1887 and the ban against Texas cattle because of the fever, no one used the old trails anymore.

She missed those times of roundup and getting the cattle ready for market, but she'd never admit it to her family. Pa's trail boss now was the overseer for the herd getting to Kansas by train, but they still needed the cowboys to keep watch on the herds and round them up for transport. What good times she'd had when she'd been allowed to participate in the roping and branding of the calves.

At the store, she tied Danny Boy's reins to the hitching rail and headed inside with her list. Mr. Grayson glanced up from an order he entered into his account book. "Good afternoon, Kate. Come for Mae's supplies?"

"Yes, and I have a long list again today. Brought the wagon to help me carry it home."

He turned his head and called, "Millie, Kate's here with Mae Sullivan's order."

Mrs. Grayson stepped from behind the shelves and smiled. "Hello, Kate. Let's see what's on that list of yours." She studied it a few moments then began collecting items from the shelf near her. "This is as long as the one you brought in a few weeks ago. Your guests must be eating a lot at the house."

"With the extra tables at noon and for supper, Aunt Mae is cooking more than ever. Of course Cory, Daniel, Frank, and Henry eat like each meal is their last."

"That's young men for you. When our boys were at home, it seemed like I could never get enough food on the table." She set a sack of flour on the counter then added one of sugar.

"I'm going over to pick up the mail bag from the Dallas train. If you'll wait, you can take the boardinghouse mail back with you." Mr. Grayson headed out the door.

It'd probably take that long to get the order filled and the wagon loaded. Then she remembered the letters in her pocket. "Oh, here's the mail from our boarders. All of them are already stamped and ready to go out on the eastbound train."

"Just put them on the counter, dear. I'll add them to the outgoing mail bag." She set two cans of peaches on the counter by the flour and sugar. "I don't want to be spreading gossip or anything, but did you know that a number of our men are sending advertisements for wives back East?"

Kate had heard rumors but so far hadn't heard what men were involved. "Yes, but none of the men at the boardinghouse have said anything about it, so it must be some men I don't know."

Mrs. Grayson grinned. "But you do know them. For a fact, Allen Dawes and Frank Cahoon sent off letters a month or so ago, and they got several inquiries last week, or at least I think they were."

"They're good men. Some girl will be lucky to nab them for a husband." Allen and his brother Philip were two of the nicest men in town. Both in their thirties, they had come to Porterfield and opened the freight office two years ago. So far they had a very successful business. Philip had shown some interest in Kate last year, but she didn't have time to mess with courting, so that relationship died before it really began.

Mrs. Grayson tallied up the bill and peered at Kate. "Seems to me you'd be finding you a husband with all the eligible men around town. A pretty girl like you should be having fun and not spending so much time studying books."

There it was again. Why did everyone think a girl's only lot in life was to find a husband and settle down? "I enjoy my studies, and I like working with the doctors," Kate responded as she glanced out to the street and saw Daniel step out of his building and turn toward the sheriff's office. As angry as Kate was with him, she had to admit that if any man could entice her into a relationship, it would be him. Right now, though, she had to get the wagon loaded and out of town before he returned.

∞

The heat hit Daniel in the face like a blast from a furnace and took his breath away when he stepped outside his office. At least he had a cross draft upstairs that cooled the rooms somewhat, but the sun glaring down caused perspiration to form on his brow and neck before he'd walked two feet.

Right away he noticed Aunt Mae's wagon and Danny Boy at the mercantile. Kate must be in town buying supplies for her aunt. That girl had a done a good job of avoiding him all week, but that was fine with him. Even so, she filled his thoughts at times he least expected it.

At the moment he needed to talk with Cory, so he pushed Kate from his mind and stepped into the sheriff's office. "Cory, I need to speak with you about a matter I've discussed with your pa. Do you have a few minutes to spare?"

"Sure. Everything's pretty quiet now, so have a seat." He shoved a chair out from the desk with his booted foot.

Daniel removed his hat and sat down. All the talk and

discussion from the association meeting last Saturday now led to questions. "Tell me what you think about your pa's ideas."

Cory leaned forward. "I agree with him that it's in the best interests of all concerned to sell those timber rights. His ideas about using fences to divide up the ranches isn't so bad now either. That seems to be the trend."

"The smaller ranchers aren't sure. They're afraid men like your pa will take more than they're entitled to. I've discussed this with the land commissioner, and he's assured me that his surveyors will be as accurate as possible according to the descriptions he has in his office. How can I reassure the smaller ranchers that the divisions will be fair?"

"I think they trust you and will listen to what you have to say."

"Good, because I plan to represent them and make sure they get all that's rightfully theirs. Callum and your brothers agree that's what should be done, so I'll be out with the surveyors making sure they follow the property lines." If only he knew more about the lines around here, he'd have more confidence that all the ranchers were getting their rightful acreage. Even with the Muldoons' support, Daniel didn't feel qualified enough to take on the task they expected.

In addition to the property lines, he had to make sure the contract with the lumber company benefited all the ranchers and not just the Muldoons.

Cory tapped his desk. "Another good reason for the fences to go up is to keep rustling down. We've had reports from down south that several hundred head have been lost to rustlers. We've been told to keep an eye out and warn the ranchers."

Rustlers? Another aspect of the West he'd read about. From what he'd heard, rustlers were a bad lot and didn't care who they hurt in the process of getting what they wanted. Stories about how they sneaked up in the middle of the night, took the cattle, and shot anyone who got in their way filled his mind now. A shudder passed through his body. This was a bunch of men he wanted nothing to do with.

"Then your pa and the others ought to get those fences up right away."

"They've ordered the barbed wire they want to use, and Pa had his men making fence posts to be ready. Fences might slow the rustlers down some, but when men like that want what's not theirs, they'll cut through the wire like a knife through warm butter. Mark my words; thieves are prepared for anything that might get in their way."

That was one thing Daniel didn't need to hear. He could defend himself in fisticuffs, but he'd have no chance against a gun. Handguns were one weapon he'd never conquered, although he could hold his own with a rifle. However, as long as he stayed in town, he'd be less likely to be anywhere near the thieves. "What else is your pa doing to safeguard his herd?"

"With my three brothers and their ranches, we have a lot of territory to cover, but they also have cowhands who can patrol it for them. Of course Pa will be right out there with his men. I'm riding out to show him the messages we received from down south. Maybe they won't come up this far north, but I don't want to take any chances."

Daniel nodded and stood. "I'm going to get on back to my office. I still have some research to do regarding the timber rights. You've helped a lot, and I do hope the rustlers stay south." He planted his hat back on his head and headed back outside.

When he stepped onto the boardwalk, he glanced down the street. He saw Kate shove a box onto the bed of her wagon and dust her hands together. That must mean she was ready to leave. His stomach knotted up worse than a snarled-up ball of string. His feet glued to the spot even though he had an urge to rush over to greet her before she left.

Why did Kate Muldoon have to be so stubborn and independent? She was beautiful, talented, and strong, but some of her qualities left a lot to be desired. No wonder no man in this town had grabbed her up and married her before now.

She clicked the reins of the horse and turned toward home. Just as she did, she locked gazes with Daniel. She was too far away for him to see what her eyes held, but her body stiffened and she jerked on Danny Boy.

Obviously Daniel was the last person Kate wanted to see. Remorse filled his heart. How could he ever get her to forgive him if he couldn't get near her?

Chapter Twelve

It was September 24, two days after the first day of fall, but summer made its last stand with the promise of more of the hot temperatures that left Daniel sweltering. He removed his jacket and hung it on the hat and coat rack in his office. He had yet to hire someone for the reception area, but he had furnished it with a few chairs and a table. He'd added a few more bookshelves and books as well. Perhaps he wouldn't need a clerk for a while. The timber rights contract he was working on for the ranchers was about the most business he had.

He read over the contract once again. The surveyors should be finished soon, and he could add the last details to the document. If he planned to see what progress had been made, he'd better ride out there now. He'd learned that to get anything done in this heat, one had to get started early in the morning or wait until near sundown.

Daniel retrieved his coat and headed to the livery for his horse. Once in the saddle he rode out to the Johnson ranch, the last one to be surveyed. As he rode, he observed the landscape. Dust from the trail filled his nostrils and covered much of the area near the trail. By this time in Connecticut, the trees would have begun their turning, and within two or three weeks, the horizon would be filled with the brilliant colors of orange, red, yellow, and gold. The air would be cooler and much fresher with a hint of the winter ahead.

Not so here in Texas. The great pine trees were still as green as they were in the spring, and the oaks, sweet gum, and pecan trees still sported leaves that trembled only slightly as a gentle wind touched their branches.

Daniel reached for his canteen and swallowed a mouthful of water. He replaced the cap then swiped his sleeve across his mouth.

The Johnson property came into view, and Daniel followed the cloth flags set out by the surveyors to mark the boundaries. In a few minutes he came upon the crew. He alighted from his horse and sauntered over to the men.

"How's it coming?"

One of the men folded up his tripod. "We've just finished this section, and it's our last. We have all the boundaries set now." He handed Daniel a stack of papers. "I think Mr. Muldoon wanted to see these."

Daniel grasped the papers and rolled them before placing them in his saddle bags. "You've done a great job in a short amount of time. Mr. Muldoon will be glad to get this information. I'm sure he'll be calling an association meeting soon to make final plans."

"Well, our job here is done. We're packing up and heading back to town." He turned back to the task of stowing his gear.

Two other men with him helped load it all onto the spare horse they had.

"I'll be on my way to the Circle M and take these surveys to Mr. Muldoon. Thank you for a job well done." Daniel tipped his hat and reined his horse around to follow the trail to the Muldoon ranch.

By the time he arrived, Mrs. Muldoon stood on the porch ringing the dinner bell. The rumble in Daniel's stomach reminded him he hadn't eaten since early morning at Aunt Mae's. Although he hated to intrude, he sure hoped Mrs. Muldoon was in a hospitable mood and would invite him in for the meal.

When she saw him riding up, a big grin split her face. "Hi, there, Mr. Monroe; you're right on time for lunch." She rang the bell again.

Ranch hands burst through the doors of the bunkhouse across the yard. As they filed into the house, Callum Muldoon rode up and dismounted. He removed his working gloves and reached out for Daniel's hand. "I'm figuring you must have brought me some information unless this is a social visit."

Daniel climbed down from Black Legend. "I have the surveyors' reports, sir." He removed the packet from his saddle bag and held it up.

Mr. Muldoon clamped his hand on Daniel's shoulder. "Good. Now come on in and eat with us. We can look over the papers afterward."

Daniel followed the man inside, where the aroma of fried steak and berry pie sent his stomach to rumbling again. Mrs. Muldoon had set another place, and he joined the men already there. As he glanced about the table, he realized this would be only about half of the crew at the ranch. The others must still be out on the range.

After the blessing, food passed around and disappeared faster than the sun melted ice on a warm day. One thing for sure, the men in Texas could outeat most men he'd ever met. Not much conversation flowed as the men filled their bellies after a long morning of hard work. Even Erin and Mrs. Muldoon didn't have much to say, although he caught Mrs. Muldoon staring at him several times.

He turned to speak to Erin. "I do appreciate the time and effort you spent on my office. That other furniture we ordered arrived, and Mrs. Bennett came and put up the drapes you picked out. It's beginning to look more finished already."

"Thank you. I enjoyed doing it. Anytime you need any help with decorating or such, just let me know." She pinched off a piece of bread. "By the way, Ma and I are planning a trip to Dallas soon, so I can look into getting those paintings we discussed."

"I look forward to seeing them. I'm sure whatever you decide on will do fine." If the pictures were anything like the ones in the Muldoon home, then Daniel would be most happy with the selections. He was anxious for his office to take on even more décor that typified Texas.

As soon as Mrs. Muldoon and Erin started clearing the table, Mr. Muldoon rose. "Mr. Monroe and I have business to discuss. You boys stay here and have some of that berry pie I smell. Mr. Monroe and I will take ours in my office." Daniel followed the big Irish rancher. He might be over six feet himself, but Mr. Muldoon was a good inch or two taller and broader. Daniel had learned Callum Muldoon had served in the army here in Texas and had been an officer. He still had that bearing, and not many men stood up to him. He had a way of making requests that sounded more like commands, and when he did, people listened. Daniel had come to respect Muldoon and was glad to do business with him.

Daniel handed the rancher the surveyors' report. "They finished up on the Johnson land today."

Callum Muldoon sat down in his leather chair and waved at Daniel to take a seat in one of the cowhide chairs across the desk. Daniel did so and waited for him to read through the documents and study the boundaries. He had gone through the reports as the surveyors did them, and he had found them to be quite accurate and matching what the land office had. At least none of them had tried to encroach on the other.

"These look good, and they're almost exactly like I expected them to be," Callum declared. "I'll call a meeting of the association, and we'll take the next steps. I understand the wire and posting for the fences arrived. It'll take several loads and maybe more than one day to transport it out here. I sent a couple of my men in with two wagons to bring back whatever they can load. That should give us some idea of how long it'll take."

"Yes, sir, and I'll have the contract ready as soon as I add the numbers from the surveyors, but I'll need those reports to do it."

Mr. Muldoon looked down at his desk and hesitated. "You'll have them ready for the meeting?"

"Of course I will. You can take my word for it." Daniel wasn't about to let these reports out of his sight. Someone with know-how could alter them and throw off the figures for every one of the ranchers.

Mr. Muldoon handed Daniel the papers, and Daniel left to get back to Porterfield. If he made good time, he'd have a chance to do a little work for the ranchers before supper at Aunt Mae's.

Although the wide brim of his cowboy hat kept some of the sun out of his eyes, the reflection from the landscape almost blinded him. The sun beat down on his shoulders, and soon his shirt glued to his back with perspiration. Once again he reached for the canteen he'd learned to take with him every time he rode out of town.

Never had he seen such large expanses of land with nothing on them but grass and trees. Back in Connecticut, towns, farms, and orchards had dotted the landscape. Texas was truly the land of wide-open spaces, and the longer he lived here, the more he liked it.

When he neared the town, a large gray and black cloud rose from the horizon. He sniffed the air. Smoke. Something in Porterfield burned. Daniel dug his feet into Black Legend and raced into town to find the source.

ↀ

Kate ran down to the infirmary. Men ran toward the Davis house where flames leaped through the roof. Four of the family had been injured in the fire, and Doc Jensen needed her help. She dodged those in a hurry to help at the house and bounded up the steps and into the infirmary.

"Where do you need me, Doc?"

Doc Jensen peeled the shirt off Joe Davis while Elliot

tended to Mrs. Davis. "Take care of the children. Both have burns."

Kate hurried toward the sounds of crying from the next room. Four-year-old Carrie and three-year-old Lenny Davis were each sitting on a cot with tears streaming down their cheeks. The burns on their hands and faces were immediately evident. At least no blisters had formed, but the redness indicated the pain the little ones must be suffering. The odor of smoke permeated their clothes. Kate checked their breathing and examined their throats. No signs of their breathing in a lot of smoke. That was good.

She grabbed the bottle of sweet oil that would soothe the burning and began applying it to the wounds. As Kate gently spread the oil, she crooned to the children. "This will make it feel better. Just be real still and let the medicine do its work. Burns do hurt for a while, but this will help. See, it's sweet oil, and it will take away the pain in no time."

First the little girl then the boy stopped sobbing long enough for Kate to treat them. She wrapped their hands lightly with wool strips. "This will help keep the ointment on and take the burn out."

An older boy yelled from the next room. "Ma, Pa, what happened? The house is burned down."

That must be Pete, the oldest Davis child who would've been at school. His sister called right behind him. "Where are Carrie and Lenny?" Doc must have pointed Kate's way because Sally burst through the door and ran to them. Tears filled the ten-year-old girl's eyes. "Oh, I'm so sorry."

She wrapped her arms around her siblings and cried. Kate reached over and patted Sally's back. "It's OK. They'll be fine.

I didn't see any burns anywhere else, and I don't think they breathed in much smoke. Stay here with them and sing or tell stories. I'll check on your ma and pa."

Satisfied Sally could handle her brother and sister, Kate returned to the room where Mr. and Mrs. Davis both lay on cots. Pete stood by his pa's side. At twelve years old, the boy stood straight and tall. Although his lips quivered, he wouldn't shed a tear.

Doc Jensen had removed the man's shirt to reveal the burns on Joe Davis's chest and arms. Elliot had removed Mary Davis's shirt waist, but found no burns on her other than her hands and arms. She stirred on the table, and Kate rushed to her side.

"Where are my children? Are they all right?" Her eyes darted right and left until they settled on Kate.

Kate reached over and smoothed back the woman's hair. "Carrie and Lenny are fine. They have burns on their hands, but they'll be OK. Sally is with them now."

Mrs. Davis visibly relaxed then turned her head toward her husband. "Joe! Is he OK?"

Elliot wrapped Mrs. Davis's hands. "He's unconscious and has more burns than you, but he'll be all right. You both are very lucky."

Pete came to his mother's side. "Ma, what happened? We were in recess at school when we saw the smoke and someone said our house was on fire. I ran to the house, but flames were everywhere and men were pouring buckets of water on it."

"I was outside feeding the chickens when a log fell out of the woodstove and started the rug on fire. Carrie and Lenny were upstairs when they smelled smoke, and they got their hands burned when they tried to put it out. They screamed for me, and I came in and tried to put it out, then your Pa came, but the flames had grown too big. He fought it for a few minutes while I ran out with the babies to holler for help." Tears welled in her eyes, and she bit her lip.

Kate hugged Pete. "The important thing to remember now is that everyone is safe. Doc Jensen will take care of your pa, and Dr. Elliot here has your mother all fixed up."

Pete shrugged away and stepped back. "But what are we going to do for a house to live in, and who's going to take care of Carrie and Lenny while Ma's sick?"

All were good questions, and Kate didn't have an answer at the moment. She sensed someone in the doorway and turned to see Daniel standing there. What was he doing here? Maybe he had news about the Davis place.

Daniel removed his hat and entered the infirmary. "I just got back into town and saw the Davis house." He placed his hand on Pete's shoulder. "I'm afraid it's destroyed. You won't be able to live there until it's rebuilt, but I'm sure the good people of Porterfield will help you do just that. The good thing is that the fire didn't reach your pa's shop. That's still intact."

Doc Jensen raised his hands. "Now all of you need to get out of here. These two need some rest. Since Mrs. Jensen isn't here right now, Kate, can you take Pete and Sally to your aunt's and get them something to eat? I think the little ones oughta go with you too, so you can stay with them and make sure their burns are OK. "

"Of course, Doc." Kate hurried to the other room and picked up Lenny. "Sally, you and your brothers and sister are coming with me. We're going to my aunt's house and get you something to eat and drink."

"Here, I'll take Carrie." Daniel picked the little girl up and settled her on his arm. He patted Sally's shoulder. "Now let's go see what Aunt Mae has to offer." He grinned at Kate then headed out the door.

Kate followed, shaking her head. This man could be so exasperating. How could she stay angry at him when he did things like this? He already had Carrie giggling, her blonde curls dancing on shoulders.

If he decided to say he was sorry for his words to her after the brawl, she just might forgive him, but that didn't mean she would change her mind about seeing him.

CHAPTER THIRTEEN

DANIEL REMAINED IN the dining room with the children while Kate went to pour lemonade and fetch cookies. He cradled Lenny on one knee and Carrie on the other. Sally and Pete sat at the table, but Pete's scowl revealed the boy's inner turmoil. Nothing Daniel could say at the moment would bring a smile to Pete's face. Only if his ma or pa walked through the door good as new would that boy be happy.

Aunt Mae bustled in with a tray filled with glasses and a big plate of oatmeal cookies. "This ought to help ease your pain a bit." She set it on the table then distributed the glasses and cookies. She picked up one of Carrie's hands. "Sweetie, can you hold the glass, or would you like for me to hold it for you?"

The little girl reached for the glass then whimpered when she tried to hold it. Aunt Mae extended her arms. "Here, sit on my lap and I'll help you." Aunt Mae grasped the child under the arms and hoisted her up onto her lap.

At that moment Kate reappeared and pulled Lenny up

into her arms. Daniel didn't protest as the boy wrapped his arms around Kate's neck.

"Hey, little one, let's see how that lemonade tastes." She sat across from Daniel and held the glass while Lenny sipped. "That's good. You need lots to drink." She turned to Sally and Pete. "You know, everyone in town will be over to help clean up the mess at your house. Lenny and Carrie here need a little nap time, so you and I can go over and see what we can find. No telling what we might be able to salvage."

Even as she spoke, Lenny and Carrie both nodded and fought to keep their eyes open. "Come, let's get these two on my bed. They need sleep more than anything else right now. If their hands are hurting when they wake up, I can give them a tiny bit of laudanum to ease it."

The two women disappeared through the door. Kate had such a way with children. That's what she ought to be doing all the time, but it should be her own children. Even Pete's scowl had lessened at the prospect of going to his house to look for anything he could save.

Daniel leaned forward. "You know, I bet people are already getting together and finding things for your family. People love you and want to take care of your family." Daniel had already come to respect Joe Davis as a fine wheelwright who repaired wagon wheels in his shop behind his house. If the shop was spared, then Joe could continue to provide for his family.

Kate returned and grabbed Sally's hand. "Let's go see what we can find."

Pete stood, as did Daniel. He gripped the boy's shoulder. "This may be difficult, but we'll be with you. If you don't want to do it, then we won't."

"It's OK, mister. I want to see what's left."

"All right." He followed Kate and the others out the back door. The walk to the Davis home took less than five minutes. Many citizens of Porterfield still milled about the ruins making sure no new fire would start up. The chimney and part of a room still stood, but the rest was mostly rubble. The acrid smell of smoke and burned wood filled the air and caused Daniel's eyes to water. Maybe this wasn't such a good place for the children. They didn't need to be in the smoke.

Beside Daniel, Pete stood with his hands in fists at his side. The boy's lips trembled before he clamped down on his bottom lip to keep from crying.

Daniel gripped the boy's shoulder. "I think it's too hot for you to do much right now. Do you want to walk over and check on your parents at the infirmary?"

Pete nodded, and Daniel turned to Kate. "I don't think it's a good idea to stay around here with the smoke, so why not head back to the infirmary?"

Kate peered down at Sally. "Do you want to go see your ma and pa?" When the girl nodded, Kate said, "OK, we'll walk over there with your brother and Mr. Monroe."

Sally grabbed Pete's hand, and the two children walked a few steps ahead of Daniel and Kate.

Daniel glanced down at Kate's hand. How nice it would be to hold hers like Pete held Sally's. He regretted now that he allowed her to avoid him and that he had not sought her out to apologize for his words three weeks ago. Perhaps it wasn't too late.

"I watched as you helped Doc Jensen," he began, keeping his tone conciliatory. "You have a way with your hands. I'm sorry I railed against you that day of the celebration, but the foul language really got to me. No woman should ever have to hear that kind of talk."

She looked at him with a question in her eyes, as if to gauge his sincerity, then shrugged. "I understand your feelings about that, and I accept your apology. You must realize that I grew up on a ranch, and although Pa frowned on the cussing, cowboys sometimes can't help it. Especially when they get thrown by a horse they're trying to break or get tangled up with an ornery calf. Pa scolded them if Erin or I were around, but even then they'd sometimes forget."

"I've noticed that with some of the other men in town." He stooped to pick up a rock and bounced it between his hands. "I also saw how good you were with the children. You seem to know just what they need and how to talk to them to bring them comfort."

She grinned and shook her head. "You didn't do so badly yourself. You had Carrie giggling when we went to Aunt Mae's. That helped her to forget the pain in her hands."

Kate would make a fine mother, but if he mentioned that now, she'd up and stalk off again and not speak to him. If he wanted to get to know her better, he'd choose his words very carefully so as not to rouse her temper.

They reached the infirmary, and the children ran on inside. When Daniel stepped through the door after Kate, both Pete and Sally were by their mother. Mrs. Davis hugged first one and then the other. "I'm so glad you two were at school and didn't get hurt too."

"But Ma, if I'd been there, I could've helped Pa. I'm strong, and we could have put out that fire."

Mrs. Davis reached up and stroked Pete's face. "No, it was too big and spread too fast, and that's how Pa and I got hurt. He fell and hit his head. The doctor says it's a concussion, and he'll wake up soon."

Pete's lips formed a firm line across his face. Such a burden for a twelve-year-old to bear. Daniel tried to think of what could be done to help but came up empty. This was not his field of expertise.

Seth burst through the door. "There you are. I've been looking for you two." He went to Pete and Sally and hugged each one. He stood back with a huge grim spread across his face. "I have good news too."

He placed his hand over Mrs. Davis's. "You and your family will move into my house. It's all furnished and has three bedrooms and is already stocked with food. It's too much for one man to live in. I'm moving in with Reverend and Mrs. Blackman for the time being, so you all can go back to the parsonage as soon as Doc releases you."

The doctor's wife, Maggie Jensen, strode through the door. "I heard part of what the parson said, and I want you to know, we've already started working on clothes for you and your family. Mrs. Bennett is making Pete and Joe new shirts right now, and Mr. Grayson picked out a couple of pairs of pants for you. I'll take care of Sally and your ma, and Mrs. Grayson is finding some things for Lenny and Sally."

Daniel listened in amazement. He'd expected the town to help, but not to this extent. Of course with their only wheelwright hurt and needing help, they didn't hesitate to pitch in even more than usual.

"Mrs. Davis, I'm Daniel Monroe. I'm new in town, but I'm

here to help in any way I can too. We just came from your place, and I'm glad to say that the workshop out back wasn't touched by the blaze. Soon as Joe heals, he can go right back to work."

This time when Mrs. Davis smiled, it filled her eyes. "I can't begin to thank everyone enough." She turned to her children. "Pete, Sally, you won't have to miss any school. Everything will be all right, you'll see."

Daniel admired this woman who had suffered so much today. Her family had survived, and she could go on taking care of them without the worry of where they would live or where they would get food. At the moment, gratitude to God for sending him to this place filled his heart. He glanced at Kate. Now if he could only make things right with her.

∞

Daniel had tried to apologize and make things right, and he'd almost succeeded, but then Kate remembered his ideas of what a woman should do with her life. He may be good with children, and he certainly charmed Mrs. Davis, but he wasn't going to fool Kate Muldoon.

Reverend Winston and Mrs. Jensen left to attend to the business of getting things ready for the Davis children that evening. Kate would stay with them until their ma came home. She could tend to Carrie's and Lenny's wounds more easily if she was with them. Maggie Jensen may put up an argument, but she'd have to give in to Kate.

Funny, she hadn't even noticed the workshop wasn't burned. Her mind had been completely on the children. Daniel's reassurance that it was intact seemed to make a big difference with Mrs. Davis. As long as her husband had his livelihood, she seemed to believe things would be fine. Clearly, the woman was truly dependent on her husband to provide everything she and the children needed. Kate shook her head. Never did she want to be that dependent on anyone, much less a man.

She glanced at the clock and jerked back. "My gracious, I didn't realize it was getting so late. I need to be there when Carrie and Lenny wake up from their naps, so they won't be frightened. Pete, you and Sally can stay with your mother as long as Doc Jensen says it's OK. Then you come on back to the boardinghouse for supper."

Both children nodded, not taking their eyes off their mother. Kate glanced at Daniel and tilted her head toward the door. He understood and followed her outside.

"Do you want to come on back to the boardinghouse now?" she asked. "Won't be long till suppertime." His clothes emitted the odor of smoke and the outdoors, and his hair clung to his forehead in damp curls. Her heart raced with indecision. Did she want to walk with him all that way alone? What would they talk about?

"No, I can't." He smoothed his hair back and set his hat on his head. "I have to get back up to my office and fill in some figures on that contract I drew up for the ranchers and the lumber company."

Kate gasped. "You mean they're really going through with that?" She hadn't heard her father mention it anymore, so she'd believed it was only talk.

"Yes. I have the contract all drawn up. The surveyors

finished today, and I have to add their information. Your pa is calling a meeting of the association to go over it all."

Her hands drew into fists on her hips. "I suppose that means they're going to put up fences too. I can't believe you're promoting these ideas. This has been cattle country for a long time, and we don't need any more lumber camps and sawmills coming in to spoil the beauty of our piney woods. And we don't need fences carving up our land."

"It's called progress, Kate, and your pa is a smart man. He knows he can't stop the lumber camps from cutting down trees, but we can stipulate just how it's to be done on his property and that of the other ranchers. As for the fences, they're for the protection of the ranchers."

"I've seen what sawing down those great trees can do to the landscape. It'll be barren as the desert and twice as ugly." Her eyes narrowed, and she used all the control she could muster for her next words. "I don't like the idea, and I'm going to do everything in my power to talk some sense into Pa. He can't let them ruin our land like this."

Let Daniel protest all he wanted. He'd shown another side of himself that she didn't care for. He wasn't from around here and had no idea about open lands and piney wood forests, or the deer, squirrels, rabbits, and all the other creatures that lived there.

"I'm sorry, Kate, but his mind is made up. You'll see. It'll be a good thing for all the ranchers. It will bring them more money to improve their herds."

"I don't agree, and don't bother trying to smooth-talk me into believing you. In fact, don't even talk to me at all. You don't know anything about our way of life, but in less than a month you've sure turned it upside down. You're a traitor." With one last glare, she marched down the steps and headed for the boardinghouse. Her hands clenched and unclenched at her sides as she stomped along the hard-packed street. Hot tears flooded her eyes.

How could Pa agree to a contract giving up the beautiful trees? True, life on the ranch was changing, but that didn't mean the land had to be fenced off or the trees destroyed.

Her head spun with all the events of the day. She had assumed responsibility for four children, had another argument with stubborn Daniel Monroe, and learned her pa was willing to give up trees to appease the lumberjacks. The only one she didn't regret at this point was taking in the children. She had to put the other issues behind her. Right now, Carrie, Lenny, Sally, and Pete had become her priority. Only the Lord could give her the strength she'd need in the days ahead.

Chapter Fourteen

With the older two in school and the two little ones with Miss Perth, Kate rode out to the ranch. She didn't intend to visit her mother and hoped she wouldn't run into anyone along the way. She wanted some time alone to think about what Pa and Daniel had done. Anger still roiled her insides, but the flame had cooled since yesterday.

The association planned to meet later this evening to discuss what they wanted to do. If Kate had her way, she'd be at that meeting telling the ranchers why they shouldn't sell the timber. Pine trees, oaks, sweet gums, and the cypress trees along the creeks were all God's handiwork, and together they all made a glorious landscape for everyone to enjoy.

Even now as she rode across Muldoon range land, the magnificent trees in the distance lent a beautiful backdrop for the prairie grasses that provided fodder for the cattle now grazing all about her. Plenty of rain this past summer kept the trees green and lush and the grasses growing in abundance.

She remembered summers past when drought had plagued the land and everything dried up, even the creek through the Muldoon property.

Although the temperature was still in the low eighties, a hint of fall filled the air. Kate loved this time of year. In other parts of the country the foliage would be changing from summer green to brilliant hues of autumn. She didn't care so much about that but would enjoy the cooler temperatures that would eventually come.

She breathed deeply of the fresh air that filled her lungs with the promise of the season ahead. A clear blue sky and scattered clouds should have made her heart fill with peace, but not today. She regretted calling Daniel a traitor, but if he'd been around this area as long as she had, maybe he would understand.

The one thing buzzing in her head at the moment concerned her pa more than Daniel. She could live without the young lawyer, but she loved her father too much to stay angry with him, even though she hadn't yet figured out why he would sell the timber.

The sun moved lower in the western sky. If she didn't hurry, she wouldn't be there when Sally and Pete got home from school. The ride had helped calm her anger, but it hadn't cleared up her doubts or answered her questions. She reined in Red Dawn and turned the mare toward Porterfield. If Cory attended the meeting tonight, he would tell her what went on. She'd have to be satisfied with that, but her curiosity only grew deeper, as did her desire to be at that meeting.

When the outskirts of town came into view, Kate nudged Red Dawn to go faster. A few minutes later she pulled up to the barn at the boardinghouse. Pa's horse was hitched to the side railing of the house. Kate jumped down from Red Dawn and led her into a stall.

"I'll be back to take care of you later, my girl, but right now I want to see why Pa is at Aunt Mae's." She removed the saddle and dropped it by the door then hurried up to the house.

Pa sat in the dining room drinking coffee and eating a slice of custard pie. He glanced up when he saw her and beckoned her to have a seat.

So many questions skittered around in Kate's mind, but she'd wait until Pa had his say before asking.

Aunt Mae poked her head through the door opening into the kitchen. "I have the little ones in here drinking milk, and Pete and Sally will be coming here from school for a snack, so you can visit with your pa for a bit."

The children had flown completely from her mind. She'd have to make a better effort to remember if she planned to take care of them for a few days. Having such a responsibility turned out to be a little more work than Kate first imagined.

Pa swiped across his mouth with a napkin then laid it on the table. "It's a fine thing you're doing to help the Davis children, but I'm glad Mae is here to help you." He paused a moment and peered across at her. "I understand you're not entirely happy with our decision to sell the timber rights on our land."

Kate's eyes opened wide. He must have been talking to Daniel because she hadn't said a word to Cory. "Yes, that's right. Those trees are what make our land so beautiful. They've been there as long as I can remember, and I can't bear the thought of them being chopped down and the land left bare."

"That's not going to happen. Daniel Monroe knows what he's doing. He's been around the lumber camps and sawmills up in his part of the country and knows what should be done to preserve the forests."

That did put a new wrinkle in her ideas, but she still didn't trust the lumber company. "How do you know it will be done like you want?"

"Mr. Monroe is a good lawyer and knows exactly what he's doing. He's drawn up an airtight contract they will have to follow or forfeit all rights to the timber."

Trust didn't come easy, and it didn't come now. So many things could go wrong. She worried with a napkin and made creases with her fingers.

Pa leaned over and raised her chin to gaze into her eyes. "I tell you what. If you promise to keep quiet and just listen, I'll let you come to the meeting tonight. You can sit in the back, but the first sound you make, I'll send you out fast."

Kate sat silent for a moment. She wanted to attend the meeting, but keeping her mouth shut and listening might try her patience a little too much. Still, being there for even a little while would be better than not at all. "Thank you, Pa. I promise to do my best to keep still and listen to what you and Mr. Monroe have to say."

He pushed back his chair and stood. "That's all I ask. I'm going over to the law offices now for one last conference before tonight. I'll be back for supper. Your ma and Erin came in with me to see about getting Erin a new dress. They'll be here too." Pa strode toward the door then turned back to her. "Remember, no talking."

She nodded, and he went out.

One thing for sure, she understood why the other ranchers followed Pa's lead. His height, demeanor, and experience all gave him an air of authority few other men in town possessed. She remembered how he'd only had to scowl once at her brothers to get them to behave or do what he wanted. None of them ever argued with him, but they had learned their lesson before Kate came along. Kate rebelled against her pa only twice when she was a child, and after the second time, she realized she never wanted her father angry or upset with her again.

She wouldn't put up a fuss. But still, the meeting tonight couldn't come soon enough to suit her.

Daniel gathered up his papers and the contract and placed them in his satchel. If all went well this evening, each rancher would put his name on the dotted line in agreement with conditions set forth for the lumber company. Mr. Muldoon had left for the meeting already, and Daniel would be right behind him.

The respect the other ranchers held for Mr. Muldoon amazed Daniel. Never had he seen such a man with so much command and power. Still, he didn't abuse it. He used it to make things better for all concerned. However, Daniel hoped to never be on the side of the man's wrath that was displayed weeks ago at the infirmary.

Once again Kate had made no appearance at suppertime. Of course she had to feed the Davis children, so that accounted for her absence, but she probably wouldn't have shown up anyway. Mrs. Muldoon had taken over Kate's duties and helped serve the meal to the boarders and guests.

In just a few minutes he'd join Cory and head over to the town hall for the Cattlemen's Association meeting. He reached for his coat and hat. Although he didn't really need it in this weather, it was important for him to look like a lawyer. The more comfortable clothes he saved for the weekends, but he did give in to wearing cowboy boots with his suits. He never thought he'd be wearing such shoes for everyday, but he loved them and planned to order more.

Fifteen minutes later he joined Callum Muldoon at the front table. He sat down and removed the documents from his satchel. Also at the table were two representatives from the lumber company. They were there to answer any questions the ranchers had about the contract.

A movement in the back caught his attention, and his mouth dropped open. What was Kate Muldoon doing here, and what would her father say? Daniel glanced up at Mr. Muldoon, but the man simply nodded in her direction with steel in his eyes.

Daniel stared at her for a few moments, but she didn't raise her head to look at him. Her pa must have threatened her to keep her mouth shut before allowing her to attend the meeting.

At that moment Callum called them to order. "All of you have your surveyors' reports, and as you can see, we've all been pretty much right in our boundaries. That will give the exact places we need to put up our fences. The supplies have been delivered, and some of you, like me, have started transporting them to your land. Dawes Freight Company is willing to haul large loads out for a fair price if you so desire. Any questions about the surveyors' reports or the fences?"

One rancher to the side stood. He rolled the brim of his hat in his hands. "I've heard tell of rustlers to the southwest. These fences ain't gonna stop them if they want our cattle. What do we plan to do about that?"

Callum rubbed his chin. "No, the fences won't keep out rustlers if they're bent on stealing, but it can slow them down. It'll be up to the individual ranchers to patrol their own property and protect their herds. The fences are mainly for our benefit. Open ranges are no longer needed since we have more efficient ways to round up our herds and take them to market."

The man sat down and nodded as though satisfied with Muldoon's answer. No one else stood or raised their hand in question, so Mr. Muldoon turned to Daniel. "Since that seems to be all the questions, I turn the meeting over to Mr. Daniel Monroe, who will explain the contract we've drawn up with the lumber company. All of you who are willing to sell your timber will have to sign it. If you're not sure, the contract will be in Mr. Monroe's office until next Monday. Those not signing by then will not have any timber cut from their land."

He nodded to Daniel as the signal for him to present the contract terms. Daniel stood. "Gentlemen, Mr. Muldoon and I have spent some time with the representatives from the lumber company interested in your land, and we've reached an agreement that will benefit both sides."

Daniel unfolded the document and began explaining the terms.

∞

Kate listened to every word Daniel said, but she wasn't sure she understood all the legal terms, and certainly some of the ranchers wouldn't either. Why didn't he just talk straight? If he'd just explain what the company was planning to do, then maybe she'd know what was going on. Questions popped into her head like corn popping on the hearth, but she remembered Pa's warning and kept silent.

Daniel paused then began talking again. "Now, those were the legal terms. What that means is that the men will not saw down all trees. The ranches will be divided so that one-third are cut each year. Jacks will come through and mark which trees they'll take. They'll pick them at random and not all in one spot. This way you'll still have the beauty of the trees, but they won't be as thick as they were. Wildlife like the deer, squirrels, raccoons, and rabbits won't be dislocated. They'll still be there for hunting when the cutting is done. In addition, new trees will be planted to replace those cut down. They will come in every three years to check for trees to cut on the designated land. Between times, they'll be left alone."

What he said sounded good, but wariness still filled Kate's heart. What if they cut down more than they were supposed to? What if they ruined the timberland at the Circle M?

The room became stifling with so many bodies creating more warmth to add to what was already there. The odor of unwashed bodies almost overwhelmed her, but nothing would stop her from hearing every word said. She breathed through her mouth, but that only made it dry and in need of a cool drink. Finally she held her hand over her nose and breathed in the lingering smell of the food she'd helped Aunt Mae prepare.

At last Daniel opened the floor for questions. Some of the very ones that had popped into her head were now being asked by the ranchers. Daniel stood tall and answered each one without hesitation. For some, he turned to the men from the lumber company to answer.

"Mr. Farnsworth, tell the men what will happen if the contract is not followed to the letter by your company."

The man rose from his seat. "We lose all timber rights in this area and pay for all that is listed in the contract even if we don't cut it. Our company is proud of the way we've left the forests after going through them. There's plenty of forest land in this part of Texas to take care of our needs for many years to come."

A round of applause followed as he sat down. His words sounded good, but would the company keep them? Kate shook her head. She'd heard enough. Daniel might believe he'd drawn up an airtight document that would protect the forests, but she'd reserve any judgment on that until the cutting and hauling actually started.

Kate jumped up and left the hall, still disappointed that her father and the other ranchers had given timber rights to the lumbermen. None of this would be happening if that fancy-pants lawyer hadn't come to town.

Chapter Fifteen

Kate sat at the table with the Davis children as they ate breakfast. Sally's sunny personality had returned in the week since the fire, but Pete still scowled at everyone. His sullen demeanor did nothing to help Kate's mood concerning the contract with the lumber company. Every rancher had signed it, and yesterday, Daniel had taken it over to the lumber camp. It was all a finished deal now, and there was nothing she could do about it. She may be helpless in stopping it, but that didn't mean she had to like it.

Kate listened to Carrie and Lenny chattering away like the squirrels out back, but she kept her eye on Pete. "I have good news for you. Today I'm bringing your ma home from the hospital, so she'll be here when you get home."

Sally and the little ones clapped, but Pete bit his lip and frowned deeper. "Peter Davis, aren't you happy your ma's coming home so you can be together as a family again?"

"The parson's house ain't home."

Kate gasped. "You will need a home until yours can be rebuilt, and Reverend Winston's home is perfect for your family."

Sally sat back, her little face bursting with something to tell. "I know why he don't want to live there. The boys are teasing him about living in the parson's home. They say Pete can't do bad things no more because he'll get into trouble with God. Will he really, Miss Kate?"

Stifling a laugh took every bit of Kate's strength. Striving to keep her face straight, she patted Sally's hand. "Now why would Pete want to do bad things in the first place?" She moved her hand to rest on Pete's arm. "And living there doesn't mean you have to quit being a boy and doing some of the things boys are going to do. Remember, I have four brothers, so I know the kinds of mischief boys can get into. You just remember that your ma and pa are as anxious as you to get back into your own home."

Pete jumped from the table and grabbed his book bag. "It's just not the same. C'mon, Sally. We don't want to be late for school."

Sally picked up her bag and the two lunch pails. She scurried out the door after Pete. Well, that certainly explained Pete's behavior the past few days. If the boys at school were teasing him, then the boy just might do something to prove to the others that it didn't make any difference where he lived. She'd have to warn the teachers. Without a doubt, Miss Perth and Miss Chambers would be able to handle any problems that came up.

Kate cleared the table then checked Carrie's and Lenny's

hands. "Well, I think these are healing quite nicely. You didn't have any trouble holding your spoon for cereal this morning."

Carrie's blonde curls bounced when the child hopped down from her chair. "Is Mama coming home today?"

"Yes, and while I go get her at Doc's place, you're going to be with Mrs. Blackman. Soon as I get your ma settled in, I'll come get you and bring you back for a visit."

Lenny's bright blue eyes peered up at her. "Papa come home too?"

Kate knelt beside the boy and hugged him. "Not for another day or two, but he's OK, and he will be just like his old self before you know it." She grasped his hand and Carrie's. "Now let's get the two of you washed up so we can go to see Mrs. Blackman."

Being with these two little ones for the week had shown her how much she would enjoy children of her own, but she had also neglected her responsibilities at the infirmary. She'd hardly had any time at all to study or work. At least she'd been able to keep the children occupied while she helped Aunt Mae with chores around the boardinghouse. As much as she enjoyed taking care of Carrie and Lenny, having them around reminded her of how much work children required.

After she dropped the children off with Mrs. Blackman, Kate headed for the infirmary with the wagon. Mary Davis was as anxious to get home as any mother would be after being separated from her children for a week, and she didn't need to be walking any distance.

Kate waved at the doctors and headed for Mary Davis's room. "Good morning, Mrs. Davis. Doc told me I could take you home to the parsonage today."

The petite woman sat on the edge of the bed dressed in a blue calico print Mrs. Bennett had dropped by. She held up her hands for Kate to see. "My hands are about all healed. They don't hurt anymore, and my lungs are much better. I don't have any problem with breathing at all now."

Kate smiled. "That's good news indeed." She helped the woman down from the bed.

Doc Jensen came in and handed Kate some papers. "These are her instructions for what she needs to do at home. You can go over them with her when you get her there." He grinned and placed a hand on Mrs. Davis's shoulder. "Joe is doing fine. He'll be able to go home tomorrow. I understand the lumber is here for the house building. You'll be back in your own place in no time, and Joe will be fixin' wagons and wheels just like always."

"Thank you, Doctor. I don't know how or when we can pay you, but we will. Joe always takes care of his debts."

"I know he will. You just concentrate on getting stronger and taking care of those young'uns of yours."

He left them, and Kate hugged Mrs. Davis. "See, everything will be fine. Carrie and Lenny are waiting for you to come home. I'll get them from Mrs. Blackman as soon as I have you settled in the parsonage."

Out on the boardwalk, Kate helped Mrs. Davis to climb aboard the wagon then joined her on the seat. They had gone only one block when her father and several other men rode into town at a fast clip. Something had happened at the ranch. Kate wanted to stop and find out what was going on, but her duty lay with her patient and taking care of her.

Whatever it was, the pace of their ride didn't bode well for whoever was in trouble. Since he didn't go to the infirmary, something else must be wrong. She turned in the wagon seat to see the quartet of men head for the sheriff's office. Now Kate's curiosity ran rampant. What in the world was going on? Whatever it was, she'd have to wait. She guided the horse toward the parsonage, but her feet and hands both itched to race back and find out what had happened.

~

Daniel was sitting in the sheriff's office talking with Cory when the thundering of hooves filled the room. Sheriff Rutherford jumped up from his desk. Daniel peered through the window and spotted Callum Muldoon and several other ranchers. Something must have gone wrong. Worry nudged him into action, and he ran out to meet them right behind the sheriff.

Dust flew as the horses pulled to a stop. Callum called out, "We've had rustlers out at the ranches. They cut the new fences, and we lost about fifty or so head each. Got my boys doing a search now. I picked up a trail, but decided you needed to be with us, Sheriff."

Cory grabbed his gun belt as well as Sheriff Rutherford's and brought them outside. He handed the lawman his guns, and both strapped them on. Sheriff Rutherford went back in and grabbed several badges. When he returned, he handed one to each man. "I'm deputizin' you into a posse to bring those rustlers in." He turned to Daniel. "You're the only other man of law around here, so I'm deputizin' you to take care of the town until the marshal returns tomorrow."

Daniel gulped as the sheriff pinned the badge to Daniel's coat. "Yes, sir, but what if something happens, and—"

"Don't worry about that. This town is usually as quiet as they come." The sheriff and Cory both swung up into their saddles, and moments later the entire group had disappeared around the corner.

Daniel glanced down at the badge pinned to his coat and sighed. Nothing to do now but to sit in the sheriff's office and wait for their return. First he needed a few papers from his own office. He could work on them down here as well as he could up there. He headed down the boardwalk to the building housing his firm. Soon he'd have to think about getting someone to sit in the front office and handle his mail and appointments. Besides a few wills and the timber rights contract, he'd managed to rouse up a few more clients who would keep him busy and help him pay the rent.

At ten in the morning, Porterfield was a sleepy small town like hundreds of others to be seen along Texas trails. The people were friendly, the food and accommodations at Aunt Mae's more than satisfactory, and business was picking up. All in all, a satisfying move. He did miss his sister and parents, but many others here were becoming like family.

He reached the stairs to his office but stopped when Kate Muldoon pulled up on Red Dawn. "What was my pa doing in town? He sure left in a hurry."

Wonders never ceased. Kate Muldoon was talking to him. "Your pa and some of the other ranchers had some cattle stolen. Cory and the sheriff took a posse out to track them down."

"Cattle rustlers? I heard they were having problems south of here, but I didn't expect them to come up this way." Her forehead wrinkled in a frown, and she bit her lip. Red Dawn danced around as though sensing Kate's unrest. "I don't like the sound of that. You say Cory and Rutherford went with them?"

From the indecision that filled her face, he'd wager that Kate was itching to ride out after the posse, but common sense and her responsibilities with the Davises would keep her from doing so. Or at least he prayed they would. Chasing outlaws was no job for a woman.

She glanced down toward the sheriff's office. "And who's taking care of the town? The marshal isn't due back until tomorrow." At that moment she must have seen the badge, for she gasped and then laughed. "You're a deputy? And what is a fancy lawyer from back East going to do to protect our fair town?"

Heat rushed to Daniel's face, and his hands clenched at his sides. How dare she laugh at him. "Sheriff Rutherford seems to think I'll be able to handle things until the posse or the marshal return. After all, I am a lawman too."

"Maybe so, but I hope nothing happens. Sure would hate for you to get hurt and need a doctor. You might have to put up with my treating you, and I know how much you'd hate that."

He frowned at her teasing and turned away. "If you'll excuse me, I want to get some work from my office to take down to the sheriff's office. I don't plan to waste my time sitting around doing nothing."

"Oh, and are you insinuating that's what Cory and the sheriff do with their time?"

His stomach knotted, and he breathed deeply. Frustration with this ornery girl was going to get the best of him yet. "No, I am not, but I don't do what they do in the office and—" He stopped, reminding himself he didn't owe her an explanation. In fact, he didn't owe her anything. He tipped his hat. "Good day, Miss Muldoon. I have business to take care of."

Once again her laughter rang out as she turned Red Dawn and trotted away, her back straight as an arrow, but her shoulders shaking. Daniel blew out his breath. How could one woman be so exasperating and beautiful all at the same time? One of these days he hoped to figure out a way to tame the fire-haired Irish lass, but until then, he had to learn to hide his frustration.

CHAPTER SIXTEEN

AFTER A HEARTY dinner at Aunt Mae's, Daniel changed into his denim pants and cotton shirt, deciding he may as well look the part of a Texan since he'd been deputized. He sauntered back to the sheriff's office to watch over the town for the rest of the day. At two o'clock in the afternoon, all was quiet. People greeted him as they passed, and at the infirmary, he spotted the younger Doctor Jensen talking to a patient with his wrist in a new cast. He waved at the men then continued on his way.

Since the posse wouldn't be back until nightfall, if then, Daniel decided to stay on duty at the jail until their return. Of course if the men found tracks, they might not return until they captured the rustlers and brought them in. Until one or the other, he wouldn't take his duties lightly.

The sun beat down, and horses riding in stirred up the dust in the streets. Hard packed from so much traffic, the street had no ruts and bumpy places. It was unusual for a dirt road, but the continuous stream of horses and wagons up and down Main Street managed to keep the street comparatively smooth; however, the street still threw up dust.

He stopped in front of the saloon, which was open with a few customers ambling in and out. He'd heard rumors about some of Jim Darnell's ladies, but that was a matter for the sheriff and not Daniel's responsibility. There'd been a couple of disturbances since the saloon opened, but so far Darnell had managed to take care of things himself.

A train whistle sounded in the distance. The train from Dallas ran late today. He ambled over to the station to greet any passengers who might be stopping off in Porterfield. No telling where he might drum up a new customer, so it paid to stay in circulation.

He stepped up onto the platform just as the train puffed into the station. Four green cars held passengers, and three men and two young women stepped down. At first Daniel assumed they were together, but the men headed off toward town, and the women stood staring about. They clung to each other like they were best friends and whispered to one another. One was petite and blonde, while the other had dark hair and stood several inches taller. Both were very attractive women.

"Excuse me, ladies. I'm Daniel Monroe, attorney and acting deputy of Porterfield. May I help you?"

The brunette stepped forward. "Oh, yes, please. I'm Suzanne Pruitt, and this is Penelope Simmons. We're looking for these men." She handed him a slip of paper with the names Allen Dawes and Frank Cahoon.

Daniel pushed his hat back on his head. "I see. Are you friends of theirs?"

The girls giggled, and Miss Pruitt said, "No, we're their brides. I'm to meet Mr. Cahoon."

Brides? He'd heard that some of the men might be advertising for brides since girls were so scarce, but this was the first time he'd seen any proof of the talk. "Now that does make a difference. Do the men know you were to arrive today?"

Miss Pruitt looked at Miss Simmons then shook her head. "No, I wired that I'd be here tomorrow, but the train for Dallas hadn't left when I arrived in St. Louis, so I was able to come a day early."

Miss Simmons added, "The same thing happened to me. Miss Pruitt and I met on our way here."

"Well, Mr. Dawes is out of town making a freight delivery, but I think Frank Cahoon is down at the livery. I'll take you ladies to the hotel where you can rest out of the heat, and I'll go let Frank know you're here." He needed time to get Frank prepared to meet the lovely Miss Pruitt. What would she think of the burly blacksmith?

The ladies picked up their satchels. Miss Pruitt pointed to the baggage cart. "Will it be all right to leave our bags there for now?"

"I don't see a problem with that. I'll have one of the men at the hotel come back and get them for you." The ladies fell into step with Daniel. The aroma of honeysuckle filled his nose and reminded him of his own sister. Miss Simmons didn't even look to be as old as Abigail, who had just celebrated her twenty-first birthday.

Daniel led them to the Lone Star Hotel and rang for the

clerk, who hurried from behind the key rack. His face lit up like a Christmas tree at the sight of the two pretty girls. "My, my, what do we have here? Welcome to the Lone Star." He ran his hands over his graying hair and grinned like a schoolboy at his first dance.

"These two ladies need a room for the night. They're here to meet Frank Cahoon and Allen Dawes." He turned to Miss Pruitt. "If you will both sign in, Clarence will give you the key to one of his best rooms. Right, Clarence?"

Red flushed the man's face as he reached for a key. "Oh, yes, nothing but the best. That'll be room eight at the top of the stairs. It's a large room and looks out over Main Street."

Miss Pruitt and Miss Simmons both smiled and thanked him.

"While you're getting settled, I'll run over to the livery and let Frank know you're here, and Clarence, you need to send someone to the depot to pick up their bags."

"Yes, sir, Mr. Monroe. I'll take care of it."

Leaving the scent of honeysuckle and gardenia in their wake, the ladies ascended the stairs. Clarence leaned over to watch them. "Prettiest girls to come to Porterfield in a long time. Are they mail-order brides? I heard rumors some of the men were advertising for such."

"I believe they are. Take good care of them, and I'll be back with Frank later." First he had to find him and make sure he cleaned up. Mucking stalls, grooming horses, and blacksmithing didn't leave a man with a pleasant odor, and if Frank wanted to impress Miss Pruitt, he'd need to smell better than horses, sweat, and manure.

When Frank heard the news that Miss Pruitt had arrived,

he dropped the hammer he'd been using on a horseshoe and stood with his mouth gaping open. "She ain't supposed to be here till tomorrow. What's she doing here now?" He wiped his hands on his apron. The whites of his eyes shown like snow-balls against his tanned skin.

"She caught an earlier train and is down at the hotel with the little lady who came to marry Allen Dawes. I came to tell you so you could get cleaned up and go down to meet her."

Frank stood an inch taller than Daniel but a heap sight wider in the shoulders and chest. The muscles bulged on his arms as he clenched and unclenched his fists. His dark black hair shone with the sweat of his labors. He reached for a cloth to wipe his hands. "I–I don't know what to say. Suppose I best get on down to the boardinghouse and have myself a bath."

Frank's hands shook as he untied his apron and hung it on a hook. "Is she purty, Daniel?"

"About as pretty as they come. Dark hair and brown eyes that sparkle give her a nice-looking face." Her figure was also comely, but Daniel wouldn't mention that to Frank. No sense in getting the man heated up any more than he was.

A big grin spread across Frank's face. "I knew it. She didn't lie to me. Yeehaw! I got me a girl." He slapped his hand against his thigh and ran from the building.

Daniel chuckled and followed him back out to the street, where he ran smack into Kate.

∞

Kate steadied herself against Daniel then stepped away as fast as she could. The shock of hitting his chest like that sent waves of heat through her. She smoothed her skirt with her hands. "Where was Frank going in such a hurry? He was running faster than a hound after a coon."

"His mail-order bride arrived in town a day early, and he's heading to Mae's to clean up."

"His what?" Mrs. Grayson had said some of the men had sent letters advertising for brides, but she'd never thought they would actually come.

Daniel headed back toward the sheriff's office, and Kate swung into step beside him. "Oh no, you don't. You can't make a statement like that then just walk away. Where is the girl, and what does she look like?" Curiosity filled her faster than a platter of Aunt Mae's fried chicken. She wanted details, not a simple fact.

"Miss Suzanne Pruitt is at the hotel waiting for Frank to arrive. But that's not all. There's another one named Penelope Simmons waiting for Allen Dawes to get back."

Kate lifted her head and laughed out loud. "I can't believe it. Frank Cahoon actually sending off for a bride. Wonder why he didn't tell us."

Daniel frowned and stopped in the middle of the boardwalk. "For exactly this reason. They knew everyone in town would be laughing at them."

Kate sobered up and nodded. "You're right. I'm sorry. I shouldn't have laughed, but you have to admit it is pretty funny to think those two had enough gumption to actually advertise for a wife." She'd never marry a man she didn't know, sight unseen. No telling what kind of scoundrel she'd wind up with. "So what do they look like?"

"Both of them are pretty. Allen's girl has light-colored

hair and eyes as blue as the sky. Frank's has brown hair and brown eyes."

Jealousy sent its tentacles into Kate's heart as Daniel described Allen's bride-to-be. He'd looked hard enough to know the color of her eyes. Kate stiffened her shoulders and cut out the jealousy vines before they had a chance to entwine themselves into a snarl in her heart. Let Daniel admire whoever he wanted to because it certainly made no difference to her.

"I think I'll mosey on over to the hotel and meet these ladies. I might be able to fill them in on a few things they don't know about Frank and Allen." She lifted her skirts and turned toward the hotel.

"Don't you go stirring up trouble, Kate Muldoon. Those ladies came here in good faith, and they deserve a chance to find out about their men for themselves."

Kate stopped dead in the middle of the street and whirled around to face Daniel. Heat rose in her face. If he didn't think any more of her than that, he wasn't worth the dirt he stood on. "Mind your own business, Mr. Monroe. I'm not stirring up any trouble."

At that moment Mr. Grayson came running and shouting from his store. A shorter figure ran in front of him. "Stop that thief, Monroe. He stole food from my store."

Daniel reached out and grabbed the boy. Kate gasped and grabbed one of the boy's arms. "Pete Davis, what are you doing out of school and stealing from Mr. Grayson?"

"I ain't stealin' nothin'. I jest forgot I had it in my hand when I left."

"That's not true. I caught him stuffing some apples in his

pocket, and he had a handful of beans." Mr. Grayson panted beside Kate and pointed at Pete.

Daniel held tight to the boy. "I think we need to go down to the sheriff's office and talk about this." He glanced back at Mr. Grayson. "Did you get your merchandise back?"

"Not yet, but I don't want them after they've been in his pockets. Just do something with him." The merchant spun on his heel and marched back to the mercantile.

Daniel shoved his hat back on his head and rubbed his chin. "Seems to me you have some explaining to do, young man. Let's go talk about it." He grasped Pete's shoulder and turned him in the direction of the jail.

Kate forgot her mission to talk to the brides and followed Pete and Daniel to the jail. No way was Daniel going to put that boy in a cell. There had to be a logical explanation for what he'd done. He might be more willing to talk to her too.

"Thought you were going to the hotel to meet the new ladies in town." Daniel's voice dripped sarcasm. She could play that game.

"And leave you to question Pete all alone? Not on your life. I want to be there to make sure he gets a fair hearing."

Daniel said nothing but set his mouth in a firm line. Well, she could be just as stubborn as he was. She didn't like the idea of having to go back and tell Mr. and Mrs. Davis that their son was in jail. They'd had all the misery they needed for a year.

Her shoes clomped across the boardwalk as she marched into the sheriff's office behind Daniel and Pete. The boy's lip stuck out a mile. If he didn't watch it, he'd trip over it. It reminded her of his sullen looks at breakfast the past week.

Something was eating at the boy, and she aimed to find out what it was.

Daniel sat Pete down in a chair in front of the sheriff's desk. Kate stood behind him with her hands on his shoulders. His muscles were as taut as the chicken wire Aunt Mae used to fence her hens. The urge to massage his neck and help him relax itched in her fingers, but she kept them still. No need to embarrass the boy in front of Daniel.

Wanted posters behind Daniel shouted with faces of criminals on the loose, but Pete was no criminal. This was all a misunderstanding. He belonged in school, not jail.

Two men burst through the door of the office. Frank Cahoon shouted at Daniel, "You gotta come quick, Mr. Monroe. Two men got to fighting at the Branding Iron, and when they headed outside, one of them grabbed his gun and shot the other feller. Doc Jensen's with him now."

Daniel jumped up and grabbed his hat. "You stay with Pete, Kate. I'll go see what's happening." He muttered something about so much for a quiet afternoon.

Kate's first impulse was to run after Daniel to see what was going on in the streets. Doc might need her help, but she had an obligation to Pete. She pulled over a chair and sat beside the boy. "Now, do you want to tell me what this is all about? I'd understand if you needed food, but we've been cooking good meals for you." There had to be some logical explanation for Pete's actions.

He sat with his arms crossed and his lip curled without answering. Kate tapped her foot and glared at him. This boy tested every bit of patience she had. Finally Kate stomped her foot. "If you don't tell me what's going on, I'm going to tan your hide myself unless you prefer Mr. Monroe locking you in a cell." Surely Daniel wouldn't put him in jail. A twelve-year-old had no business locked up in a cell, and it wasn't going to happen if she had something to say about it. But she wouldn't tell Pete that.

Kate blinked her eyes. The parsonage. That was the problem. Memory of what Sally had said at breakfast rolled through her mind. "Peter Davis, did those boys at school have anything to do with this?"

Still he sat, but now his chin rested on his chest. Kate grabbed his chin and lifted it so her gaze locked with his. A hint of tears glistened in his eyes. "Tell me the truth. Did those boys have anything to do with this?" She'd expected him to cause mischief at school like most other twelve-year-olds, but something like this had never entered her thoughts.

His bottom lip quivered, and his shoulders shook. "I just...I didn't want my friends laughing at me no more and making fun of me living in the parson's house. I–I had...I had to prove I could do whatever I wanted. Bobby and Billy Duncan dared me to steal something from Mr. Grayson's store, so after school I came to do it."

The Duncan twins were always into mischief, and Kate suspected as much in Pete's case. It wasn't really Pete's fault, but he should have known better. "Some friends you have, daring you to do something wrong like that. I'd say you need some new friends. Your pa is sure going to be mighty disappointed in what you've done."

"I know, Miss Kate, and I'm so sorry. I won't ever do anything like that again."

"I don't think you will." She knelt beside him and hugged

him. All the bravado he'd shown in the past few days lay shattered like so many shards of glass as he leaned against her shoulder. Now if only Daniel would listen to reason and let the boy off with a lecture and warning. If he didn't, she might never speak to Daniel Monroe again.

Chapter Seventeen

Daniel handcuffed the shooter and looked down at Doc Jensen. Two men lifted the wounded man to take him to the infirmary, but Doc shook his head. Blood stained the ground where the injured man had been, and Daniel recognized the fact that too much spread in a circle. Now Daniel had a murderer on his hands.

He shoved the cuffed man in the back. "Let's go. You can cool off in the jail until Marshal Slade or Sheriff Rutherford return."

As he headed down the street, all about him the good citizens of Porterfield murmured and shook their heads. It'd been a long time since anything this deadly had happened in their town, and now they looked to Daniel, a temporary deputy, to take care of justice.

When he marched into the jail with his prisoner, Kate jumped up from her chair. "What happened?" Her hands rested on Pete's shoulder as though protecting him.

"We have ourselves a murderer, and I'm locking him up." Daniel snatched the keys from the hook behind Sheriff Rutherford's desk. The man in custody snarled at Daniel and leered at Kate as Daniel led him back to the cell area.

When Daniel shoved the man into his cell, a loud cackle burst from his mouth. "You ain't gonna keep me here. I got friends, and they won't let me rot here."

The door clanged shut, and the key scraped in the lock. "You won't be here long enough to rot. The marshal will take care of you tomorrow, but you're not going anywhere until then." This time the defiant laughter sent a chill down Daniel's back. He'd be more than glad when his deputy duties ended and silently prayed that would be very soon.

Fire blazed in Kate's eyes when he closed the door to the cells behind him and placed the keys back on the hook. Now it was time to deal with Pete. Kate looked as angry as a mama bear protecting her cub. This was one matter he wanted to resolve quickly.

Kate launched into a torrent of words that threatened to drown him with their intensity. None of it made sense to him. He grasped Kate's upper arms. "Whoa there. Slow down and tell me what's going on to have you so fired up."

"For one thing, you can't keep Pete here overnight. Not only does it smell like a pigpen, but you have a murderer back there. Pete needs to go home to his ma."

Daniel hunkered down in front of Pete. He'd learned that eye-to-eye contact worked much more quickly than towering over a person like a giant. If he kept his voice quiet and calm, Pete should respond. "Can you tell me exactly what happened at the store? Did you take the apples and beans like Mr. Grayson said?"

The boy glanced up at Kate, who nodded her head, then faced Daniel again. The boy's eyes were moist as though he'd been crying or maybe trying not to. "Yes, sir, I did, but I didn't really want to do it, and I'm sorry."

"I see. If you didn't want to steal, what made you do it?" Just as he figured, there was a lot more to Pete's story than swiping a few apples and beans.

"Billy and Bobby have been teasing me about living in the parsonage. They said God would get me good if I did anything bad while living there."

Daniel let out his breath. That sounded like something the Duncan twins would do. He'd heard enough tales from Miss Perth to know Pete's story held the truth. Two years older than Pete, the twins were just short of being bullies. "So you were going to prove them wrong?"

"Sorta, they dared me to do it. Said I'd be proving that I wasn't afraid of anything or anyone." The boy's head drooped, and he wouldn't look at Daniel.

"See, I told you there would be a logical explanation." Kate planted her hands on her hips and jutted her chin out toward Daniel.

At the moment he wanted to paddle her and send her on her way for her attitude, but she'd stayed here with Pete instead of running out in the street to see what was happening out there. He had to give her credit for that.

Just then Mr. Grayson entered the office. Daniel shook his hand and explained the situation. After he heard the story, the merchant strode over to stand before Pete.

"Now I know you're a good boy, Pete Davis, so I'm going to make a deal with you. You come to my store the rest of the week for an hour or so after school and on Saturday for a couple of hours, and we'll call it even."

Mr. Grayson's plan would be a valuable way for Pete to learn his lesson without severe punishment. Daniel pinned Pete with his gaze. "I'll let you do that, Pete, but you have to promise me that you won't do anything like this ever again. Next time you won't be so lucky."

"Yes, sir, I understand. I won't ever do it again."

Kate beamed and knelt beside Pete. "What do you say to Mr. Grayson?"

Pete looked up at his accuser and benefactor. His lip trembled, but he said what needed to be said. "I'm sorry, Mr. Grayson. I promise to work hard and pay off my debt."

The storekeeper reached down and shook Pete's hand. "So it's a deal. I expect to see you tomorrow afternoon as soon after three as you can get here." He turned to Kate and Daniel and nodded before heading back to his store.

Kate reached for Pete's arm. "Now, let's get you home. If your ma hasn't already heard about this, I'm not telling her, but you need to do it right away. Understand?"

The boy nodded, and Kate led him to the door. She turned back to Daniel. "Thank you. You handled that quite nicely." A smile flitted across her face, and then she was gone.

Daniel slumped down in his chair. His stomach rolled and pitched worse than a raft on the rapids. Every time he was around Kate, his emotions roiled. *Lord, give me patience, and help me understand what's going on in my heart.* What made Kate so attractive when she wasn't what he really wanted in a wife? She was so demanding and independent. On top of that, things had to be her way or else. She drove him crazy, but he didn't know what to do about it.

The reports on his desk stared back up at him. As much as he'd like to think about her now, he had reports to write and have ready for the sheriff and the marshal when they returned. He tossed his pen aside and massaged his temples with his fingers. At this rate, he'd never get anything done.

∞

Kate went with Pete to his house but let him go in alone. It was up to him to explain what happened in town, and she trusted him to tell his parents. Then she chuckled. By now Sally knew it all, and if Pete didn't say anything, magpie Sally would. She sincerely hoped Pete did it first. Her brothers had told on her more than once, and it was never a good thing.

She consulted the watch pinned to her shirtwaist and decided she had enough time to go meet the two brides who'd come to town. As Kate walked toward the hotel, she heard snippets of conversation all around her. Most all of it concerned the cattle rustling, the shooting, the mail-order brides, and even Pete's escapade at the store. She couldn't remember when the town had had so much happen in one day. And the day wasn't even finished yet.

Mrs. Bennett came running from her shop and stopped Kate. The plump little woman's eyes were wide open, and she panted from her run. "Kate, is it true that two mail-order brides arrived this afternoon? I heard tell they were at the hotel."

Clarence must have been blabbing his mouth. Nothing

was sacred in this town, and Kate was happy that she didn't have any secrets to keep. "Yes, it is. I'm on my way there now to introduce myself and get to know them. It's hard to come to a strange town and not know anyone, so I aim to give them a welcome."

Mrs. Bennett's gray head bobbed up and down. "Yes, you do that, and you can let us know at supper what they're like." She picked up her skirts and scurried like a mouse back to her shop.

Kate glanced up above the dress shop and stared at the sign on Daniel's window. That was one exasperating man. If he could be so gentle and understanding with Pete, why couldn't he be the same with her? Of course she'd done nothing but clash horns with him ever since that first day, but he had shown he could be very pleasant at the picnic.

A breeze stirred the dust at her feet. Kate lifted her face to the cooler air blowing in. It had come from the northwest and had the feel of autumn in it. Maybe the brisk air would cool some tempers and nothing more would happen in town for Daniel to handle. Much as she hated to admit it, he had done a decent job this afternoon. But what if something more happened? Could he handle it?

She crossed the street and headed for the hotel. A giant of a man and young woman stepped through the door. The man looked familiar, but she'd never seen the girl before. Then she gasped. The man was Frank Cahoon all spruced up and wearing clean trousers and shirt. He even sported a string tie at his collar. Kate shook her head. She had to admit the blacksmith cleaned up very nicely.

"Kate, come here. I have someone I want you to meet."

Frank beamed brighter than the sun on a summer morning. "This here's Miss Suzanne Pruitt. She's just arrived from Ohio, and she's gonna be my bride. Miss Pruitt, this is Kate Muldoon. Her aunt runs the boardinghouse where I live now."

"I'm pleased to meet you, Miss Pruitt. Welcome to Porterfield, and I hope you find our town to be friendly." Daniel had been right. She was pretty and tall enough that Frank didn't overpower her with his size. The dark yellow dress she wore highlighted her dark hair and was of the latest fashion with just a hint of a bustle.

Miss Pruitt smiled, revealing an even row of teeth. "I'm pleased to meet you too, Miss Muldoon. I've already found the citizens of Porterfield to be very friendly. I think I'll like it here."

Frank tipped his wide-brimmed hat. "If you'll excuse us, I'm taking her down to meet Aunt Mae and then we're coming back to the hotel for supper."

Miss Pruitt hooked her hand around his arm, and they proceeded on their way. Kate observed them for a moment. Frank had talked about getting a piece of land and building a house. Now she knew why. They made a nice-looking couple, and Frank was a good man. She hoped Miss Pruitt proved worthy of his love.

There was still one more bride to meet. Kate strode into the hotel lobby. The owner had dressed it up with a dark green velvet round seating area. The back of the seats left a round portion in the middle, and someone had placed a large vase of golden chrysanthemums on it. The clank of silverware and glasses rang from the dining room. She peeked in to see the staff preparing for the evening meal. Linen tablecloths and napkins adorned each table, and a small candle lamp sat in the center of each one. It wouldn't open for business for another hour yet, but the room already looked quite festive.

She stepped over to the registration desk and rang the bell for Clarence. When he appeared, he nodded and said, "If you're looking for Miss Simmons, she's up in room eight."

Kate thanked him and proceeded up the stairs carpeted in the same green as the round sofa. Room eight was on her right, and she knocked on the door.

A petite blonde girl opened the door a crack. "Yes?"

"I'm Kate Muldoon, and I've come to welcome you to Porterfield, Texas. My aunt runs the boardinghouse in town. May I come in for a visit?"

The girl opened the door for Kate to enter. "I'm Penelope Simmons. Suzanne left a few minutes ago with Mr. Cahoon."

"Yes, I met them on my way into the hotel. She's from Ohio, but where is your home?"

Penelope sat down, and Kate joined her on the settee in the room. "I'm from a little town in Illinois. It's not much bigger than Porterfield, but it's full of old people, so that's why I've come West to find a husband."

"Well, Porterfield is full of men, but I understand you're here to marry Allen Dawes. He's a fine man and owns the freight company with his brother. They're out on a run, but I believe they'll be back tomorrow." Although not as handsome as Frank, Allen still turned the heads of a few girls in town. He was kind and generous and would take good care of Penelope.

"Yes, Mr. Monroe explained that to me. He was quite nice in helping me and Suzanne find the hotel and register. He told us he was acting deputy. What does that mean?"

"It means the sheriff and his real deputy are out with a posse trying to round up some cattle rustlers that hit last night. Daniel is a lawyer here in town and will give up his badge when the marshal returns tomorrow." Once again Kate had to squelch jealousy as she heard Penelope talk about Daniel. This girl was here to marry Allen Dawes. Kate had to get her mind off Daniel.

"So how long have you and Allen Dawes known each other?"

"Mr. Dawes has written me several letters over the past few months. He says he is working to make a house ready for us."

Several months wasn't long, but it had been long enough for the young couple to find romance. Daniel had been here less than two months, and she hardly knew anything about him. Whose fault was that? She had only herself to blame for the way the relationship with Daniel was going. A shiver ran down her spine. She had to forget him. Kate turned her attention back to Penelope Simmons, who continued talking.

"I'd heard that Texas might be dangerous, but I never expected a shooting and a cattle rustling on the same day Suzanne and I arrived. Is it always like this?" A shudder and quick shake of her head indicated Miss Simmons's distaste for violence.

"No, we're usually a very quiet town with only a few drunks to contend with. Today was most unusual." Of course everything had to happen on the day Daniel was left alone to care for the town. The more she thought about it, the more she believed he needed help. With a murderer in jail and rustlers on the loose, there was no telling what might come up yet.

She turned to Penelope. "Miss Simmons, it's been wonderful to meet you, and I'm sure Allen will be delighted to know you're here. I must go now, as I have a few errands to run."

"Thank you for dropping by, and please call me Penelope. I do hope we can be friends."

"I think that would be nice. Good-bye." Kate hurried out the door. If she left now, she'd have time to get out to the ranch and send one of the hands after Cory and bring him back to town. Daniel wouldn't admit it, but she could bet he would gladly surrender his duties as deputy.

Chapter Eighteen

Because a prisoner sat in a cell, Daniel didn't leave the jail to go back to the boardinghouse for dinner. He filled out the report for the sheriff and ate at his desk. Mrs. Bennett had delivered his meal and one for the prisoner. Daniel savored the beef, potatoes, and peas that he learned were called purple hulls. Another thing he had learned to like was Aunt Mae's version of cornbread. Back home Ellie had made a corn cake that was yellow and sweet. Aunt Mae's was lighter, almost white, and had buttermilk. It actually tasted better with beans, peas, soups, and stews than the yellow kind did. One thing he hadn't found in Texas, though, was asparagus. Aunt Mae said she'd never tried to grow it. Daniel missed it, but not to the point he'd want to go back home for some.

The empty dishes now sat on the floor on a tray and covered with a napkin. If no one came to retrieve them, Daniel would take them back tomorrow when the sheriff or the marshal arrived. He yawned and leaned his chair on its two back legs. What a day this had been. All these weeks and the town had been relatively quiet with only a few rowdy men ever locked up, and now he had a murderer in the back, a thief on probation, two mail-order brides arriving to claim their husbands, and rustlers on the loose.

At least the murderer could sit in his cell until the real lawmen returned. He read over his report once again and let pride creep in. He'd done a good job considering he was not a real deputy, but he had to thank the Lord nothing more had happened.

He stretched and then sauntered to the door to observe the goings-on in town as dusk settled in and the orange and lavender skies turned dark. Lights and noise from the Branding Iron drew his attention. Daniel prayed nothing else would happen over there tonight.

Just then Miss Perth and Mrs. Jensen stormed out of the establishment. His mouth dropped open. What in the world were those two women doing in a saloon? By the way they marched down the street, they must have had some argument with someone.

They spotted him in the doorway, stopped, and conversed between themselves. Miss Perth shook her head and glanced back at Daniel. She grabbed Mrs. Jensen's arm and headed the other way. Daniel breathed a sigh of relief. He didn't want to deal with those two ladies at the moment.

Just as he turned to go back inside, a horse and rider thundered around the corner. Cory pulled his gelding up to the rail and dismounted. "Came back to give you some help. The posse found the rustlers' camp, but not the men or the cattle. They stayed there, and I came back here to relieve you. What's been going on?"

More relief flowed through Daniel. Now he wouldn't have to spend the night in a chair watching over a killer, and if the two women decided to come back, they could talk with Cory.

"We've had some excitement today. Come on and I'll fill you in."

Half an hour later, Cory shook his head. "If we'd known anything like this would happen, one of us would have stayed here. You did a good job."

"Thank you, but I'm still glad to see you. Now why didn't you stay with the posse?"

Cory's face turned red, but his expression remained bland. "One of Pa's men rode after us and said there was trouble in town, so I came on back."

None of Muldoon's men had been in town since the posse left this morning. How could one of them have known about the killing and the rest? "Well, it's good you're back." Daniel bent down and picked up the tray of dishes. "I'll take these back to Aunt Mae's. I'm sure she'll send a plate down for you, since I figure you haven't eaten."

"Right about that, but I stopped and told her I was here, so it should be on its way. The sheriff and posse may be back tonight as well. It all depends on what happened after I left. They're about an hour's ride from here up by the river."

Daniel gathered up the papers he'd brought from his office and placed them in his satchel. "Then I'll be on my way. Sure glad I don't have to sleep here tonight."

The prisoner in the back began yelling for the sheriff. Cory shook his head. "I guess I oughta see what he wants. Thanks for your help today. Sorry there was so much commotion."

Daniel waved, picked up the dishes, and headed out to the street. Music from the entertainment at the Branding Iron floated in the air. Something in there had riled Miss Perth and Mrs. Jensen earlier. Maybe he could get Miss Perth to talk to him when he got back to Aunt Mae's.

The noise gradually faded as he walked farther down Main Street. All the other shops and stores were dark and quiet for the night. Up ahead the light from the boardinghouse windows beckoned him home. He still had one question on his mind. How did a cowboy from the Muldoon ranch know what was going on in Porterfield today?

Kate!

He hadn't seen her since she left with Pete Davis earlier in the afternoon.

Riding Red Dawn, she could have gotten to the ranch in less than half an hour and told them he needed help. Maybe he had, but if Kate didn't have more confidence in him than that, her estimation of him was not what he had believed. Anger soured his stomach, and the supper he'd eaten burned in his gut. He needed to have a few words with that young lady, but if he did it with this anger building, he'd end up saying something that would drive her even farther away. What was it about her that always drove him to say the wrong thing and find himself in deeper trouble than he already was? Kate Muldoon was a puzzle he had yet to figure out.

Kate slipped out the back door with supper for Cory when she heard Daniel talking in the dining room to Aunt Mae. He was the last person she wanted to see, even though the sound of his voice sent her heart aflutter.

If she hadn't sent for Cory, Daniel would have had to spend the night at the jail, and no telling what would have happened. Mr. Fancy Pants had handled himself well this afternoon, and the shooting at the Branding Iron was serious, but a lot more could have happened, and she wanted Cory there to protect Daniel.

Of course, he may not see it that way, and as smart as he was, Daniel had probably figured out she was the one who sent for Cory. It'd been easy to avoid him the past few weeks, so she could do it again. If he was angry with her, she didn't want to hear it. It'd only get her riled up, and words would spew forth that neither one of them had any business saying. Never had she met a man who could exasperate and frustrate her like Daniel Monroe.

She walked the five blocks to the jail in record time. No sense in Cory's dinner getting cold by her lagging along.

Cory stood when she entered the office. "That sure smells good. I'm hungry as a bear after hibernation." He reached for the tray and set it on his desk.

Kate sat across from him while he said a short prayer over his meal. Her brother spread his napkin and peered at her. "What's on your mind? You don't seem to be in a hurry to get back to Aunt Mae's."

"I'm not. I thought I'd wait for you to finish then take

things back with me." She didn't plan to tell him that she wanted to avoid seeing Daniel. Cory already made such a big deal of his being single and handsome. No sense in giving him any fodder for his talk.

Cory broke off a piece of cornbread. "Daniel did a fine job while we were gone. I don't know why you were so concerned. He took care of those brides and Pete without any trouble, and he managed to arrest the man responsible for the shooting."

"I was worried that something would break out that he couldn't handle. We've never had such a day as this."

Cory laughed. "I admit Porterfield is usually a quiet town, and we had no idea anything would happen while were gone. If we had, I would have stayed behind in the first place."

"I'm pretty sure he's probably figured out that I sent out after you, and it's going to make him angry with me again. It seems I can't do anything right in that man's eyes."

"Do you want to do what's right? From talking with him, he has some old-fashioned ideas about women and their role in society."

That was the same question pestering Kate, and Cory's assessment of Daniel's ideas were the truth. He'd voiced his opinion enough that she was sure she'd never be acceptable as marriage material for him. "Well, I don't really like him being angry with me all the time, so I just stay out of his way. It's easier than watching my words every time I'm around him."

Cory scooped up the last bite of his peas and eyed her as he chewed. He swallowed and nodded his head. "You don't want to hear this, but I think you both care about each other more than you want to admit. I've seen a look in his eyes that tells me that, and you carry it in yours when he's around."

Before she could protest, hooves pounded outside. Cory grabbed his rifle and strode to the door. Sheriff Rutherford burst through the entrance followed by three dirty, mangy-looking characters and one of the ranchers.

"We caught these three men at the camp, but the cattle and the other men are across the river. Your pa has gone after them with several of the other ranchers. I'm going to lock up these fellows then head back out to join the others. Don't think they'll move the herd far in the dark."

Kate swallowed hard. That was like Pa to take out after the thieves. She prayed he wouldn't be in any danger, but of course he would be if these men were any indication of what the others were like.

Cory grabbed the arm of one of the men and led him back to the cells. Sheriff Rutherford and Mr. Oberlin brought in the other two. Sheriff Rutherford stopped short. "What have we here? Who's this other prisoner?"

Kate picked up Cory's empty dishes and covered them. She'd let Cory explain all that had happened today. She wanted to take the tray home and then pop over to the Davis place and talk with Mary Davis about the house-raising being planned. She left without saying good-bye and hurried out to the street to be greeted by Miss Perth and Mrs. Jensen.

Miss Perth pursed her lips and stiffened her back straight as a rail. "I see the sheriff's horse, so he must be back. We have something we'd like to report about the Branding Iron."

Kate frowned and shifted the tray to hold it on her hip. "Sheriff Rutherford is busy right now putting three of those rustlers in jail. What's the matter at the saloon?"

Mrs. Jensen narrowed her eyes. "My doc went in there to

get some whiskey to use on his patients, and he told me he saw a girl in there much too young to be working in a saloon. We went in ourselves to confront Mr. Darnell, but he wouldn't talk to us and had one of his men escort us out."

"Yes, and we wanted to tell the sheriff but saw that Mr. Monroe was here, so we decided to wait until the sheriff returned. That's what we want to tell him now, so he can go over there and get the truth for himself." Miss Perth lifted her nose in the air. "I don't like the idea of those girls being here at all, and if he has one who's too young, he needs to be arrested."

"They're pretty busy with the cattle rustlers right now, and I think they plan to go back out to help the posse track down the others. Maybe this can wait until tomorrow." Kate doubted anything would be done tonight anyway. If the ladies had already been to the saloon, Jim Darnell was too smart to let a girl too young to be working be seen tonight.

The two women turned their backs and whispered to each other. Kate strained to hear, but their mumbles made no sense to her. All Cory and the sheriff needed now was a run-in with Darnell. Kate didn't like the thought of an underage girl working at the saloon, but there wasn't much she could do about it right then.

The ladies turned back around. Miss Perth said, "All right, we'll wait until morning. Good night, Kate."

Kate watched as they marched back down the boardwalk toward the infirmary, staying on this side of the street and steering clear of the saloon. She didn't doubt for one minute they'd be camped on the sheriff's doorstep first thing in the morning.

Music from the saloon started up, and Kate gasped. When

had it gotten so late? She'd have to wait until tomorrow to see the Davis family. She hoped Daniel would be so tired after today that he'd already be in his room and she could reach hers undetected.

A brisk walk took her past the saloon where the noise of the men and music gave her pause. She stopped a moment and eyed the establishment from across the street. Men from the lumber camp came in and drank and gambled away their earnings just about every weekend. Why men thought they could make money gambling with the odds so high against them had always puzzled her. As for drinking whiskey, not only did it waste money, but it also led to more problems.

Leaving the raucous sounds behind, Kate headed on to the boardinghouse. The church steeple came into view, standing straight and tall under the moon. There was the answer to all their problems. God had a plan for His children, and when they listened to Him, life was much better. Why couldn't the men in the saloon see that?

Kate swallowed hard. God had not been on her mind lately. What was His plan for her? She'd always believed it was to be a nurse, but she'd never really consulted Him. She should pray every day and not just when she needed something.

She tiptoed into the kitchen and set the tray in the sink, then headed to her room. The time had come for some serious talk with the Lord. She needed to get her thinking straight about a lot of things, including one Mr. Daniel Monroe.

Chapter Nineteen

KATE STOOD OVER the autoclave, waiting for the surgical tools to be sterilized. Her thoughts dwelt on her father and brothers. They hadn't returned with the posse as yet, and here it was Friday. Something must have happened for them to be gone so long, and it couldn't be good.

The town had gone back to its usual quiet self, but Cory spent all his time at the jail guarding the prisoner accused of murder. Marshal Slade had taken the captured rustlers up to Dallas to stand trial because the men were part of a gang that had been stealing cattle all across Texas.

Two good things had happened to warrant celebration. Both Allen Dawes and Frank Cahoon had weddings planned next month. Those two gals had taken to Porterfield like they'd lived there all of their lives, and the ladies at the church welcomed them and offered all kinds of advice and help. It made Kate proud to see her town live up to its reputation for friendliness and hospitality. As for her own prospects, she continued to avoid Daniel after her prayers about him Tuesday night yielded no new wisdom.

She checked the time on the new autoclave and saw it wasn't ready to open yet. Doctor Elliot worked on a patient in the other room. She had taken to calling him that to distinguish him from his uncle. Two Doctor Jensens would be confusing.

A ranch hand had come in with a carbuncle, and it needed to be drained properly to prevent the infection from spreading. One thing for certain, those instruments would have to be boiled and sterilized after the lancing. This was another time she was thankful for the doctors' careful attention to cleanliness.

Since Doc Jensen was out at the Watkins' place delivering Mrs. Watkin's third baby, Kate and Elliot were alone in the infirmary. He had given the patient a swig of whiskey before cutting into the sore, but the man's screams and curses still echoed in the room.

Kate shook her head and continued to check the supplies in the treatment cabinet. She'd heard more foul language in the past few months than she'd heard in most of her lifetime. The pain the men suffered was understandable, and those who didn't know the Lord found curses to be the only way to endure it.

A few minutes later the doctor had the man sit up on the edge of the bed. "Keep it bandaged with this ointment on it, and change the dressing every day for a few days. Don't get it wet, and come back to see me next week. If it gets infected and swells or gets red all around the sore, you come back immediately. I showed you how to change the dressing, so be sure to wash your hands and burn or bury the soiled bandages. Understand?"

"Yeah, Doc. I'll take care of it."

No sooner had he left than another man ran in holding a sobbing boy in his arms. "Where's the doc? This young'un fell out a tree and broke his arm."

Kate looked up and saw that it was one of the Duncan twins. "Land sakes, Billy, what were you up to?"

"It hurts, Miss Kate!"

She nodded to the front room. "I know it does, but we'll take care of you in two shakes."

Doc Elliot washed his hands and dried them. "I'll look him over while you get the supplies ready to make a cast." He followed the other two into the other room.

Kate prepared the supplies the doctor would need. Young boys were forever getting into things and getting hurt. It's a wonder any of them lived to manhood. Memories of her own brothers and their pranks that sometimes ended with injuries brought a smile to her face. No matter what the consequences, boys thought they had to prove themselves to be bigger, stronger, and smarter than all the rest. Come to think of it, that didn't change much when they became men.

She turned around and almost dropped the tray. Her heart thumped in her chest. Daniel Monroe marched toward the infirmary like a man on a mission. He didn't wear his hat, and his usually well-groomed hair was ruffled from the breeze blowing down Main Street.

He stomped into the waiting area. "Kate Muldoon, you've been avoiding me all week, and it's time we had ourselves a talk."

Her palms grew damp, and a lump formed in her throat. "I–I can't. We're busy right now. Billy Duncan broke his arm, and we're treating him."

Before Daniel could reply, Frank Cahoon ran inside. "Where's the doc? Ebenezer fell off his mule and hit his head on the hitchin' post. Blood's everywhere."

"Doctor Elliot is treating a patient and Doc Jensen is not here. Daniel, go help Frank bring Ebenezer in here and put him in that second room over there. Be sure to put him on the bed on the far side. We just drained a carbuncle on the other one, and I have to boil those sheets."

Daniel and Frank rushed out to get the old man while Kate went in to help the younger doctor. Ebenezer would have to wait a few minutes. What was happening to this town? First all the things that happened on Tuesday, and now everyone in town was needing the doctor at the same time. It never rained, but it poured.

Daniel and Frank clomped back inside with their burden. Ebenezer groaned loud enough to be heard clear across town. Elliot looked up from the cast he plastered on Billy's arm. "You go help the old man, and I'll finish up here."

Kate washed her hands and hurried in to check on Ebenezer. Daniel stood to one side, but Frank had disappeared, probably back to his shop. She stepped to the bed and examined the elderly man. Although he groaned, he didn't open his eyes, and his pulse was weak.

She found the wound to be a deep cut on his forehead. It would need stitches. That she could do. After cleaning the wound and cutting away some of the greasy hair around it, she prepared her tray for sutures.

Daniel said, "You aren't going to sew him up, are you? Do you know how to do that?"

Kate gritted her teeth before turning to him. "Yes, I am, and I do know how it's done. If you don't want to watch, I suggest you step outside and let me do my work."

He raked both hands through his hair. "I suppose that would be for the best. I still think you should—" He stopped, shook his head, and said, "Never mind." Then he left.

Good riddance. The nerve of him to think she couldn't handle a simple cut to the scalp. She tied a kerchief over her nose to help alleviate the stench from the unwashed, filthy body on the bed. A good bath should be in his instructions on taking care of the wound.

Her thoughts turned back to Daniel as she inserted the needle into the loose skin. No matter what she or Daniel felt about each other, they'd never see eye to eye over her love of nursing. This was her calling, and she didn't plan to give it up for any man, even a man as handsome as Daniel Monroe.

∞

Daniel stepped out onto the boardwalk in front of the infirmary and slapped his forehead. He'd almost done it again. Why couldn't he keep his mouth shut? Every time he spoke, he managed to say something that triggered Kate's anger. The way her shoulders had straightened and her eyes had narrowed, he knew he was in trouble...again.

With her will as stubborn as his, they'd never be able to agree on anything. A life with Kate would be a life of arguments and trouble. Kate tested and defied every notion he'd ever had about women and how they should spend their lives. Why couldn't she be more like Abigail or Rachel?

He ambled down the street, too tensed up at the moment to think about clients and work. When he passed the Branding Iron, all was quiet this early in the morning. In another few hours it'd be open and noisy. That reminded him of Miss Perth's accusations against the owner of the saloon.

She had told Cory that Jim Darnell had a girl working for him who wasn't old enough to be working, but when she and Mrs. Jensen checked for themselves, no such girl could be found. Nor had Cory seen her when he'd gone in to check the following day. Could be Darnell was having her lie low awhile. Maybe Cory should check again.

He walked with purpose now to the jail. Not only did he have questions about the saloon, but he had also become concerned because Callum Muldoon and his boys hadn't returned yet with the missing cattle. At least some of the rustlers had been caught, but none of the cattle returned or the other members of the gang found.

Cory sat at his desk rifling through a stack of wanted posters. He glanced up when Daniel walked in. "What brings you down here so early? Thought you were going to stop by and talk to Kate."

"I tried to, but she was busy. Doc Jensen is out, and just she and Elliot are handling things. One of the Duncan twins broke his arm, and old Ebenezer fell off his mule and busted his head. I'll talk to her later." He would if he ever found her alone again. She managed to find all sorts of excuses to elude him when they were at the boardinghouse. This morning had been the first time he'd been able to catch her at the infirmary, and then she was too busy to talk.

He sank into a chair and shook his head ruefully. "I don't know about that sister of yours. She's as stubborn as they come and gets angry faster than a bullet finding its target. Sometimes she frustrates me no end with her attitude, but other times when I see how she handles children, I can't believe she's the same person. I know she loves nursing, but I worry about the things she sees and hears at the infirmary."

Cory laughed. "All I can say is that Kate has a mind of her own and always has. Being only a year older than she is, we locked horns on more than one occasion as we were growing up. It's the Irish in us, so I'm told." Cory leaned back in his chair, his hands behind his head. "If you decide to try and court my sister, it's going to be like carrying a wildcat in a feed sack. She'll be fighting every step of the way, and you might end up getting scratched."

He knew what that felt like already. Courting Kate would be far from boring, but would he ever get a chance to be more than a friend?

Just then Brody Muldoon burst through the door. "Cory, we've got the rest of the rustlers, and Pa's been hurt. He's down at Doc's right now."

Cory jumped up and grabbed his hat. "What happened?"

Donavan Muldoon pushed two men through the door, followed by Ian Muldoon and the sheriff shoving two more. Ian spoke up, "We got the rest of the gang and recovered most of the cattle, but one of the bulls charged Pa and gored him in the leg. He's got a pretty deep wound."

Cory relieved Ian of his two men. "Brody, you and Ian go see about Pa. Has anybody ridden out to tell Ma?"

The two brothers headed out the door along with Donavan. Ian called over his shoulder, "I sent Kate out to fetch Ma and the rest of the family. You come when you can."

Cory and the sheriff led the four men back to the cells, and Daniel sat down hard. The wound must be serious if Ian had sent for the whole family to come. Kate would be devastated if anything happened to her pa. His insides churned. As much as he wanted to go to the infirmary, he'd only be in the way. Kate didn't need him either. Her large family would be more than enough support.

He blew out his breath and grabbed his hat. Callum Muldoon was Aunt Mae's brother. She'd want to be with the family. He quickened his pace and headed for the boardinghouse.

He reached the front door and stopped to read the sign posted. "No dining room today" was all it said, but that told Daniel enough. He opened the front door and called for Aunt Mae. Mrs. Bennett opened the kitchen door. "She's not here. Her brother is hurt, so she's gone to the infirmary, and Kate's gone out to the ranch to fetch her ma. I'm getting things ready for lunch, although I suspect you, Mr. Fuller, and I may be the only diners. Frank is eating at the hotel with Miss Pruitt, and the dining room is closed."

"Yes, I saw the sign, and I was with Cory when Brody came in and told him about his pa. Is there anything I can do to help you with the meal?"

"It's going to be light today. I found some of that roast beef from last night for sandwiches. How are you at slicing tomatoes and cucumbers?"

Daniel grinned and rolled up his sleeves. "I'm not sure, but I do know how to use a knife." He followed Mrs. Bennett into the kitchen. Maybe cutting tomatoes and cucumbers would take his mind off Kate.

He sighed. He was only kidding himself. Kate would be all that was on his mind the rest of the day.

Chapter Twenty

Ada's heart pounded in her chest with all the fury of the horses' hooves now driving them toward Porterfield and Callum. Ada gripped the reins harder and glanced behind to check on Erin, huddled in the back of the wagon, her head bowed in prayer. Behind them her daughters-in-law Megan, Sarah, and Jenny were in another wagon. Kate rode alongside on Red Dawn, her own red hair flying behind her in the wind. Ada's husband and their father lay injured, and Ada couldn't get to him soon enough.

The urge to spur the horse to go even faster rose like a wave, but they were already riding faster than was safe for the wagons. Better to spend extra minutes getting there than to have a wagonload of casualties to add to the doctors' burdens. Clouds came in to cover the sun as though acknowledging the fear raising bile in Ada's throat.

Kate had told few details about the injuries, only that Callum's leg was badly hurt and he'd lost a lot of blood. So many prayers had gone up in the last half hour that the words were coming to her mind like gibberish, but all with the same goal...Callum had to be all right. They'd endured hardships before, but never had anything happened to either of them that threatened life like this injury.

With the cloud cover, the wind grew cooler as they approached Porterfield. Fall was arriving at last to relieve the heat of the past few weeks. The air sang with the autumn breeze and would have lifted her spirits, but not with her husband lying injured. Nothing would be the same. Not until her husband was back at home in his own bed would anything be right again. She shivered slightly and pulled her shawl tighter about her shoulders.

Finally the buildings on the edge of town came in to view. Only a few more minutes and they'd be at Callum's side.

When they arrived at the infirmary, Ada jumped down and ran inside before the others could help her. She raced through the waiting room, but Brody grabbed her arms and stopped her. "Wait a minute, Ma. Talk to Doc Elliot."

"I don't want to talk to him. I want to see Callum." A cry escaped her throat. "He's not dead, is he?" He couldn't be. He was still too young, and they had too much living yet to do. She tried to wrench her arms out of Brody's grip, but he held firm. She glared at him with all the fury she could muster.

The doctor gripped her shoulder. "Ada, Callum's not dead, but I want to tell you exactly what is wrong and what to expect before you go in."

Ada clenched her fists but waited for the doctor to continue. "The bull ripped into Callum's calf with its horns and made a deep, long gash in Callum's leg, almost from knee to ankle. I've cleaned and stitched the wound, but he's lost a lot of blood. You can go in, but I gave him some laudanum to relieve the pain, so he may not be able to respond to you."

Ada opened her hands and rubbed them together. "I understand, but let me see him now."

Doc Elliot nodded his head, and Brody let her go. She entered the treatment room, where Callum lay quiet and still just as the doctor had said. His pale face only accented the redness of his hair. A week's worth of orange-red stubble covered his chin and jaws. Tears streamed down her face as she stroked his hair and gripped his hand. The thunder in her heart slowed to a quieter thumping.

"Callum Muldoon, you scared the living daylights out of me. What am I going to do with you since I certainly can't live without you?" She bent over and kissed his cheek. "You have to get well. We have too many grandchildren yet to be born and too much life yet to live."

Doc Jensen joined her. "I just got back, but Elliot filled me in. He's going to need a lot of care and rest in the next few days. I want to keep an eye on him here to make sure no infection appears, because gangrene can set in and he could lose his leg if we're not careful with this wound. He's not going to die, but he came close to it with all the blood he lost."

Ada's shoulders shuddered. She couldn't go home without him. He needed to be in his own bed where she could take care of him. "No, I want to take him home."

Brody placed his arm around his shoulders. "Listen to the doctor, Ma. He knows what's best for Pa. Here he can keep everything clean and make sure Pa's wound is treated correctly." He moved back the sheet. "Here, see for yourself how bad it is."

Ada gasped at the sight of the foot-long row of stitches. She'd never seen anything uglier. Taking care of something like this went beyond her capabilities. She had no choice but to leave him here.

Brody led her to a chair. "You can stay here in town with Aunt Mae. Kate will be here every day with you. The boys and I will go back to the ranch and see to things there. If you need any of our wives to stay, just say the word."

Ada pondered the situation. Doc could take better care of Callum, and if she was at Aunt Mae's, she'd be only a few minutes away from the infirmary and Callum's bedside. Kate would take good care of her pa too, and the boys could handle the Circle M as well as their own herds. This plan would work; it had to. She had no other choice.

She strode out to the reception room where the rest of the family waited. "I'm staying in town with Aunt Mae. Erin, you go back with Megan and take care of our home. Kate will be here to help if I need her, as well as Aunt Mae. Doc can take better care of him here than we can at home."

Her children murmured among themselves for a moment. She searched for Erin and found her with Reverend Winston. With all the others in the room, Ada had failed to notice the young minister's presence. Erin hadn't missed him, and they stood hand in hand talking. Reverend Winston turned to the others.

"If you don't mind, let's join hands and voice a prayer for Callum Muldoon."

As their hands joined in the circle, Ada caught Aunt Mae

staring at her. Callum's sister blinked her eyes then nodded her head as if to say it was going to be all right. And it would be...when Callum healed and she had him at home once again.

The preacher's soothing deep voice filled the room and Ada's soul with peace. God would see them through this as He had so many other times. He was her rock, her strong tower, her deliverer, and He was faithful to keep His promises. Even amidst the smell of alcohol and blood, she had no doubts at all that their prayer would be heard and answered in a mighty way to show God's power and mercy in their lives. He'd never let her down in the past, and He wouldn't now.

∞

After he ate lunch, Daniel drifted back outside and down Main Street. He had to work this afternoon or count the day as a loss. When he reached the infirmary, two wagons as well as Kate's horse had been added to those already there. He itched to know what was going on inside, but he wouldn't intrude on a family's private time.

As he came to the Branding Iron saloon, an idea sent Daniel across the street and inside. He'd find out for himself if Jim hired any underage girls. None of the patrons looked up when he came in, but the bartender reached down and hid something below the counter. "Anything I can get you, Mr. Monroe?"

"No, I'm fine. I just came to let you know the marshal will be here tomorrow to take our shooter over to Panola County for trial since we don't have a courthouse as yet and the judge will be over there."

"That's what I'd heard." His eyes darted to the left.

Daniel spun around just in time to see Jim grab one of the girls and hustle her out the back door, but not before Daniel got a look. She was just a girl. If he had to guess, she was maybe sixteen if that old.

"I guess Darnell's in a hurry. Hoped to talk with him a moment." Daniel tipped the brim of his hat. "I'll be leaving now. Got some work to do at my office. I'm glad to know you're up to date on the shooter and everything's good here."

Once out in the street, thoughts and images swirled through his mind like a whirligig on a windy day. He stopped and pondered whether he should go on down and report what he'd seen to the sheriff or leave it until later.

He sensed someone watching him from behind, but he didn't turn back to see. Better to go to his office and let whoever watched him think he hadn't seen anything, or if he had, nothing would be done about it. If they thought he might go to the law now, no telling what might happen to the girl.

Daniel climbed the stairs up to his office with a heavy heart. Kate's father was injured, and he had learned Jim Darnell might be holding a young girl captive for his own use. The idea sickened Daniel. When he reached his desk, he opened his Bible. No one but the Lord could cure his heavy heart and give him wisdom as to what to do next.

⁂

Kate gazed about the room at her family. Aunt Mae had left to go back to the boardinghouse. She wanted to prepare a place for Ma and make sure all was well with her tenants. If nothing else, Ma could sleep in Cory's room, and he could sleep down at the jail. He would be spending most of his time there anyway guarding the prisoners.

"I'm going back to the jail to help the sheriff. We have five prisoners now, and I don't want to leave all the responsibility to him." Cory spoke so only she could hear.

"I understand. I'll bring supper down to you both later on." She kept her eyes on him until he disappeared from view. She hugged herself and shivered. Everyone had someone to comfort them. Ma was in with Pa. Each brother stood with his wife, and even Erin had Reverend Winston by her side.

Kate bit her lip. Here she stood all alone. This was one time she wouldn't mind having a man's arms around her shoulder assuring her all would be well. The Lord was with her, but sometimes it helped to have someone with flesh and bone to hold her hand and comfort her.

That someone could be Daniel if she let him into her heart, but they had too many differences of opinion for any kind of relationship to work. Still, all his good qualities marched before her, and she found it difficult to think about the things that stuck in her craw and brought on her anger. She shook her head to clear it and went to clean the examining room.

Was she being wrong in pursuing her ambition? Once again the seeds of doubt planted themselves in her mind. What did God want her to do? No answer had come from Him, only confusion and now doubt. Daniel Monroe was a man any woman would cherish as a husband, but she wasn't any woman. She was Kate Muldoon with a future ahead in medicine.

She grabbed the sheets from the bed where the cowboy had slept and tore them off then piled them in a basket to take to the laundry. With Ebenezer in one bed and her pa in the other, at this rate they'd have to have the laundry done twice instead of once this week. Kate retrieved clean sheets and began remaking the bed.

Doc Jensen laughed and Kate jerked her head up. "Kate, you're attacking those sheets like an enemy. You're stretching and pulling and tugging until they're tight as a drum. Your pa's going to be OK. I guarantee I'll do everything in my power to keep him from losing his leg."

Of course he would. Pa wasn't the reason for her attack on the sheets, but Doc didn't need to know that. Every bit of extra work she could do would take her mind off Daniel. "Thank you. I know you and Elliot will do your best."

"I think it's time for you to go home and get some rest yourself. You've been here most of the day, and then you had that hard ride to the ranch and back. Elliot and I will take turns staying with Callum tonight, and your ma will probably stay here until late. Maggie will bring us down some dinner, so you go on and help your aunt."

"She'll appreciate that. I have to take supper down to the sheriff and Cory because they can't leave the jail with that many prisoners there." Helping Aunt Mae and then going to take supper to the jail would keep her out of Daniel's path. With her confused feelings he was the last person she wanted to see tonight.

Chapter Twenty-One

In the second week of October cooler weather finally arrived, and Kate wrapped her shawl tightly about her shoulders as she left Aunt Mae's Thursday morning. She enjoyed this time of year when the temperatures called for a wrap of some type but not the heavy coats of winter. The air smelled fresh and full of promise for the colder months ahead.

Her morning session at the clinic finished and her duties with Aunt Mae fulfilled, Kate walked out to the Davis house to check on the progress there. The community had come together last Saturday for a house raising, and they had made remarkable progress. Just about everyone in town had helped in some way, and she had managed to stay busy and out of Daniel's path all day. His prowess with building tools had come as a surprise, but so had his way with horses and his understanding of children.

Staying clear of him was the only way to keep her emotions in check. Whenever he was close, she let all sorts of notions and ideas enter her head, and she didn't want to keep having to fight them off. Better to keep her mind occupied with other things than to let Daniel keep messing up her thoughts.

Doc Jensen had finally decided Pa's leg was past getting infected, so Ma had taken him back to the ranch yesterday. That had been something to see. As big as Pa was, it had taken all four of her brothers to get him out to the wagon. He had insisted he could walk, but Doc threatened to have Ma tie him to the bed if he didn't stay off his leg for another few days.

In her experience in the infirmary she had come to the conclusion that women were much better patients than the men. Men either didn't want to stay in bed and fought any treatment, or they took advantage and became babies expecting to be waited on hand and foot. Both were a handful and demanded more of a caregiver's time and attention than did any of the women.

The Davis house came into view. All four walls were framed. The lumber for the outside walls had been delivered and sat covered by the side of the house ready to be added when Joe and the men from town had time to come out and do it.

Out back, the carriage works was open for business. She strolled toward the noise of hammer on iron and found Joe forming a new rim for a wagon wheel. Coals glowed red in the forge he used for making the wheel rims, and a barrel of water stood ready to cool down the red-hot metal he forged. Her shadow fell across his work, and Joe glanced up. He stepped back and wiped his brow with a kerchief. "Good morning, Kate. What brings you out here?"

"I just wanted to check on you and the house. I see you're

using your hands again." Even in this cooler weather, sweat rolled down Joe's face and glistened on his arms. Shaping iron with hot coals kept the space hot, no matter what the season.

"Yes, and I only have a few scars, and they don't hinder the use of my hands to work with the tools I need for repairing wagons. The Lord was merciful when He delivered my family from serious harm and spared my business from the fire."

The children and Mrs. Davis were back on their daily schedules, although it was at the parsonage instead of here. She counted it a true miracle the children hadn't suffered more damage than burned hands.

Joe turned to check the fire for his forge. "I've never had the chance to tell you how sorry I was about what Pete did. I went down and thanked Mr. Grayson for not pressing charges and putting Pete in jail. Thankfully the boy was good about working off his debt."

"He's a fine boy, Joe, and I don't think he'll be doing anything like that again anytime soon. The other boys were disciplined too, so it all works out." Pete had indeed carried out his responsibilities well, so much so that Mr. Grayson had hired the boy to stock shelves and sweep two days a week.

"I'm glad to see you're back at work. I'm going over to the parsonage now and see if Mary needs any help. I'm sure Carrie and Lenny can be a handful."

Joe laughed and picked up his hammer again. "That they can, and they talk about how much they liked your taking care of them while Mary was laid up. We both appreciate your willingness to step in and help."

"I was glad to do it and enjoyed being with them." She turned to leave, but he stopped her.

"Kate, did you know Frank Cahoon is building a house for him and Miss Pruitt? I heard at church on Sunday that they're getting married soon. If you ask me, he's mighty lucky to have someone like Miss Pruitt answer his ad for a bride. He sure took a chance, he and Allen both. No tellin' what kind of women they could have ended up with."

"Frank told me about the house. I met both ladies the first day they came to town, and they struck me as very nice ladies. I agree with you, though. I've heard some horror stories about mail-order brides. Guess it's just the luck of the draw, and those two men were mighty lucky." She waved good-bye and headed toward the parsonage. Never in her lifetime would she take such a chance on an unknown man.

Daniel isn't an unknown man. The words echoed through her mind.

∞

Ada pushed Callum back on the pillow. "Now you heard what the doctor said. No walking on that leg for another day or two. Since you wouldn't let me bring the wheelchair from the infirmary, you'll just have to stay in bed." And she'd tie him down if she had to.

"Horsefeathers, Ada. I feel fine. I didn't want the wheelchair because it's too hard to get around in." He sat up again and tried to swing his legs over the edge of the bed. Although he tried to hide the pain, it shouted from his eyes and from the firm line of his mouth.

Such a stubborn man, but that was the way with all the Muldoon clan. She'd put up with it all these years, but now Callum was about to rouse her own anger. If he thought Kate was a spitfire, he'd think different by the time Ada Muldoon finished with him. She poked her finger in his chest.

"If you don't lie back on that bed and do what you're told, I just might have to use my skillet and knock you out cold. I don't mind having you laid up for several days, but I don't want to put up with your whining and complaining if something goes wrong and your leg don't heal."

"Woman, you try my patience." He stared at her for a moment then managed to get his legs back under the covers.

She'd try more than his patience if he didn't listen to her threats and do what he was supposed to do. She just might have had to follow through on her threat. As big as Callum was, it would take more than one whack too. She grinned at the idea of using her rolling pin or skillet on his head.

"I don't know what you think is so all-fired funny." He grabbed her arm and pulled her down on his chest. He glared at her almost nose to nose. "Remember, I'm bigger and stronger than you are." His arm tightened around her as though to prove his strength. Then his head bent toward hers and his lips came crushing down.

She didn't move for a moment, in shock from his move. Then her arms went up around his neck. He hadn't kissed her like this for a long time, and she wasn't going to let it end too soon. Embers caught fire in her belly, and she returned his passion with her own.

Later she returned to the kitchen pinning up the hair that had escaped the past few minutes. Heat still flooded her body, and her fingers touched her lips that still bore the imprint of Callum's. He might be stubborn as an old mule, but she loved him with every particle of her being.

Ada filled a bowl with steaming stew and sliced up the cornbread. This would feed his body and give him more strength. With everything on a tray, including a hot cup of coffee, she headed back to their room.

Callum again sat on the edge of the bed. At her gasp, he looked up and grinned like a boy caught with his hand in the cookie jar. "I wasn't going to get up. I'm just stretching my shoulders."

"And why don't I believe that?" Looked like she was going to have to watch him every second until he could be up and around. "I've brought your lunch. Lie back on your pillow so you can eat, and I'll sit here and we can talk a while."

"You really don't trust me, do you?" But he did as she asked and reached for the tray. "Um, this looks as good as it smells, and I know it'll taste the same." He scooped up a spoonful of stew and savored it in his mouth. He swallowed and grinned. "Yep, it's good."

Ada pulled up a chair and sat beside the bed. "Reverend Winston came by, and Erin went with him for a ride. I expect those two will be setting a wedding date before too long." Her baby had grown up and fallen in love. That it was with the preacher pleased Ada no end. She'd always thought a preacher would be good for the family.

"I think you're right. I like the young man even if he is from the North. He's a good preacher, and he'll take good care of Erin."

Ada sighed and slumped her shoulders. "Now if we could only find mates for Kate and Cory. Those two don't seem to have any more interest in marriage than flying a kite. I thought maybe Daniel Monroe might spark Kate's interest, but they don't even talk to each other." The whole time she'd stayed with Mae, she hadn't seen Daniel and Kate talking to each other even one time. She could have sworn she'd seen a spark of interest in both of them when Daniel first came, but whatever had been there must have died out.

"I thought I saw sparks there too, but our Kate has a mind of her own and isn't going to be controlled by anyone. I watched her at the infirmary. I don't mind her nursing sick people, but some of the stuff that comes into Doc's, she has no business being around."

Ada nodded. "I agree with that, but she has her heart set on a nursing career. She does have a way with patients, and Doc Jensen has bragged on her often enough with me." Ada had observed Kate talking with small children and their parents. Pride had filled her heart at the sight of her daughter taking charge of the sick and injured with such a caring, concerned attitude. She continued, "As long as she stays with Doc Jensen, I see no real harm in her helping out. He's a good man and will watch out for her."

Ada couldn't deny her daughter's dreams, but she'd be much happier if some young man came along to sweep Kate off her feet. If Kate fell in love, then she would forget about nursing. Until that day came, though, she'd have to be content planning Erin's wedding and praying for her unmarried children.

~

Cory slammed through the door to Daniel's office. "I just found out that the rumors about Jim Darnell having an underage girl at his saloon are true."

Daniel groaned and frowned. "In all the excitement and turmoil of the few days, I forgot to tell you about that. Last Friday I saw Jim hustling a young girl out of the saloon when I came in."

Cory's mouth gaped open. "You actually went into the Branding Iron? Why didn't you tell me or the sheriff right away?"

Daniel grimaced and shook his head. "I started to, but I sensed they were watching me, so I went straight to my office. I was afraid Jim might do something to the girl if he thought I was going to the sheriff's office. What with charging the rustlers, the whole incident slipped my mind." How could he have forgotten something as important as that? He had, and now it might be too late to do anything. "How did you find out?"

"One of the men who goes there a lot told me. He was all fired up and accused Darnell of being a fraud. He said that Darnell had promised him a special treat that night, and she was waiting for him in the usual room. When the man got there and was going to have his way with her, he realized she was just a child and high-tailed it out of there, demanding his money back."

Anger with himself rose with heat to Daniel's face. "I should have done something right away. What do you want me to do now?"

"You look up all the laws you can find that have to do with children. The girl can't be over fourteen, and there's gotta be a law somewhere we can enforce to get her out of there."

Daniel shook his head. "I don't know of any. Children are used as labor all over the country, and our government is only now beginning to do something about that. I will look into it, but I think maybe you and the sheriff can just take her out of there on your own because it's the right thing to do even if it isn't against the law for Darnell to hire her." Daniel didn't like the situation any better than Cory, but until laws changed, they had no legal recourse against Darnell.

"I'll tell Sheriff Rutherford. He's as angry as I am about it. Clem said the girl had on lots of rouge and her hair done up to make her look older, but everything else indicates she's younger." He started for the door then turned back around. "Any ideas where we can take her when we do get her?"

Daniel smiled with relief. They really were going to do something about it. "I'd say your Aunt Mae's is the best bet. She and Kate will take good care of her."

"Of course, I should have thought of that. Thanks."

After he was gone, Daniel remembered Miss Perth and Mrs. Jensen. Those were two more ladies who'd be willing to take care of the girl. Porterfield may have its scoundrels, but most of its citizens were law-abiding, God-fearing people who hated cruelty and injustice.

Then he chuckled. Kate would be right in the middle of this one. He could see her now with her green eyes flashing and her red hair shining. Oh yes, if she tangled with Jim Darnell, that man may wish he'd never set foot in Porterfield. That was one of the things he loved about her.

Loved? When had that happened? He had to admit the truth to himself, but until the good Lord told him what to do about it, he sure wouldn't admit it to Kate.

Chapter Twenty-Two

Friday arrived, and Daniel met with the sheriff and Cory to carry out their plan for rescuing the young girl in the saloon. Daniel waited in the shadows with his heart pounding like a hammer on an anvil. The time he had gone into the saloon, Darnell had whisked the girl out the back door to get her out of sight. He now stood at the corner in the shadows to signal Cory when the sheriff entered the saloon.

Cory had a horse ready at the back entrance. The plan was for him to overpower whoever brought the girl out and to get her on the horse. Then Daniel would get her to Aunt Mae's while the sheriff kept Darnell busy. Daniel prayed no one would see them in the dark of the cloudy, moonless night, so Darnell would have no idea where she'd been taken.

Sheriff Rutherford clomped up onto the boardwalk, and Daniel signaled Cory, who took his place at the back door. As soon as the sheriff pushed through the doors, Daniel ran around to join Cory. Just as they expected, a man ran out the back with the girl. Cory hit him with the butt of his gun, and Daniel grabbed the girl, stuffing a handkerchief in her mouth to keep her from screaming. Together they hoisted her onto the horse, then Daniel swung up behind her.

In less than a minute they were gone from the saloon and racing behind the buildings on Main Street toward the boardinghouse. Every hoofbeat matched the thumping beats of his heart. The girl wiggled and squirmed, but Daniel held her tight. She must be scared out of her wits, but he'd have to explain later.

When he pulled up to the back door, Aunt Mae stood there and held a lantern. "Hurry and get her inside." The other boarders were all in bed except for Miss Perth, who stood behind Aunt Mae. The lantern was the only light to be seen.

Daniel swung the girl off the saddle and dropped down beside her. Her eyes opened wide with fear, and she kicked at Daniel. "Be still. We're not going to hurt you. We're here to help you," he grunted.

He carried her up the stairs and into the kitchen. She couldn't weigh more than a hundred pounds, but she was a fighter. Even now she squirmed and tried to get loose from his grasp. A sharp heel drove into his thigh, and a hand got free and hit him in the nose. He dropped her with a thud into one of the chairs and grabbed his nose. "Why did you have to go and do that? We're only trying to help you."

Kate stepped out of the shadows and grasped the girl's shoulders. "He's right. You're safe now. We only wanted to get you out of that place and find out why you were there."

Daniel knelt in front of her. "Look, if Mr. Darnell hired you, and you want to go back there, we can't legally stop you, but from the way he's been hiding you from the sheriff and me leads us to believe otherwise. Now if you'll promise not to scream and yell, I'll take that handkerchief from your mouth."

The girl nodded, her brown eyes still filled with fear and doubt. When Daniel removed the cloth, she gulped and swallowed hard but didn't scream. "Who are you?"

Kate now knelt beside the girl. "I know you're frightened, but we want to help you. Did Mr. Darnell hire you to work for him?"

The girl's eyes moistened with tears. "No, ma'am, he came to my school and offered to take me home. He'd been at my house for dinner before, so I didn't think anything of it. I went with him, but he didn't take me home. He put something over my face, and the next thing I knew we were out in the country, and I had no idea where I was. He's going to be so angry that I'm gone."

Kate gasped and glanced up to Aunt Mae. "He kidnapped you?"

"He told me that my parents had sold me to him and that I had to come with him, or he'd make sure I never saw them again. I–I was afraid, so I went with him. Please, he might do something to them if you don't take me back."

Daniel's brain went into overdrive. Surely there must be some law about selling children into prostitution, but he couldn't remember ever seeing one, and many parents did sell their children to work in factories. If selling children into prostitution wasn't against the law, it ought to be. Imagine selling a child to a man like Darnell! He wanted to find those parents and string them up by their toes.

He patted the girl's hand. "No one's going to hurt anyone. We'll keep you safe here."

Aunt Mae tapped his shoulder. "Let me clean her face up." She nodded to Miss Perth. "Fix a cup of hot tea with those herbs I use." She then proceeded to use a damp cloth to remove the rouge and powder from the girl's face. "Can you tell us your name?"

"Trudy is what Mr. Darnell named me, but my real name is Laura Prescott."

Without the paint on her face, her youth became even more evident. Aunt Mae smoothed her hair. "How old are you, my dear?"

"I turned fifteen several weeks ago. That's when Mr. Darnell started putting me with the men."

Daniel silently thanked the Lord for men like Clem who wanted no part of being with a child. Then he groaned inwardly. He could have saved her a week of shame and humiliation if he'd reported what he'd seen to the sheriff. He would work with the mayor and town council toward establishing some local laws in Porterfield that would prevent anything like this happening again. But right now he needed more information to take to the sheriff.

"Laura, where is your home, and what are your parents' names? We need to contact them. If they really sold you to Mr. Darnell, we may not be able to keep him from taking you back."

Tears streamed down the girl's face. "Please don't take me back there. Those men are awful."

Kate whipped around to face Daniel, her green eyes flashing with anger. "You are not going to take her back. How could you even think of such a thing, Daniel Monroe? That's the cruelest thing I've ever heard."

Daniel pulled Kate aside and lowered his voice. "The law's the law, Kate, and I don't like it any more than you do. Let me get the information I need, and the sheriff can investigate and get the truth. For one thing, if her parents did sell her, they may not want her back, and you have to face that possibility." Now she'd hate him, but he was on Laura's side, and the sooner they could clear up this mess, the sooner Kate would understand that.

Kate glared at him then returned to Laura. "Tell him where you're from and who your parents are." Kate used the same soothing voice she'd used on the children at the infirmary. It calmed Laura down, and the fear left her face. Kate had a gift, no doubt about it. Admiration for her courage and compassion filled him. If only he could bring out her finer qualities instead of provoking her temper.

"My parents are Lawrence and Matilda Prescott. They live in Dallas."

Dallas was close, no more than one or two days ride. If they'd been looking for her, they should have been able to find her this close. Maybe Darnell's story was true. There was only one way to find out, and that was to wire Dallas and see if any kidnappings had been reported.

"Kate, I'm taking this information down to Cory and Rutherford. Maybe they can wake the telegrapher and get him to send a wire to the Dallas sheriff tonight and see if any kidnappings were reported. He can also find out where her parents live and contact them."

When he opened the back door, he turned with a warning.

"Darnell is going to be plenty angry. You keep her out of sight. I don't know if he'll come here looking for her, but better to be safe. I'll be back later."

Kate reached out and touched his arm. "Be careful, Daniel. Darnell's men are probably out looking for her right now."

"I'll stay behind the buildings and in the shadows." He squared his hat on his head and stepped into the darkness.

∞

Kate breathed a silent prayer for Daniel's safety as he disappeared into the black night. Darnell's men might be anywhere in town, and she didn't want Daniel encountering any of them. It must be after midnight by now, but Cory and Sheriff Rutherford would be awake and waiting for Daniel's report.

She turned back to Laura. Her job now was to make sure this child was safe and returned to her parents. Kate didn't believe for one minute that a mother had allowed a father to sell their child to a man like Darnell.

"Laura, come with me, and we'll get you out of those clothes." With her hair loose and all the paint gone from her face, the girl looked even younger than fifteen.

Aunt Mae took the cup from Laura's hands. "That should help you sleep. You'll be in Kate's room with her. Miss Perth and I are going to bed, but we'll both be alert all night. Her room looks out toward town, so she can see or hear if something goes on out there, and mine is on the back, so we have the house covered."

"Why are you doing this for me? You don't know me or anything about me."

Aunt Mae wrapped an arm around Laura's shoulder.

"You're too young to be used like that. We wanted to be sure you had no choice in the matter. Now, let's get you out of that getup and into a warm nightgown."

Kate helped Laura remove the green satin dress she'd been wearing as well as the hose and shoes. She left the room to give the girl some privacy in removing her undergarments and slipping on the nightgown. When she returned, a lump rose in Kate's throat. Laura's dark hair hung down her back in waves of silk, and in the gown she looked so innocent and sweet.

Disgust for Darnell and what he'd put this child through raged through Kate. If the man had been in the room, she'd have socked him a good one and twisted his arm behind his back until he cried to be set free. Perhaps she'd visit him tomorrow and give him a piece of her mind, but she'd wait until she found out more from Cory.

Kate laid back the covers on her feather bed. "You slip in here between the sheets and pull this quilt up. I'm going to sit up a little while and study, but you need to sleep." Kate sat on the side of the bed. "Let's say a prayer first. You can rest easy because the shades are drawn tight so nobody can see in, and Aunt Mae nailed the windows shut just a while ago so no one can climb in. She thought of everything."

Kate grasped Laura's hands in hers. "Lord, keep us safe tonight. I thank You that Daniel and Cory were able to rescue Laura. Help us to find her parents and get her safely home where she belongs. We love You, Lord, and trust our lives and well-being into Your hands. Amen."

A tear made its way down Laura's cheek. "I never had anyone pray for me before. Mr. Darnell said I was a piece of trash that could be discarded if I didn't do what he said."

Kate swallowed a sob in her own throat. "Honey, you are not a piece of trash. You are one of God's children, and He loves you too much to leave you where you were. He let us find you and get you out of that place."

Laura yawned and blinked her eyes. "I don't know much about God. Ma and Pa never talked about Him except at Easter or Christmas."

This girl needed help in more ways than one, but tonight she was tired and needed her rest. Kate pulled the covers up under Laura's chin. "Go on to sleep now, and we'll talk more about it in the morning."

She carried the oil lamp over to her desk and turned it down to where she could still see her books, but the light wouldn't carry far into the room. This would be a long night, and she'd probably pay for it tomorrow by being sleepy at the infirmary. Maybe it would be a slow day, and she could come home for a nap.

After reading one page three times and still not getting the words, she closed her eyes and strained to hear the sound of Daniel returning from the sheriff's office. It shouldn't have taken this long to deliver the information and come back. Perhaps he'd decided to stay and visit with Cory, or maybe they were even able to waken the telegrapher and get a wire sent tonight. No matter, she wouldn't be able to sleep or concentrate until he returned, but even as the thought crossed her mind, her eyelids grew heavy once more.

Daniel delivered the message and waited until Rutherford returned with the news that he'd sent the wire to the sheriff in

Dallas, and they should hear back early in the morning. Only a few hours of sleep remained until then, but he wanted to get back to the boardinghouse and make sure the women were safe. Mr. Fuller, Wilder, and Frank may be there, but they wouldn't be much help against men with guns.

He stood and yawned. "I'm going back to Mae's and watch things there. Maybe I can grab a little sleep too. If Darnell did kidnap Laura, will you be able to arrest him right away?"

"Soon as we find out exactly what happened, I'm sending for Slade and letting him take care of Darnell, but I may be able to arrest him based on what Laura told you." Rutherford shook his hand. "Thanks for your help tonight. I think we were able to throw Darnell off track."

"Good, I'll be careful. See you two later." He slipped again into the inky black of night and made his way around to the back of the jail then turned toward the boardinghouse.

Twice he stopped. Once when a rock slithered under his foot, and once when a creaking sound came from behind the livery. He had just reached the corner of the livery when another sound like a thud made him stop and turn. This time a dark figure loomed up. Before Daniel could speak, something whacked him across the head. He fell into a heap but tried to rise to his knees. A second blow hit him, and he slumped to the ground, surrounded by silence and darkness.

Chapter Twenty-Three

Kate awoke with a start. Slivers of sunlight slipped around the edges of the shades. Although still dim, enough light showed Laura to still be sleeping curled up under the quilt. Kate rubbed her eyes. She must have fallen asleep before Daniel came in because she never heard him.

A dull ache spread from her temples to the back of her head. She'd slept with her head on her book, still in the clothes she'd worn yesterday. She massaged her temples and rolled her shoulders to loosen them.

The clang of pots and pans echoed from the kitchen. Aunt Mae was up and getting breakfast ready. Kate jumped to her feet and hurried out to help. "What time is it, and why didn't you wake me?"

"I figured you needed to sleep. I can get by on a lot less these days." Aunt Mae retrieved eggs from the icebox and proceeded to crack them into a bowl.

Kate found the slab of bacon and placed it on a chopping

block on the table. She picked up a large bladed knife and began slicing. "Did you hear Daniel come in? I went to sleep and missed him."

"No, but I imagine he decided to stay down with Cory and Sheriff Rutherford. You'll need to take them some breakfast."

"Perhaps I should go check to see if Doc Jensen needs me this morning. Since I slept later than usual, he's probably already there with Elliot and wondering where I am." She placed the slices of bacon on the counter by the stove. "I'll just run over there now, but I'll be back to get breakfast for the men."

Kate grabbed her shawl from the hook by the back door and stepped out into the cool morning air. The clouds had begun to dissipate, and the sun colored what remained with the pinks and orange of a new day. She stopped and breathed deeply of the fresh air. It would be the first day of new life for Laura, and Kate intended to make sure the girl stayed safe.

When she rounded the corner of the house, Frank raced down the street. "Miss Kate, you gotta come quick. Doc needs you. Mr. Daniel is hurt bad."

Kate's heart skipped a beat, and fear clutched her in its vise. Daniel hurt? She drew in a deep breath, picked up her skirts, and ran behind Frank the few blocks to the infirmary, praying as she ran. *Please, Lord, don't let anything bad happen to Daniel.*

When she entered the infirmary, the smell of ether, alcohol, and blood filled the room. She spotted Doc Jensen and ran to help. She skidded to a stop and a sob escaped. "Oh, no, Daniel."

Daniel lay on the bed, his face as white as the sheet beneath him. A nasty, long wound slit his head from the temple to the middle of his forehead.

"Help me with these sutures. He's got another deep gash on the back of his head, but this one is more serious. I sent Elliot down to get Cory. This was no accident."

She washed her hands and grabbed an apron. Then she cut lengths of black thread and laid them across the clean towel on the tray. She carefully threaded another needle to have ready for the doctor. "What happened?" she asked as she worked.

Frank still stood in the doorway and said, "I found him, Miss Kate. He was lying behind the livery when I got there this morning. I almost didn't see him 'cause he was behind some crates. Blood was all over his head, and I thought he was dead until I bent down and could see him breathing."

"He's lucky to be alive, Kate." Doc Jensen was solemn. "I think whoever did hit this boy thought it was hard enough to kill him and just left him there to die. Good thing he's a strong young man, or we'd be at the undertaker's instead of here."

Kate could only nod. How had this happened? It had to be one of Darnell's men. But how did they know Daniel had helped Laura escape? Questions whirled thorough her mind faster than she could think. Doc reached for a new needle, and Kate shook her head to clear it. She had to concentrate on the job in front of her and ask questions later.

"I think he fell so that his head pressed against his hat and stopped the flow of blood from this gash. The one on the back of his head is clotted with blood, and I haven't had time to clean it yet. We'll get to it when Elliot gets back."

The doc worked slowly, his fingers sure and steady as he made each stitch. Someday she hoped to make sutures like that. They'd leave a scar, but it wouldn't be as noticeable as some she had seen on others. Her heart continued to thud in her chest as she helped the doctor.

Cory came roaring into the room with Elliot right behind him. He took one look at Daniel and blanched. "What's going on? Elliot told me Frank found him behind the livery with his head busted open."

Frank retold his story then backed out of the room. "I got to get back to work. Somebody come and tell me how he's doing later."

Cory stepped closer to the bed. "Are you sure he's alive?"

Kate's teeth clenched. "Yes, he's alive, but barely. Did he get our message to you?"

"Yes, Rutherford sent the wire to Dallas, and we should be hearing back later this morning. We sat talking for a little while until Daniel decided he'd better get back to the boardinghouse. He left a little before two."

"Frank said he found a shovel with blood on it. I think that's what made this cut here so deep." The doctor tied up the last suture. "OK now, Elliot, we need to turn him over and see about that place on the back of his head."

Another sob caught in Kate's throat, and her hands trembled when she saw the bloody mess. Dried blood matted Daniel's hair. Doc Jensen dipped a rag in warm water and began cleaning the wound.

"This one isn't nearly as deep, but it looks like the initial blow may have been done with the butt of a gun. The second one near his temple is the one the attacker hoped would kill him." As he cleaned, it became more evident that the blood came from a surface cut, and a large knot was revealed. "Don't think I'll even need to stitch this one up."

Kate removed the bloody pillow where Daniel's head had rested while Doc tended to the more serious wound. Her stomach churned with fear and concern. If Darnell's men believed Daniel had been a part of the snatching of Laura, then they most likely would be snooping around the boardinghouse.

"Cory, go warn Aunt Mae to be careful this morning and keep an eye for anything unusual going on. Darnell's men might be planning to surprise her and grab Laura back."

"I'm going. I'll stay there with her for a while. Rutherford's gone over to see Darnell. Fat lot of good that'll do him." He loped across the waiting room and headed for Aunt Mae's.

A bit of relief shut out some of her fear, but a large part remained for the man on the bed. As long as he remained unconscious, he would feel no pain, but the more serious his condition would be. All the feelings and emotions she'd kept in check for the past months came roaring to the surface. Daniel had to be all right. He meant more to her than she'd been able to admit to herself or anyone else, but seeing him so pale and helpless brought it all cascading into her heart. If only he didn't have such old-fashioned ideas about women, she could see the possibility of a future together.

Who was she trying to fool? He'd shown no interest in her, and they hadn't even spoken to each other in weeks. Whose fault was that? If he really cared about her, wouldn't he have made more of an effort to seek her out? She shook her head. All she wanted to do now was to take care of Daniel and make sure he got well. She'd sort out the rest later.

Replacing a bowl of bloody water with a clean one, she breathed a prayer for the man stretched out before her.

∞

Someone pounded on the back door, and Mae grabbed her rifle from its place by the door.

"Aunt Mae, it's Cory, let me in."

She dropped the rifle and unlocked the door. "Land sakes, son, you scared me halfway to eternity."

He stepped into the kitchen and wrapped his arms around her shoulders. "I'm sorry. I didn't mean to frighten you, but I have some grim news."

Eloise Perth pushed through the door from the dining room. "What's going on? Oh, it's you, Cory. I hope you have good news for Laura."

Cory shook his head, and worry furrowed his brow. "Good morning, Miss Perth. Afraid I don't. Someone attacked Daniel last night on his way back here. Frank found him this morning behind the livery. He's at Doc's now."

Mae gasped and grabbed her throat. Daniel must have been lying in that alley all night. "How bad is he hurt?" No wonder Kate hadn't come back yet.

"He has a bad gash on his forehead and a big lump on the back of his head, and Doc says he's lucky to be alive."

Eloise clicked her tongue. "Who could have done such a thing to that nice young man?"

Cory cut his gaze to Mae. "We think Darnell and his men are behind it because of Laura. Daniel saw Laura in the saloon last week and realized she was too young to be there. Anyway, we think Darnell suspects Daniel had something to do with last night, and he may come here looking for Laura. I came to warn you to be extra careful today."

If Darnell was behind this, then that could explain the noises she'd heard last night. She'd sat in the dark by the window with her rifle in her lap. She'd heard rustlings and creaks, but no voices, and she hadn't seen anything either. That didn't mean they weren't out there. "Laura is in Mrs. Bennett's room trying on some clothes to see what might fit. We'll take extra precautions to keep her out of sight."

"I know you will, but to be on the safe side, I'm staying here with you. The marshal is due in this morning to take our prisoners, and the sheriff will pay Darnell a visit. This is my duty for the day."

Mae could handle things herself, but Cory's presence would lend an air of more security for the other ladies. Mae had to admit even she felt much safer with him here. "That's fine. Now I know you haven't had breakfast, so pull up a chair and I'll fix it up for you."

"But Aunt Mae, it's halfway to lunchtime. I can wait."

"Humph, I'm sure you think you can, but you need all the strength you can get if Darnell's men show up. A plate of my eggs, bacon, and biscuits will fill you up good, and I bet you'll still have room for lunch later." She'd seen her nephew eat too many times not to know he'd be starving about now and that he'd have plenty of room for more later.

Six biscuits were left over from breakfast and just needed heating. Mae busied herself with the preparations. Dozens of questions danced in her head, but she'd wait to ask them later.

"Is that more bacon I smell frying?" Henrietta Bennett entered the kitchen with Laura in tow.

Mae turned the slices of meat in the skillet. "Yes, it is. I'm fixing breakfast for Cory. He—" She stopped short. Laura didn't need to hear all that happened last night. "Um, he hasn't had time to eat yet, so I'm taking care of him."

"That's nice. Young men need their food, especially breakfast." She pushed Laura to the front. "Now what do you think of our Laura? Took a little altering, but the dress fits nicely, don't you think?" She twirled the girl around to show off the dark blue linsey-woolsey dress with a white collar and cuffs. Henrietta had combed Laura's hair back off her face and tied it with a matching blue bow at the nape of her neck.

Cory's eyes opened wide. "She doesn't look anything like she did last night, and she's a lot younger than we were told."

Mae reached out to hug Laura. "You are positively lovely." The girl eyed Cory with a mixture of fear and uncertainty. "Oh, Laura, this is my nephew Cory. He's a deputy and is one of the men who helped you last night."

"Oh, yes, I recognize you now. You're the one who hit Buck over the head and grabbed me."

Cory's smile stretched clear across his face. "We were glad to do it. Mr. Monroe told us that you're fifteen and your real name is Laura Prescott. Sheriff Rutherford wired Dallas last night to inquire about your parents. We should be hearing something soon."

"What if my parents did sell me to Mr. Darnell? Will I have to go back to him like Mr. Monroe said last night?" Laura clasped her hands in front of her so hard her knuckles turned white.

Mae placed her arm around Laura's shoulders. "I don't think that will be the case, but I promise you, I don't intend to let you go back there no matter what the law or your parents say."

The smell of burning bacon grabbed her attention. "Oh, dear, I forgot what I was doing." She lifted the strips from the grease and laid them out on a plate. "They're a little crisp, but you can eat them. I'm sorry, but I'll have these eggs scrambled up in no time, and the biscuits are all ready for buttering."

She intended to keep her promise to Laura, but at the moment she better pay attention to her cooking or she just might end up with a fire in her kitchen.

Chapter Twenty-Four

On Sunday, Kate dressed for church with a heavy heart. Daniel still lay unconscious in the infirmary. She had spent most of the day with him yesterday, but there had been no change. Doc Jensen said his heart rate was good and steady but wasn't sure why he wasn't waking up.

So many people from town had dropped by the hospital to check on him. Kate had no idea Daniel had made that many friends in the few short months he had been here. Most of them commented on his friendliness and willingness to help those in need. Even Miss Pruitt and Miss Simmons stopped in with Frank and Allen, saying how much they appreciated Daniel's help on the day the brides had arrived.

Laura had already dressed and was in the kitchen with Aunt Mae. No reply had come as yet from her parents in Dallas, but the sheriff there had wired to say he was checking into the alleged kidnapping as he had no record of it. That couldn't bode well for Laura, but all of them had prayed about the situation last night, and Aunt Mae assured Laura that God would take care of her.

Kate joined the boarders in the dining room. Only Daniel's chair sat empty. Laura occupied Cory's. He had gone back to the sheriff's office to see if any new information had arrived. Grim faces greeted her. No one smiled, and they simply nodded their heads to acknowledge her presence.

In the kitchen Aunt Mae flipped more pancakes in the black iron skillet. "Cory said he'd be back soon as he could, and he'd stop and check on Daniel too."

Kate donned an apron. "I'm so worried about Daniel. I haven't been exactly nice to him in past weeks, and now I can't talk to him at all. What if he doesn't wake up?" She had pushed that thought from her mind several times, but it kept rearing its ugly head. She had to face reality in that Daniel's injuries could be more serious than any of them realized.

Aunt Mae slipped her arm around Kate's waist. "It's in the Lord's hands, sweetie, and I believe the Lord will heal Daniel. You'll see; he'll wake up real soon."

If only Kate could believe that and have Aunt Mae's faith. First Pa had been injured and now Daniel. Two men who meant so much to her had faced life-threatening wounds. She bit her lip and filled a platter with pancakes. She had to admit now that she cared about Daniel far more than she liked to think about.

Back in the dining room, conversation halted when she entered. "More pancakes for everyone." She set the plate on the table and gazed around at each one of them. "Daniel will be all right. He has to be."

Miss Perth reached out to grasp Kate's hand. "We believe that too, my dear. I've decided to stay here with Laura, and

Frank is going to stay. I know how to use a rifle and won't hesitate if it's necessary."

"Yes, Miss Kate, I'm good with a gun too, and if any man tries to get into this house while y'all are at church, they'll have to come through me." The big burly blacksmith sat up to his full height, his muscles evident through his shirt sleeves.

"Thank you, Frank." He'd put up a good fight with any man who tried to come through that door. Just knowing he'd be here with Cory relieved much of her apprehension and her doubts about going on to church. "I know Aunt Mae and I both want to attend church this morning, so we appreciate your offer to stay here. Cody will be back before we leave, and maybe he'll have some good news from Dallas and from the doctor." She held on to that belief through the meal.

Cory joined them just before she and Aunt Mae were ready to leave for the church. "Nothing from Dallas as yet, but Doc Jensen says Daniel is getting stronger and should be waking this afternoon."

Joy filled Kate's heart and soul as she smothered her brother with a bear hug. "That's the best news I've heard in a while." She stepped back and placed her hand on Laura's shoulder. "Listen to Miss Perth and stay out of sight in our room. No one can get in there without coming through here first. Mr. Cahoon and Cory will take care of you, and Daniel will do everything he can when he's well to make sure you don't have to go back to Darnell's." Kate had to believe her own words, or her mind would go crazy with worry.

After assuring Kate that all would be well, she and Aunt Mae left to walk to the church. When they reached the church yard, several people greeted them and expressed their concern for Daniel. Their kind words and well wishes warmed her heart, and she planned to tell him how all the good people of Porterfield had expressed their appreciation for him.

Someone called her name, and she turned to find one of the most welcome and encouraging sights her heart could hope for today. Ma and Pa rode up in their carriage. Pa was driving, so he must have improved greatly. She waved and ran to greet them.

"Ma, Pa, how glad I am to see you. Are you sure you're well enough to be handling the reins?"

"Of course I am, lassie. Take more than a bull's horns to keep me down."

Ma stepped down from the carriage. "Help me get him down. He's still not supposed to put full weight on that leg, so he's using crutches."

Pa didn't complain when Ma and Kate reached up to assist him as he hopped down from his seat. He grabbed the crutches and positioned them under his arms. "Well, now, I'm almost good as new, but we need to hear all about what happened here yesterday. Brody gave us his version, but we want to hear it from you."

The church bell rang out across the yard. "It's time for service to begin, Pa. I'll tell you everything after. Aunt Mae will expect you and Ma to stay for dinner after church. Then you can see for yourself how things are."

Pa frowned and hobbled toward the church building. "I don't like it, but I figure I'll have to live with it. Let's see what the Reverend Winston has to say this morning."

The pastor didn't disappoint with his message. He spoke of how good triumphs over evil and God works everything for good, even the bad things that happen in our lives. He offered up a special prayer for Daniel and welcomed Pa with praise that God had spared his life.

Afterward, Reverend Winston came out to assist Pa into the carriage for the ride to Aunt Mae's. No sooner was he settled with Aunt Mae riding in the back seat with them than gunshots rang out, blasting the Sunday morning peace. It had come from the direction of the boardinghouse.

Kate took off running, her heart once again pounding faster than Red Dawn galloped across a pasture. She beat the carriage by only steps and ran into the house.

Cory had a man handcuffed and on the floor. Miss Perth stood with her rifle at her side and a grim expression on her face. Frank's pistol hung from his hand by his side.

Kate panted and tried to catch her breath. "What–what happened? We heard a gunshot."

Cory shoved the man in front of him. "One of Darnell's men tried to get in. He fired through the window, and Frank and I both fired back. He ran for cover but didn't get far when Miss Perth let go with her rifle and shot him in the knee. Perfect shot if I ever saw one."

The man in custody vented his anger and tried to wrench free of Cory. "That old witch could have killed me. I was just coming to visit. You had no cause to shoot at me."

Cory tightened his hold. "Just come to visit, huh? I don't know of any business you might have here, so we'll march on down to the jail and see what you have to say for yourself." Cory led him to the door.

"My boss will hear about this and be down to get me out quicker than you can lock me up."

Cory shoved a hat down on the man's head. "We'll just

see about that. He was arrested last night and is in jail himself right now." He pushed the man through the door and called back over his shoulder. "Save some of that roast beef for me. I'll be back to eat soon as I take care of this vermin."

Pa sank down onto one of the chairs with a thud. "Now this is what I call an interesting situation. Care to fill us in on what's going on?"

Kate went to check on Laura and let Miss Perth and Frank do the explaining. Laura sat huddled on the bed, her knees drawn up to her chin. Kate sat beside her and hugged her. "It's all over now, and Darnell and the intruder are in jail. See, we said you'd be safe here. Come on out to the dining room. I want you to meet my folks."

"Miss Kate, I was so scared. I heard noises outside and then Mr. Cahoon yelled something and then I heard gunshots. I just knew somebody had been killed."

"Well, they weren't, and Cory has taken the man who tried to break in down to the jail to lock him up. Aunt Mae is getting Sunday dinner on the table and is expecting you to join us. OK?"

Laura nodded and swiped at her cheeks with her fingers. Now that she was taken care of, Kate wanted to get over to the infirmary. She could eat later.

She left Laura in the capable hands of Ma and the amazing Miss Perth. Never would she have believed the elderly teacher would shoot a rifle and hit a man. Some things were just too much to comprehend—like her feelings for Daniel. She prayed as she hurried the three blocks to the infirmary. He had to wake up this afternoon.

∞

Pain thundered through his head. He hadn't felt this much agony since he fell off his horse when he was a young boy. He knew he hadn't fallen from a horse this time, but what caused this dull throbbing escaped his memory.

He tried to open his eyes, but they may as well have been glued shut. A moan broke the silence, and he realized it was his own. Footsteps clicked across the floor and stopped near him.

"Daniel, it's Doc Jensen. Can you hear me?" The doctor gripped his hand.

Another groan was all that Daniel could manage. He must be at the infirmary if Doc was with him. Daniel attempted to move his head, but the hooves of a thousand horses thundered across his skull. Each throb matched a heartbeat. Finally he managed to squeeze the hand that held his.

"Good, good. You're waking up. Elliot, go get Kate."

"I'm here. I just came from church."

Daniel heard more footsteps, and another hand rested on his arm. "Daniel, I'm here. Please wake up."

Kate's voice, the one voice that had echoed through his mind and kept him fighting, was now beside him. How easy it would have been to just let go and give into the pain, but the idea of never seeing Kate or his family again strengthened him and gave him the will to keep struggling for his life.

Daniel attempted a few words, but only moans came out. Once again he tried to open his eyes and managed enough to see light and fuzzy figures. He waited, his lids half open, until the haze began to clear. With great effort, he opened them all the way and focused on Kate's beautiful face.

Memories of last night came flooding back like rushing water over a dam. They'd rescued a girl from the saloon, and he'd gone to the sheriff's with the information about her. Then someone had attacked him on the way back to the boardinghouse.

"Laura?" he asked, his voice rough.

Kate placed a finger on his lips. "She's fine. Don't talk now. Let Doc examine you. I'll be right here too."

As the doctor checked his stitches, he spoke to Kate. "I sent Elliot down to the jail to check out the man Miss Perth shot." He chuckled a bit. "Cory said she aimed for his knee and hit him on the kneecap, and she didn't even flinch when the gun went off."

Daniel struggled to speak. "Who...shot?"

"Just one of Darnell's men trying to break into the boardinghouse, but Frank and Cory took care of it." Kate squeezed his hand.

As long as the girl was safe, the rest of what happened didn't matter. Any pain he suffered now was worth the effort of rescuing Laura from Darnell's clutches. Daniel relaxed into the pillows.

Doc Jensen held a spoon to Daniel's lips. "Here, I'm giving you something to ease the pain and help you to sleep. Your body needs plenty of healing rest, so lie still and relax."

The liquid tasted bitter on his tongue, but if it relieved the awful pain, he didn't care what it tasted like. He closed his eyes again. Plenty of time for questions later. Hands examined his head as Daniel's body began to relax and the pain began to subside. Now it was almost bearable.

Kate's voice penetrated his consciousness once again. "You

do what the doc says. I'm going to tell the others you woke up, and you're now sleeping naturally. You really gave us a good scare."

She caressed his hand a moment then he heard her departing footsteps. He wanted to call her back but could only mutter her name.

Doc's voice floated above him. "She was here with you all day yesterday and helped me get you stitched up. I finally got her to go home last night and get some rest for herself."

The doc's hands now lifted Daniel's head, causing him to yell out in pain and his muscles to tense. "I'm sorry, but I had to see about that wound on the back of your head." He gently returned Daniel's head to the pillow.

Once again Daniel relaxed, but his mind raced ahead with questions and speculations. If Kate said she'd been at church, this was Sunday. He'd gone down to the jail Friday night. That meant he'd lost a whole day. Whoever had hit him had intended to keep him quiet. The realization that the man wanted him dead swept over Daniel with a wave of nausea. It all had to do with Laura and Darnell. It had to be. He'd done nothing to anger anyone else, but how had Darnell known who had taken the girl?

He wanted to get out of the hospital and see that Laura was all right. How could Kate and Aunt Mae defend themselves against the ruthless man who wanted the girl for his own? Then his mind became fuzzy, and the noise of the room dimmed to nothing as the pain reliever took over his consciousness. His body completely relaxed as he slipped into healing sleep.

CHAPTER TWENTY-FIVE

On Tuesday Daniel sat on the edge of his bed at the infirmary. He'd just finished one of Aunt Mae's meals of hot chicken soup, cornbread, and berry cobbler. His stomach satisfied, he lay back against the pillows. The antiseptic smells no longer bothered his nose and certainly had no effect on his appetite.

He'd tried to stand before lunch, and his head spun crazier than a top. He'd try again in a little while, but he was content to sit and rest after his hearty meal. It had been a welcome relief after yesterday's parade of broths and hot tea for each meal.

Cory stuck his head through the doorway. "You up for visitors?"

Daniel sat up straighter. He'd be ready for anybody and anything if they brought good news. "Tell me you have something to cheer me up."

Cory came in with his hat in his hands. "I think you'll like what I have to say. First off, we're holding Darnell on suspicion of kidnapping a minor. He's hired a lawyer to come down from Dallas, but he hasn't arrived yet. The marshal took the rustlers off our hands, and that shooter in the saloon fight will go on trial tomorrow in Panola County."

Daniel blew out his breath in exasperation. Good news, but not exactly what he wanted to hear first. "I hope you have more than that."

Cory shook his head and chuckled. "I know. You want to hear about Laura. The sheriff in Dallas has no record of a kidnapping in that area around the time Laura says Darnell abducted her. They haven't located the parents as yet but are working on it."

That was not the news he wanted either, but it would have to do for now. If no kidnapping had happened, then that meant Darnell may have told the truth about buying Laura from her parents. Daniel still couldn't wrap his mind around the idea that any parent would be so in need of money that they'd sell their own child, especially to someone like Darnell. He picked at the sheet, searching his memory for any other cases like this in the law books he'd studied. Slavery was against the law, but men still tried to get around it and own slaves. In his eyes, Laura was Darnell's slave to do the work he commanded her to do, and that was illegal in any man's book.

Kate swept into the room, her petticoats rustling under her dark brown skirt. Her presence lit up the room, and any pain he might have been feeling disappeared with her smile.

She studied his tray a moment then moved it aside. "I'm glad to see you're eating well. That'll help get your strength back."

Daniel's eyes never left her form as she straightened the bedclothes. "Cory was just telling me about Laura."

Kate stopped her work and bit her lip. "Ma and Pa took her out to the ranch where it'd be harder for Darnell's men to get to her. Ma and Erin will take good care of her. I'm afraid it won't bode well for Laura if they can't find her parents or find out they really did sell her to Darnell. That would be awful."

"I'm going to study my books and find something that will help me free her from the bargain if her parents really sold her to Darnell. I'm hoping the judge will give us an injunction so she won't have to go back to Darnell, but he may side with the man."

Kate planted her hands on her hips and narrowed her eyes. "Daniel Monroe, if you let that snake Darnell get his hands on Laura again, I'll–I'll never speak to you again."

Daniel couldn't help but burst out with laughter at the weak threat. "Well now, that wouldn't be such a bad thing since you haven't spoken to me for weeks anyway. I think Friday night was the first time, and then it was only because we were helping Laura."

Kate grabbed up the tray and spun around. She headed for the doorway but glanced back at him. "Laugh all you want, but I'll think of something worse." She blew out her breath. "You are so exasperating. I almost wish you were still unconscious." With that she marched out of the room with her head high and her shoulders back, a sure sign he'd angered her again.

Daniel held up his hands. "What'd I do now? Every time I talk to her, I end up making her madder than a wet hen."

Just when he thought they would be friends again, he'd upset her, and all because of Laura. There was always something to go wrong when they were together. He wanted to be more than friends, but at this rate, they'd be enemies before long.

Cory shrugged and grinned. "Kate's always been the one to be in trouble with people no matter whether it's Ma, Pa, or one of us brothers. We put up with it because we love her. I say you'd have to love her with everything you are and with a forgiving heart if you're ever going to have a relationship with her."

Therein lay the problem. Could he love her enough to overlook her outbursts? Taking away her independence or any of her other traits would be taking away a piece of Kate herself. If he wanted to love her, he would have to take her as she was, with her independence and feistiness and steely compassion and, yes—her orneriness.

"I'm going to take that stubborn sister of mine out to the timberlands and show her what they're doing. The lumber company is keeping its word, and you can barely tell where they've already removed what they were given for this year. Maybe that will help ease some of her anger toward you for helping Pa and the others to negotiate that contract."

Daniel closed his eyes. He'd forgotten about that. Just one more thing added to the list of wrong steps he'd taken around her. That deal for the timber was a good booster for the entire community, and he prayed she'd see it didn't ruin the beauty of the landscape. "No, Cory, let me do that. Maybe then she'll see that I wasn't lying to her about the trees."

Cory shoved away from the wall where he'd been leaning. "OK, that may be better anyway. I'm going on back to the jail.

Soon as we hear anything else from Dallas, I'll come tell you. I'm hoping it'll be sometime today."

"Thanks for all your help, and I don't mean with just this case."

Cory winked and shoved his hat back on his head. "See you later, with good news, I hope."

When the deputy left, Doc Jensen returned, the odor of disinfectant and iodine clinging to his clothes. He peered over his glasses at Daniel. "Kate Muldoon made a very hasty exit, and she had that look on her face that told me something had upset her. You have anything to do with that?"

"I always upset her. I think maybe she doesn't like to be around me."

"Couldn't prove that by me the way she carried on when you were brought in Saturday morning. She about worried herself into a frazzle because of you." The doctor examined the stitches on Daniel's forehead.

Daniel said nothing but let the words sink into his brain. She sure had a funny way of showing her concern. He winced as the doctor's fingers worked with the bandage. Daniel hadn't yet seen what the cut looked like, but he did know it covered most of his forehead from the left temple to just past the middle, and that's where the pain concentrated now.

"Looks like I can take these stitches out by Friday. I'll let you go home then. Kate and Aunt Mae can take good care of you, but I'd rather you stay here until I can see for myself you're OK. A blow to the head is always a serious thing."

That suited Daniel just fine. He had no desire to be around Kate when she was angry with him. If she wanted to see him, she'd have to come here to do it.

Kate strode back to the boardinghouse, seething with anger at the idea Laura may have to go back to Darnell. Not if she had something to say about it, she wouldn't. Kate turned from the boardinghouse and headed toward the jail. She'd give that Darnell a piece of her mind and tell him just what she thought of his buying children.

The raucous music from the saloon and the laughter of men drinking and gambling even at this time in the afternoon infuriated her even more, but she marched on by to bigger prey. When she stomped past Mrs. Bennett's shop, the dear woman stepped out to say hello but took one look at Kate's face and scurried back into her shop. Kate would have to explain at supper tonight, or the poor woman might think Kate had lost her mind.

The five blocks to the sheriff's office gave her time to build up steam. She paid no mind to the people who greeted her or passed her by on the boardwalk. As if in tune with her mood, clouds rolled in and covered the sun. The air now had a chill, but it did nothing to cool Kate's temper. By the time she reached the jail, her anger had mounted to the point she might hit the man if he came close enough. She'd never lashed out in anger before, but a child needed protection from a rat like Darnell.

When she entered the office, heat filled her face. She didn't stop to speak but headed straight for the cells in back. Cory jumped up to detain her, but she yanked her arm out of his grip and pulled open the iron door and tramped through.

"Mr. Darnell, I have a few words to say to you." Her voice echoed through the empty cells.

Darnell leaped from his cot and glared at her. "What do you want? You're nothing but a troublemaker and should be arrested for hiding stolen goods."

Kate narrowed her eyes and planted her hands on her hips. "I am not hiding stolen goods. I'm hiding one scared little girl. You ought to be ashamed of yourself selling that little girl to men for their own use. You're worse than a no-good, low-down skunk, and you stink just like one. No one has the right to steal childhood away from a person, boy or girl, and that's just what you're doing."

"Now, wait a minute, Kate Muldoon—"

"I will not wait a minute. You keep your mouth shut and listen. Even if you did buy Laura from her parents, you're not going to keep her. Buying and selling people is wrong and against the law. We're going to mount up a case against you that'll make you wish you never heard of the town of Porterfield." All big words, and she didn't know if anything could actually be done, but she'd die trying, and she wanted to make sure Darnell understood that.

"Have you finished? Because you're all wrong. That girl is my legal property—"

"No, she's not. And she'll never be in your possession again as long as I have anything to say about it." She whirled around to the man in the other cell who had been shot by Miss Perth. "And you're no better than he is. Worse even to come to our house and try to break in. You'd have shot any one of us if Miss Perth hadn't hit you first. You both deserve to be hanged." She stomped back to the office with Darnell's words coloring the air with epitaphs she didn't care to hear. She slammed the door shut behind her to silence the noise.

Kate glared at Cory, who tried to disguise his amusement. "What are you looking at, big brother?"

"Nothing." He held up his hands. "Nothing. That was a good show, but you know you just put yourself and Daniel as well as everyone at the boardinghouse in more danger. If Darnell wants Laura, he has the men who will try to get her back."

Before Kate could respond, Sheriff Rutherford walked through the door. He glanced from Cory to Kate and back again. "What's going on here?"

"Nothing, sir. Kate just came to pay a visit." His glare told her to keep her mouth shut.

"I'm glad you're here, Kate. Save me a trip down to the boardinghouse. Had a wire back from Dallas just now. They haven't located Laura's parents because they're out of town, but they did find her grandparents. They have been looking for her ever since she didn't return from school. The parents are following a lead someone had given them saying they saw Laura get on a train headed West. Soon as they're contacted, I'm sure they'll be on the first train that can get them here. Looks like I'm charging Darnell with kidnapping for real this time."

Kate's breath expelled in a whoosh and she hugged the sheriff. "I knew it! That's the best thing I've heard all day. I can't wait to get back and tell Aunt Mae the good news, and then I'll ride out to the ranch and tell Laura." She kissed the sheriff on the cheek and raced out the door. As she passed the infirmary, she hesitated. She ought to go in and tell

Daniel the good news, but he could wait. He wouldn't have to do anything now. Laura was safe with Ma and Pa out at the ranch.

CHAPTER TWENTY-SIX

ADA SAT WITH Laura and Erin at the kitchen table drinking tea. The girl had told them about her home in Dallas, and it hadn't seemed like a family who would sell their daughter, weeks before her fifteenth birthday, to a man like Darnell. In fact, the Prescott family had money and prestige in Dallas. That made it all the more difficult to believe Darnell's claims.

Erin sat next to Laura as they discussed clothes and hairstyles. Ada gazed about her own home. The oak and pine of the dining table and chairs and the furniture in the parlor were probably not as elegant as what Laura had in her home. She pictured the family now at an lavish table covered with a linen cloth, fine silver, and crystal, and most likely a chandelier hanging from the ceiling. Her place may not be as fashionable, but it was home and suited the life of a rancher's wife just fine.

A dress of Erin's had needed only slight alterations to fit

Laura, and now she looked more like the girl she was. The fear had finally passed from Laura's eyes.

Ada passed the plate of sugar cookies to Laura. "How long did you say you'd been with Mr. Darnell?"

"I'm not sure, but I think it's been at least two months. I lost all track of time as he kept me under such close watch. I was in another saloon before he brought me here a week or so ago." She picked up a cookie and nibbled on it then smiled at Erin. "I really do thank you for the dress. You have been so kind to me."

Ada patted Laura's arm. "It's the least we could do for you. You'll never have to wear that saloon garb again." She sipped her tea then leaned toward Laura. "Tell me, did your parents take you to church?"

Laura scrunched up her forehead and bit her lip. "No, ma'am, at least not that I remember. We spent weekends going places or visiting friends. I never heard anything from the Bible until Miss Perth read from it last Sunday."

"That's a shame, but I believe that God has been watching over you and brought you to Porterfield so the sheriff and Cory could find you and rescue you."

"I don't understand. Why would God be watching over me? My father said that God metes out justice and punishment to those who sin, and our job was to do good and stay away from sinful activities."

Erin refilled her tea cup from the pot on the table. "Then why didn't your parents go to church?"

"Mother said that church was just a place people went to see and be seen, and Papa believed as long as we lived right and did what was right, we didn't have to go. He said we didn't have time to go anyway."

Ada shook her head. Sometimes she wondered where people's brains were when they talked about the Lord. Not having time to go to church just didn't make sense. No one could be busier than a rancher, but Callum always made sure his family was in church on Sunday and that they knew why they were going. Of course church didn't take away a person's sins, but it offered the opportunity to hear God's Word preached and to fellowship with other believers.

"What do you believe about God?"

Laura lowered her head. "I don't know. I guess I thought God was punishing me for my sins by making me do those things Darnell wanted me to do."

Ada reached over and clasped Laura's hands in hers. "Oh, honey, God wouldn't punish you like that. You've never been given the chance to know who the Lord is or how much He loves you."

"Why would God love me after the horrible things I've done?"

"Because, dear child, He forgives those things and loves you very much." Explaining God's gift of His Son to Laura was Ada's most important task today. The house could stay a mess for once. This child's life was in the balance, and Ada wanted to tip the scales in favor of a life with the Lord.

"You mean God would forgive me even after my body was used like that?"

"Oh, yes. He forgives every one of us for the things we do that are not good. But honey, you didn't choose to do those things. An evil man forced you, and you were a victim of his evil actions and desires. You see, God doesn't blame you or condemn you because of what someone else does. He knows your heart and how much you hated what happened. But whether you had sinned intentionally or unintentionally, He'd forgive you, because the Lord forgives and heals every one of us for the things we do that are not good if we come to Him."

Just then Kate burst through the door. "I have great news, everybody!"

She leaned on the table and stared straight at Laura. "You were kidnapped. Your parents didn't sell you to Darnell. Your grandparents told us, and your parents are out looking for you now. As soon as the sheriff in Dallas can get word to them, they'll come to get you. Isn't that wonderful?"

Ada gasped, and Laura cried. Ada wrapped her arms around Laura. "They're going to be so glad you're safe and so glad to have you back that they'll love you no matter what."

Laura's sobs subsided, and she sniffed then blinked her eyes. "Is that like what you said God did? That He'd love me no matter what I'd done?"

"Yes, it is. The Bible tells us that everyone has sinned and fallen short of God's plan, but when we confess our sins, He is faithful to forgive us. Take Kate here. She has a temper, as do some of my other young'uns, but Kate lets hers fly without warning sometimes and says and does things she shouldn't. She has to ask forgiveness for her anger. Isn't that right, Kate?"

Kate's face blazed with heat, and she swallowed hard. "Yes, that's true, and the latest episode happened just a little while ago." She then proceeded to tell them what had taken place at the jail. "I don't know what came over me, Ma. I've never been that angry before."

"Well, I would call that righteous anger and well deserved by those two men. It's the way you go about expressing your anger that usually gets you into trouble. I'm just glad it didn't this time."

"But that's not nearly as bad as what I've done." Laura's hands tightened to fists on the table. "I'm ruined. How can God ever fix me?"

Kate dropped to her knees beside Laura. "Honey, listen to me. You are a sinner, but not because of what you did with Darnell. You are a victim of his greed. Believe that."

Confusion filled Laura's eyes, and Kate wrapped her arms around the girl.

"All you have to do is give your life to Jesus. He paid the price for our sins long ago on a cross, and when you give your life to Him, He can turn the bad that has happened to you into something good that will heal you. In fact, I think that's what He's doing right now. He brought you to us so you could learn about Him."

"I think I understand. I've heard stories about Easter and Christmas, but they didn't mean much to me."

Ada's heart ached with the idea of parents who didn't teach their children about God's love. They may be good parents, but they were neglecting one of the most important aspects of a child's life. She picked up her Bible and turned to Luke 15, to the parables of the lost sheep and the prodigal son.

"Laura, I want you to read this, and when you're done, come and talk with me and I'll answer any questions you have." She handed Laura the Bible and prayed for the Lord to open her heart to His Word.

Kate stood. "You do what Ma asks, and I think you'll begin

to see what we've been telling you." She leaned over and kissed her mother's cheek. "I've always known you were the best Ma around, and this proves it."

She pulled on her riding gloves. "I need to get back to town and help Aunt Mae. I also want to stop in and see how Daniel's doing. He was sitting up earlier, so he's doing better. If Cory hasn't told him about Laura's parents, I need to do that too."

Ada watched her daughter leave with a hint of doubt in her heart. She could always tell when something troubled her children, and Kate was troubled now. Until Kate shared the problem with her, Ada would have to be content with praying that Kate would find the answers she needed.

∞

Kate climbed atop Red Dawn and nudged the horse with the heels of her boots. Her heart lay like lead as she remembered her mother's words. A quick temper had always been a problem for Kate, and usually she handled it. Lately her temper had become more active than usual, and it'd all started when Daniel came to town.

What hurt the most was Ma's confidence that Kate would be seeking forgiveness. Remorse set in because that's exactly what she hadn't been doing. It'd been a long time since she'd sought the Lord's help with her temper or asked for forgiveness when she let her anger fly. Advice and help she'd sought, but not forgiveness for her behavior. Maybe that's what held back God's answer to her prayers.

Why did Daniel have such an effect on her? He'd been here since August, and she'd lost her temper with him at least half a dozen times, and it was all because of his attitude or something he said about Kate's work.

She lifted her head and breathed in the crisp fall air that had finally arrived. She shivered as the cool air crept beneath her jacket, but not because her body was cold. Her soul was as barren as the fall landscape. No bright colors, only the dead brown of falling leaves and the dark green of the pines standing tall. No breeze or wind today to fill the air with the song of autumn.

Guilt nibbled deeper into her heart until Kate stopped Red Dawn and swung down from the saddle. She led him to a nearby tree and tied the reins loosely around the trunk. "I need to do some serious talking with the Lord, and I can't do that and concentrate on the road too." She patted her horse's neck then sat down by the tree.

With her knees tucked under her chin, Kate did what she had needed to do for several weeks. *Lord, why does life have to be so complicated? I know I should've been talking to You about my anger and how I've let it get the best of me, but I thought I had good reason to be angry. I realize I did with Darnell, but not with Daniel. Why can't we get along? Lord, if only we could agree on what's important. You are my rock, my strong tower, and I am waiting for Your direction. Forgive me, Lord, and help me to control my tongue in the days ahead. Help me to be an example for Laura.*

She sat in quiet solitude for the next few moments until the wind picked up to break the silence. Finally she stood and unloosed Red Dawn. Peace like she hadn't known in a while filled her from head to toe and gave assurance that whatever happened now, God was in control, and she would have an answer soon.

"Come on, girl, it's time to go home." She swung up into the saddle and nudged her horse toward town.

∞

Relief filled Daniel as he listened to Cory. Laura's story had been true, and Darnell was now charged with her kidnapping. He'd be sent back to Dallas for trial, but oh, how Daniel wished he could be the prosecuting attorney. At least he could attend the trial and testify as a witness.

"Kate must be one happy gal to be able to give Laura such good news."

Cory laughed and shook his head. "After she blistered Darnell and his man up one side and down the other, she got so excited about Laura, she kissed the sheriff."

"I wish I'd been there when she was reaming out Darnell. She's one tough wildcat when it comes to defending what's right." After the way she'd helped Pete Davis and now Laura, he wanted Kate on his side if he ever needed help. Of course that would mean getting her to at least be friends with him, but all they'd managed was to continually offend each other.

Cory nodded in agreement. "When it comes to helping people she thinks are victims, she's like a mama bear protecting her cubs. Don't mess with her."

"Yeah, I've learned that the hard way. Thanks for coming by and letting me know about Laura. I hope to be out of the hospital by the time her parents get here. I think Doc is being too cautious, but I've learned there's no sense arguing with him. He'll release me when he's good and ready and not a day sooner."

"I hope they arrive soon. The US marshal is coming to take Darnell to Dallas. He says he's had more business here in the past few weeks than he's had in several years."

Daniel could believe that. Porterfield had been as quiet as Briar Ridge until the cattle rustling, then it seemed like the town fell apart. He much preferred his lawyer's job to that of being a deputy. Now if he could figure out how to get back into Kate's good graces, this would be a much better place to live, and one where he wouldn't mind having a wife and family with him.

"Hey, can I come in?" Kate stood at the door with a rosy glow on her cheeks.

Daniel's heart jumped at the sight of her windblown hair and dusty boots. She'd been riding, most likely to the ranch to share her news with Laura. "Please come in. You're a much prettier sight than your brother. But he's been telling me about Laura and her parents. He also told me about your run-in with Darnell. Wish I could've have been there to see that."

A sheepish grin crossed Kate's face. "I'm a little ashamed of myself now, but he did deserve a tongue lashing."

Cory wrapped his arm around her. "I'm really proud of the way you stood up to him. Of course with the bars between you, you were safe enough."

Kate punched her brother's arm. "It's a good thing too, or I might have scratched his eyes out."

The banter between the brother and sister sent bits of homesickness through his heart. He and Abigail used to tease around like, and he missed it. He'd chosen to move away from his family and didn't regret the move, but it didn't mean he couldn't miss them. The Muldoon clan teased and joked with all the love a Christian family should have. And Daniel wanted to be a part of it.

Cory patted Kate's shoulder and winked at Daniel. "I'm sure you two have lots to talk about, and I need to get back to my duties."

When he'd left, silence filled the room with an expectant hush. Daniel's tongue stuck to the roof of his mouth like a stamp to an envelope. Even if he could think of what to say, he'd never be able to get the words to come out right. He didn't want to risk saying the wrong thing and getting Kate out of sorts again.

Doc Jensen treated another patient, and his voice filtered in from the examination room. Kate paced about the room, until she turned on her heel to face him.

"With Laura's parents coming and this being a kidnapping after all, you won't have to worry about Darnell getting Laura back. It's all working out for the best."

"Kate, I wouldn't have let her go back to Darnell no matter what the law said. She's just a child and has no business being in a place like that. At home she probably thought she was about grown at fifteen, but what she's been through should never have happened."

"I figured as much." She stepped closer to the bed and held out her hand. "Can we call a truce and be friends?"

Daniel grasped her hand in his, and immediately its warmth went straight to his heart. "Of course we can." She smelled of the outdoors and autumn, and all he wanted to do was kiss those perfectly formed lips. He swallowed hard and restrained himself. A kiss might ruin the moment and break the truce.

She eased her hand out of his grip, and his hand became cold with emptiness. "I need to get on back to the boarding-house as it's getting close to supper time. We'll miss you at the table, but I'm glad I can report you're doing much better."

When she had gone, he laid back against the pillow. A truce was a good place to start if he wanted more in their relationship than being friends. The future looked brighter than it had in a long while, and Daniel planned to do everything in his power to keep the light burning.

Chapter Twenty-Seven

Friday morning Kate's joy overflowed. Sheriff Rutherford received a wire from Laura's parents, and they'd be arriving on the train from Dallas today. Ma and Pa were on their way in from the ranch, and Doc Jensen would release Daniel from the hospital after he removed the stitches from Daniel's forehead. Everyone would be at the station to meet the Prescotts.

In honor of the occasion, the sun had chosen to shine and warm the temperatures to the sixty-five degree mark for a wonderful day of celebration. Darnell had already been transferred to the jail in Dallas where he'd stand trial for the kidnapping, and that was one trial Kate didn't want to miss. She even hoped she'd be called as a witness for the prosecution so she could tell the jury what that man had done.

Before they knew the Prescotts would be arriving, Mayor Tate had called a meeting at town hall, so they would attend that first. Kate had about figured out what the topic would be from the rumors and speculations around town since his announcement. Tate had been talking about a county courthouse and a park ever since the state named Porterfield the county seat. Just how he planned to do it and where would make for an interesting meeting.

Ma had sent Erin with the even better news that Laura had asked Jesus into her heart, and even if her parents were not arriving today, that would be cause for celebration.

Kate pinned the last curl into place but decided against a hat. It was hard enough to wear one on Sunday, much less during the week.

In the dining room Miss Perth, Mrs. Bennett, and Aunt Mae waited for her, each lady dressed in her Sunday finest. All of them had a part in rescuing Laura and wanted to greet her parents.

Aunt Mae pulled on her gloves. A dark blue hat trimmed with feathers and ribbon sat atop her gray-streaked red hair, and a grin as wide as all of Texas split her face. "This is indeed a great day for our town. Let's get on down to the hall for the meeting. I can't wait to hear what the mayor has planned for Porterfield now."

"As long as it doesn't hurt my dress shop, I'm all for improving the area along Main Street." Mrs. Bennett shook her head so that the feather on her hat wobbled.

"Now, Henrietta, I'm sure the mayor won't bother any of the existing businesses." Aunt Mae patted her boarder's shoulder and strode to the door. Mrs. Bennett and Miss Perth fell into step behind her. The men had already departed, so Kate latched the door behind her as the last one out.

As they strolled down to the town hall, Kate marveled at the number of buggies, wagons, and horses filling the streets.

Everyone from the smallest farmer to the bank owner would be here for the meeting, and a lot of them would then head for the station to meet the Prescotts.

Kate waved and greeted people all along the way. She probably should have stopped in to see if Daniel was ready to leave the infirmary, but it might be better if they just saw each other at the meeting. So far their truce had held, and neither had said anything to cause ill feelings to arise, but Kate truly disliked having to be so careful about her topics of conversation and her words. Otherwise they could probably be good friends, if not more.

Ma and Pa were already seated with Laura between them when Kate entered the building. They hailed her, and she hurried to join them. After she sat down and greeted Laura with a hug, she glanced over the girl's shoulder and spotted Daniel talking with Mayor Tate. From the dazed expression on Daniel's face, the mayor must be giving Daniel good news. He sat down with a thud that even she could hear and turned to see her. He waved at her but still looked stunned to his toes.

Evidence of the attack on him showed in the ugly red slash across his forehead and would always be a reminder to Kate of his bravery and willingness to help a young girl in trouble. Everyone in town considered Daniel to be a hero. Cory and the sheriff were doing their duty, but Daniel had voluntarily helped with the rescue, and she admired him for it.

The mayor called the meeting to order and proceeded to outline his plans for making Porterfield an even better place to live. "As for the courthouse, our plans call for a building on the north end of Main Street as it goes out of town. That way it can be seen from both the north and south."

The mayor placed a large drawing of the proposed building on a stand in front of the podium. From what she could see, it would be an imposing structure, one all the citizens could be proud of, and it even had a clock tower. Of course it would be brick to match some of the newer buildings in town. The print reminded her of images she'd seen of Independence Hall in Philadelphia.

"As you can see, it will be three stories so it will be as tall as the tallest building in town. It will have court rooms and offices for all the town officers. We'll relocate the jail and sheriff's office there and make the cells stronger and more secure. The US marshal will have an office there too."

Cory and Sheriff Rutherford beamed their approval. Such a structure would make things easier for them. As Mayor Tate revealed more about the new courthouse, people in the room began to smile and nod their heads. From what Kate could tell, Tate would have the backing of the whole town, and that was a good thing for Porterfield to move forward and become an even better place to live.

When the mayor finished telling about the new courthouse, the audience cheered, but the mayor held up his hands. When the crowd quieted, he said, "I have one more announcement to make. When the courthouse is finished late next spring, Daniel Monroe has agreed to become our first county attorney."

Kate gasped and leaned forward to get a glimpse of Daniel. His face burned red, but pleasure filled his smile. She joined in the thunderous ovation given the town hero. People swarmed around Daniel offering congratulations along with handshakes and claps on the back. Kate hugged her mother. "Isn't it wonderful for Daniel? He's really made an impact on our town since his arrival."

"And what about you, my dear? What impact has he had on you?" Ma held Kate at arm's length and peered into her face.

Heat rose in Kate's cheeks. "We're friends. That's all."

Ma simply shook her head. "Still my stubborn Kate." Then she turned to her husband. "Callum, it's time to get to the station. Let's go, Laura." Ma wrapped her arm around the girl's shoulder and hugged her. "Your parents will be in soon, and all this will be behind you. Just remember what you now know, and you'll never be alone, no matter what happens."

Kate stood in place as they walked away. She wanted to congratulate Daniel, but many others still thronged around him. Congratulations would have to wait until later when they met back at the boardinghouse with Laura's parents. No matter what their differences, Daniel was a good man, and happiness for his good fortune filled her heart.

From the corner of his eye, Daniel spotted Kate headed toward the door. Desire to run after her fought with common courtesy to the folks shaking his hand and offering their congratulations for his appointment. To say it had come as a surprise would be an understatement. The implications hadn't really soaked in as yet, but he would serve this town well in exchange for all the encouragement and support they'd given him in the few months he'd been here. His parents would be proud, and he'd get a wire off to them as soon as he could get to the telegraph office.

The train whistle sounded in the distance. "Thank you for your words of encouragement and your concern for my injuries, but I hear the train. I must get over to the station to greet Mr. and Mrs. Prescott."

Those still around him murmured their understanding as many of them wanted to be at the depot to meet the train as well. He looked for his hat then remembered he hadn't brought one because of the wounds on his head. The one in front still hurt to the touch and even throbbed now and again, but the doctor had said there was no infection and the pain would go away the more it healed. That couldn't come soon enough for Daniel.

He hurried out of town hall and headed down the street to the depot. He could hardly believe that they were halfway through October and the temperatures were still so mild. Back home the leaves would be falling and freezes happening each night. He'd been warned that cold weather could come in December and January, but it still would be nothing like Connecticut. The longer he was in Texas, the more he liked it.

At the station he spied Kate and her parents with Laura just as the train rolled into the station. He joined them on the platform with dozens of other townspeople who had come to welcome the Prescotts.

Laura first smiled and then bit her lip and frowned. She peered up at Mrs. Muldoon. "Do you think they'll hate me for what Mr. Darnell made me do?"

"Of course not, child. They love you and will be glad to see you safe."

Daniel placed his hand on Laura's shoulder. "From the sound of their telegram to the sheriff, they'll greet you like the long-lost daughter you are." The girl trembled under his hand. How frightened she must be after being away from home over two months. He prayed her family would be happy to see her and not blame her for what had happened.

When the train stopped, an attractive woman with the same dark hair and brown eyes as Laura stepped down followed by a man in a suit. Laura's hand went to her mouth, and she cried, "Mama, Papa."

She ran toward them, and the woman opened her arms wide then drew her daughter close. "Oh, my baby, my baby, we were so worried about you." Tears filled Mrs. Prescott's eyes and streamed down her cheeks. Laura sobbed into her mother's shoulder. Her father embraced them both, and Daniel's own eyes misted when he saw the moisture in Mr. Prescott's.

Laura whispered something to Mr. Prescott, and he looked around then stretched out his hand toward Daniel. "I understand you're one of the men who helped rescue my daughter. We can't thank you enough for all you did for her and for us."

Daniel grasped the man's hand in return. "I'm Daniel Monroe. Deputy Cory Muldoon and Sheriff Rutherford were the other two who helped. They're here to meet you too." He stepped back and introduced the sheriff and deputy to Mr. Prescott.

Mr. and Mrs. Muldoon and Kate introduced themselves, and Aunt Mae invited them back to the boardinghouse to get comfortable and spend time with Laura.

Mr. Muldoon slapped Cory on the back. "Son, help me get their bags into the carriage, and then we'll ride back to the boardinghouse." He turned to Mr. and Mrs. Prescott. "I have a carriage to take you down to the boardinghouse. If you and

Laura will come with me, you can ride together and visit on the way."

Since another train to Dallas wouldn't be through until Monday, the Prescotts had brought several bags with them. Daniel helped load them onto the carriage despite Cory's objections that he still wasn't well. "Don't worry about me. I feel better than I have in a long time."

When the carriage drove away, Mrs. Muldoon hooked arms with Aunt Mae. She turned to Kate and glanced at Daniel. "We'll see you back at Aunt Mae's when you get there." She grinned at them both. "Have a nice walk."

Kate dipped her head. "Sorry about that, but I guess you're stuck with me."

Stuck with her isn't exactly how he'd describe it, and he looked forward to the next seven or eight minutes they would have together. Now if he could only find a safe topic of conversation that wouldn't end up with anger flashing in Kate's eyes.

Kate turned to him. "I think it's wonderful that the mayor appointed you as county attorney. With the new federal judge appointed by the governor, all the cases we used to take over to Panola County or up to Dallas will come here, and that will keep you busy."

"Thank you. It's a great honor, but I have to warn you that I may not be so popular when I have to prosecute friends or family of people in town." He remembered times back in Hartford when the prosecution had been maligned for handling certain cases. If he didn't get a conviction, the citizens wouldn't like it, but if he did, then the family of the accused would yell at him.

"Do your job and do it right, and they won't have cause to criticize or complain."

Her green eyes sparkled, and the sunshine emphasized the deep red in her auburn tresses. Her beauty took his breath away, and he longed to hold her in his arms. But that would get him nothing but trouble. She had let him know more than once that she had no interest in romantic relationships.

"I've been thinking, Daniel, with your being the county attorney, we'll need us another lawyer in town. Do you suppose Mayor Tate will advertise for one, or do you have someone in mind for your current job?"

He hadn't considered that aspect of his new position, but it wouldn't take effect until the courthouse was built and the new judge appointed. However, someone did come to mind. "Yes, I think I do."

If he could persuade Nathan and Rachel Reed to come West and practice law, his life here would be complete. Well, not exactly. It wouldn't be complete until he had a wife, preferably Kate Muldoon.

Chapter Twenty-Eight

Kate had no opportunity to speak with Daniel in all the excitement at Aunt Mae's. While they ate dinner, questions bombarded Mr. and Mrs. Prescott. The first one Kate had to ask concerned how they knew Mr. Darnell in the first place.

Mr. Prescott frowned and shook his head. "I'm an investment broker, and Mr. Darnell was a client of mine. I handled a great many investments for him over the past several years. He was always polite and very businesslike in our dealings. When I learned he was not married and alone in Dallas, I invited him to our home for dinner."

Mrs. Prescott squeezed Laura's hand. "I knew something was wrong with that man. He had this look in eye when he met Laura that bothered me. He was polite enough and asked her how old she was and where she went to school, you know, ordinary questions that seemed innocent at the time. She told him her fifteenth birthday was in a few weeks, and that perked up his interest."

Mr. Prescott sat on the other side of Laura and reached for her hand also. "The terrible thing is that we didn't know she was missing until she didn't arrive home at the usual time. We figured at first she'd stopped at a friend's house, but then we found a note at our door telling us that if we wanted to ever see our daughter alive again, we must say nothing to the law about this, and that she was safe and well, but only if we followed instructions."

Laura's eyes brimmed with tears. "When he told me that you had sold me to him, I didn't want to believe him, but he was so convincing and kept such a close watch on me that I ended up believing it."

Kate's anger simmered at the idea of a man like Darnell being so evil. To take a child away from his or her parents was the cruelest act a person could commit against a family. Then to use her like he did was evil at its worst. Her heart uttered a prayer of thanksgiving that things had worked out as they did. God had protected them all when they rescued Laura.

A young boy from town pounded on the door. "Miss Muldoon, come quick, Doc Jensen says he needs you right now." The frantic tone of his voice caused Kate to jump from her seat and run for the door. "I'm on my way. Sorry, folks, but there must be some kind of emergency."

She raced after the boy, anxious to know what had happened. Several people had gathered on the boardwalk outside the infirmary. Only the words "a wagon accident" and "the Blalock family" reached her ears. The first thing to greet her inside was two young children with blood on their faces and clothes.

Doc Jensen appeared in the doorway of one of the

examining rooms. "They're only scratched and bruised. I need you in there with Elliot."

Kate headed for the second room and found the young doctor treating a baby and a young boy. "What in the world happened?" She washed her hands then tied a clean white apron over her dress.

"The boy's arm is broken. I've set it and gave him a little something for pain." All the while he talked his hands moved swiftly and carefully over the baby. The tiny girl's chest barely moved. "I can't find any external injuries, and I pray there are none inside. She was pinned under her mother, so I believe she just had the breath knocked out of her, but she does have a bruise on her forehead, so we'll watch her closely."

"What else do I need to do?" Kate was already gathering the supplies and equipment needed to put the boy's arm into a cast.

"Exactly what you're doing. We'll get this one fixed up in no time. Then we'll need to see about the parents and help Doc." His clipped, curt words spurred her into action.

While he prepared the mixture for the cast, he explained what had happened to the family. "Something spooked their horse, and he raced out of control. They must have hit a rock because the wagon went up into the air. That's when those two out there fell from the back. Then the wagon overturned and pinned the others down."

Kate's heart went out to the family and the two little ones in the waiting room whose eyes were so wide with fear. Their red, wet faces attested to the fact they'd been crying for a while. Mrs. Jensen's soothing voice now spoke to the little ones. Relief filled Kate. The doctor's wife would know exactly what to do for them.

Doc Elliot finished with the cast and went to help his uncle. A few minutes later, when Kate stepped out to the waiting room, the children were gone. Mrs. Jensen must have taken them to her place to clean them up. Kate washed her hands again and went back to make sure the baby was secure in the crib the doctor kept on hand for young patients. The boy still slept with his arm on a support.

When she entered the room where the two doctors worked on the mother and father, she surveyed the scene to see what she must do first. Doc Elliot stitched up a wound on the woman's face. Another gaping laceration bloodied the sleeve of her brown dress.

Elliot glanced up at Kate. "She has two broken ribs, but Doc couldn't find any other broken bones. These cuts are deep. She had some laudanum, so she won't be in much pain for now."

"Kate, help me with Mr. Blalock." Doc unbuttoned the man's shirt and eased it off. "I've got his leg in a splint, but we need to see about his back and head. Help me roll him over."

Once again a blood-stained pillow greeted her. She faltered a moment at the memory of Daniel in this same spot. Then instinct kicked in. This wound was much worse than Daniel's.

Doc Jensen explained while he examined the laceration. "He landed on his back, and his head hit a rock. He may be unconscious for a while, but he'll be OK. The wagon landed on top of them, and that's how their bones were broken."

Kate's heart went out to the family. What had started as a pleasant afternoon riding to town had turned into a catastrophe. Porterfield was lucky to have two doctors who knew what they were doing.

After the wound had been cleaned and stitched, Doc washed his hands. "I'll put a cast on that leg in a few minutes. Why don't you go back and check on the little boy and the baby?"

Kate cleaned up before checking on the children. Doc Jensen was a real stickler for cleanliness and washing hands before going from one patient to another. The baby's chest moved in a much smoother rhythm now, and her face relaxed as in a natural sleep.

Kate ran her finger gently across the baby's cheek. How precious this tiny life was to God. He had protected her and her family. Her heart beat with gratitude that all had been spared. How terrible it would have been for the parents to have lost one of their children or for the children to have lost a parent.

Behind her, the boy moaned. She leaned over to check on him, and he opened his eyes. Kate gulped. Never had she seen eyes that color of blue. It was as though she gazed at a cloudless summer sky. She ran her fingers through his blond hair matted with leaves and dirt."Hi, there, what's your name?"

"I'm Davy Blalock." His face scrunched up, and he cried. "My arm hurts."

"I know it does, sweetie. You broke it, and the doctor put a cast on it. Let me get you something to drink." She stepped over to the sink and filled a glass with water then returned to Davy's bedside.

"Here, drink a few sips of this. Your arm will stop hurting soon. Your parents are in the next room. They got hurt, but they'll be OK, and so will your baby sister." She wet a cloth and began cleaning his face and removing leaves from his hair.

His sobs diminished, but he breathed in spurts and his shoulders shook. Elliot came up behind her. "How's our big boy doing? That arm still hurting you?" At the boy's nod, the doctor said, "Let's see what we can do about that." There he was again, all smiles and sweet words for a patient.

A few minutes later, the boy quieted down and settled back onto the bed. Kate and Elliot stepped out to the waiting room. Elliot said, "Thank you for your help. We know we can always depend on you to come when needed."

Kate's mouth dropped open, but she quickly closed it again. That was the first compliment he'd ever paid her. "I saw the tender way you handled the baby and your gentleness with the boy," Kate said gently. "Have you thought about a family of your own? I know there aren't many women around town, but have you considered writing an ad for a mail-order bride? Worked out good for Frank and Allen."

A veil fell over his eyes, but not before she detected once again a deep sorrow and pain in their brown depths. He swallowed hard and turned away from her. "I didn't come here to find a wife. Things are just fine the way they are."

Kate drew in a quick breath at the bitterness in his voice. What could have happened in this young man's life to cause such a reaction to a simple question? All she really knew about him was that he was Doc Jensen's nephew, was twenty-seven years old, and had been a doctor back in Ohio. What secrets did he carry buried in his soul?

Mrs. Jensen stepped into the room. "Kate, I know you're worn out and you have company at your house. So go on home. The other two are upstairs sound asleep, and I'll take these two up with me and look after them. You and Doc need some rest too, Elliot."

Kate glanced at her watch and realized the lateness of the hour. What little dinner she'd eaten before she had to leave had long since disappeared, and her stomach growled in protest. "Thank you, Mrs. Jensen. I think I will go home."

She washed her hands again before setting out for the boardinghouse. With night, the air had grown colder, and Kate wished she'd taken time earlier to grab up her shawl. She wrapped her arms around her body and ran the few blocks to Aunt Mae's.

Her parents' buggy was gone, so they'd left for the ranch. The house was only dimly lit. Everyone must have gone to bed. She stepped up onto the porch and opened the door. A shadow moved, and Kate yelped.

Daniel's hands steadied her. "I didn't mean to frighten you. I...we were worried about you being gone so long. The Prescotts took Laura and went out to the ranch to stay with your parents. What was the problem that the doctor had to take you away from dinner?"

She explained the situation to him and told him Mrs. Jensen had taken the children to care for them.

His eyes shone in the dim light from the hallway. "You amaze me, Kathleen Muldoon. Most women I have known would never have been able to handle a situation like that. They'd have done what Mrs. Jensen did and taken in the babies but left the other work to someone else." He placed his hands on her shoulders. "I'm very proud of you."

Kate gulped and blinked her eyes. Had she heard him

correctly? He was proud of her and hadn't scolded her for doing what she loved to do?

Daniel dropped his hands. "I can see that you are tired, so go on and get some sleep. But tomorrow, I have something special planned for us. Will you be free?"

His touch still burned on her shoulders, and she wanted to lay her cheek against his chest, but she focused on what must be done in the morning instead. "I'll check on the Blalock family early, and then I'll be free. What do you have in mind?"

"Let's just say we're going for a ride. I'll saddle up Red Dawn for you while you're at the infirmary, so we'll be all set to go." He briefly kissed her forehead then released her. "Get some sleep now. You've earned it."

In the next moment he disappeared up the stairs and into the shadows. She reached up to her forehead where the touch of his lips still smoldered. What an odd thing to do after all their disagreements, but she liked it, and that only served to confuse her more.

Curiosity about tomorrow danced in her head, but her brain was too tired to speculate. The only important thing now was that he had spoken of his pride in her, and that was music to her ears.

As she prepared for bed, she hummed a song that always brought her joy and peace. God's amazing grace had certainly been evident in the events of the past weeks. Laura was safe with her parents, and the Blalock family had all survived a horrible accident. When she slipped under the covers, a smile formed. Tomorrow she'd be with Daniel, and it couldn't come soon enough.

Chapter Twenty-Nine

The next morning Kate carried out her duties at the clinic. The children were in Mrs. Jensen's good care. Aunt Mae had already been over to promise to take care of meals for the patients, so the doctor's wife could care for the children. Joe Davis had taken the wagon wreckage to his shop and promised to have it fixed and ready for the family to use to go home.

Mrs. Blalock was propped up in bed with a contraption Doc had rigged up. He raised the top part of the mattress with wooden blocks so the patient was in a partially raised position without actually sitting up. She held the baby to her breast. It was the most beautiful sight Kate had seen in a long time.

The young woman smiled at Kate. "Thank you so much for taking care of Grace and Davy last night. They're both fine this morning, and as you can see, nothing has affected her appetite."

After a few minutes admiring the baby, Kate excused herself. She'd already told the doctors that she was leaving early and why. She had dressed in her riding clothes this morning and ran to meet Daniel at the barn.

He brought Red Dawn out to stand beside his black horse. She stopped and observed him for a moment. Her view of him had changed so much in the two months since his arrival. Admiration for his talents, his consideration of people and how to treat them, his willingness to face danger to save a young girl, and his love of the Lord had all served to change her opinion of him as a "fancy pants" lawyer to a caring Christian man.

He spotted her and waved. "We're all set here. Are you ready for a ride in the country?"

A ride in the country? Her expectations were higher than that, but any time with Daniel would be a good time. She grinned and joined him. "All set. Our patients are well cared for and I'm free, but don't forget, we have to be back this afternoon for the weddings."

Daniel laughed and mounted Black Legend. "How could I? I'm standing with Frank. He and Allen are two lucky young men."

Kate couldn't agree more. Aunt Mae, Miss Perth, and Mrs. Bennett planned to be at the church this morning decorating with ribbons and fall flowers from Ma's garden. The whole town would turn out for this double wedding.

The sun shone from a near cloudless sky and took away the chill of the morning air. As they rode, Kate admired the way Daniel sat in his saddle. Gone were the fancy clothes, replaced with the jeans and cotton shirts most men wore in Porterfield. His tan boots fit into the stirrups of his saddle as though he'd always worn them.

Dare she admit her early opinions had changed so much that love had begun to grow in her heart and soul? Daniel evoked feelings in her she'd never before experienced. In the past if a man had even tried to kiss her as Daniel had done last night, he'd have wound up with a slap on his face that would sting for days. But that kiss she'd welcomed, and she longed for more.

Black Legend drew closer to Red Dawn. Daniel held the reins with a relaxed, confident grip. "What's on your mind this morning? I see a smile at the corner of your mouth, and I hope it might be for me."

Heat flooded Kate's face. She wasn't about to admit the truth, at least not yet. "I was just admiring the beautiful weather we're having."

"Yes, it has been nice. By now the temperatures in Connecticut would be near freezing. I already love Texas weather despite the heat of summer."

She gazed at the landscape and listened to the wind through the trees. "Hear that, Daniel? It's autumn's song."

"What do you mean? All I hear is the wind rustling the leaves."

"Listen close. In spring there's a rustle of newly green leaves, soft and comforting. In autumn, hear the slight crackle as dead leaves brush against each other and fall to the ground. It's telling us that nature is taking a rest."

"I never thought of wind having different sounds except in times of storm."

Kate lifted her head to hear the sounds. "To me, each season has its own music. In the summer the whispering pines and cicadas bring harmony and peace on a warm afternoon.

Autumn is a time of slowing down and getting ready for a long rest. Winter is the time of quiet peace even if a snow or ice storm is raging. Then spring comes with the wind through the new leaves bringing promise that the Lord lives again, and all the earth celebrates in a riot of colors and scents."

"Now that's pure poetry. Is there no end to your talent?" He pointed to the northwest. "Look at your pine forest over there. This is what I wanted you to see."

"I see the timberland on my father's property." Timber that would be ruined when the lumberjacks came in and cut the trees down.

"Did you know the sawmill has already been in and cut this year's quotient of timber from Muldoon land?"

Kate spun around in her saddle to face Daniel. "What! I thought that was happening later." She turned back to view the forest. To be honest, she could see no visible signs of cutting anywhere. "They must not have cut down very many. I can't tell if any are gone."

As they rode closer, more light penetrated and shone through the trees in some areas. She'd been told they would leave the forest with enough trees in the designated cutting area to keep it from being barren. That had been hard to believe, but now she could see it with her own eyes.

"See, Kate, they're keeping to the contract. They're over at the Bartlett place next week, and then it will be on to Brody's and Ian's properties."

"I have to admit it's not what I expected. Looks like I was wrong about how the forests would be ruined."

Once they were only yards away from the forest, the wind whispered through the pine trees almost as though assuring her that all would be well. Peace filled her heart. How wonderful and amazing God had been. Joy filled her heart until it cried out to be released. She did in the way that always increased her happiness, with her voice.

The words from her favorite hymn spilled forth into the air, telling the story of God's amazing grace toward His children.

~

As soon as the song began, Kate's soprano voice thrilled Daniel's soul. He'd only heard her sing in church, but even without a piano or organ, her notes soared clear and pure.

As Kate sang the words "I once was lost, but now I'm found, was blind, but now I see," a sense of revelation poured over Daniel. He'd been blinded to who Kate really was and her mission in life. He remembered what Doc Jensen had told him at the infirmary. Kate had the gift of a healing touch. She not only knew how to treat the wounds, but she also knew how to treat the person. Whether the patient was a child or an adult, Kate had words that lifted their fears and calmed their spirits and a soothing touch that brought strength and courage.

God had given her a talent for keeping her head in a crisis and bringing healing to the hurt and the sick. He had been selfish in wanting her to use that talent only on him and a family. Even worse, he'd wanted to thwart God's will for Kate's life. No man had the right to do that.

He loved her, more than he could ever imagine loving a woman, but how could he support her dream?

They rode on, Kate singing as Daniel continued thinking. Then another idea dawned. His mother spent her time entertaining and socializing and hired servants to take care of the home. That life had suited his father, his sister, and him quite well through the years. The same could be done here. With his new job he could afford to hire a cook and housekeeper, and Kate could spend her time ministering to those who needed her. One song, many years old, had opened his eyes to what could be in his future if he listened and obeyed God's calling.

The burning desire to tell Kate of his discovery flamed higher in Daniel's soul until he wanted to shout out his love for Kate so that all of creation could hear, but he waited until the song ended. He dismounted and then reached up to help Kate do the same.

Her eyebrows raised in question for his actions. With her feet on solid ground, he encircled her waist with his hands. "Miss Kathleen Muldoon, you are the most amazing woman I have ever known. Ever since the day I arrived, you've continued to surprise me with your unending talents." He gazed into eyes and bent his head toward hers.

"I love you, Kate, and I think I've loved you since that first day when you were so stubborn with that trunk of mine. You were bound and determined to get it into the house no matter how heavy the stupid thing was, and right then I was entranced with you. I know we've had our differences, but I want a chance to show you that I can love you and cherish you the way you deserve. Will you give me that chance?" Then his lips met hers and poured out his love in a wave that said everything he'd felt in the months since his arrival.

∞

A sob lodged in Kate's throat. Daniel's lips, so soft against her own, brought out the deep desire that had smoldered in her heart and soul, a desire she'd kept buried deep within. Now it fought to rise to the surface. She pushed back from him. "Daniel, I–I do love you, but I'm not sure this is what God wants for me. I love nursing so much." That one little piece of her heart wouldn't let go. The desire had been a part of her for too many years.

Daniel tightened his arms about her. "Kate, I don't want you to give up on your dream. I want you to continue your studies."

The idea that he'd be willing for her to finish her studies sent glimmers of hope into her heart, but what then? "And if we marry, what would you expect? I can't give up what I've worked so hard to accomplish." That sounded so selfish. Confusion reigned in her soul. If only God would tell her the answer straight out.

Daniel's hand caressed her face. "If we marry, I will expect you to continue helping Doc Jensen at the infirmary. My mother always had someone helping her with our home, and we can do the same. I was blind to what you could do with your gift of nursing. Your song opened my eyes to how remarkable you really are."

Tears welled up in Kate. This was the love God expected between man and woman. True love meant giving your loved ones the opportunity to be everything God wanted them to be. Daniel loved her like that, and in that moment God's answer burned bright. She could love Daniel with all her heart and soul.

She clasped her hands behind his neck. "Mr. Monroe, those are about the most wonderful words I could ever hear. You love me enough to give up your notions about what a wife and mother should be and what things a woman shouldn't be a part of."

"That's what I'm saying, and I mean every word. Will you marry me, Kathleen Rose Muldoon?"

Her love soared to the skies above, and the wind sang autumn's song across the pasture grasses, through the trees, and out to the rolling hills beyond. This is where she belonged, in Daniel's arms. "Yes, Daniel Monroe, I'll marry you and love you forever."

She lifted her chin, and Daniel bent once again to kiss her. This time she returned the kiss with all the flames of emotion rising within her. They may have their stormy times dealing with her stubborn streaks, but oh, the fun they'd have in the aftermath.

Coming from Martha Rogers in January 2012, ***Winter Promise,*** book 3 of Seasons of the Heart

CHAPTER ONE

Porterfield, Texas, 1890

"PORTERFIELD, NEXT STOP in ten minutes." The conductor's announcement sent the butterflies to dancing again in Abigail Monroe's stomach. Ever since they had entered the state of Texas, her mind had flitted from one thing to the next in a series of images that blurred one into the other. What she remembered from her visit last spring had been enough to give her the desire to return as a permanent resident.

All around her passengers began gathering their belongings and preparing to leave the train. Mrs. Newton, who had accompanied her on the trip, adjusted her hat and picked up her handbag. "Well, your adventure will begin shortly."

Abigail grinned at the elderly woman. If it had not been for Rachel's aunt's desire to come West to visit her daughter, this trip may have been delayed indefinitely. "Thank you so much for coming with me. You know how Father worried and didn't want me to travel alone."

"And well he should have been. It isn't safe for a young woman of your standing to be crossing the country by train without an escort." She tilted her head toward Abigail, and the feathers on the hat covering her gray hair shook with the movement.

Her parents had at first refused to even consider such a move for their only daughter, but as they began to realize that she was almost twenty-two years of age, their objections lessened. They had been in Porterfield a few months earlier for the wedding of Daniel, Abigail's brother who came to Porterfield a year ago as the town's only attorney. Now he served as county attorney and prosecutor. When Mabel Newton had said she wanted to visit her daughter and niece, Father had finally agreed.

Another factor in her decision to leave Briar Ridge had been Rachel Reed, her very best friend since childhood. Rachel's husband, Nathan, had taken Daniel's place as an attorney for the citizens of Porterfield, and now they too lived in the Texas town. As far as Abigail was concerned, God had orchestrated a great symphony of opportunities, and she had seized the score to become a part of the music.

"Aunt Mabel, do you think my plan for establishing a library is a sound one? Nathan and Daniel have found a building they think is suitable and will negotiate the purchase of it if I approve."

"Every town needs a library whether they know it or not. It will be a wonderful asset for the children as well as the adults.

Loaning books is a good way to help people read a wide variety of materials. Your brother and Nathan have good judgment, so the place must be about perfect."

A snicker escaped Abigail's throat. Daniel had always been her protector, and if the building suited him, it most definitely would suit her. She'd been so angry with him for leaving her behind in Briar Ridge last year. Of course he thought it was because she'd miss him, but it was really because she'd been jealous of his new adventure.

"I'm sorry things didn't work out for you and that young Wentworth. He seemed very interested in you when you and Rachel were in Boston."

Abigail had been disappointed at first, but when she realized what all would be expected of her as the wife a Wentworth, relief displaced the other, and now she had this new adventure ahead of her.

"It worked out for the best, but life became so dull in Briar Ridge without Rachel or Daniel that I could hardly bear it. No eligible young men my age were left in town, and I'd grown tired of entertaining with Mother and taking part on church committees."

"I see. So the fact that Porterfield has an overabundance of single men of all ages had a little something to do with your decision." Aunt Mabel's blue eyes sparkled with merriment.

Abigail's cheeks filled with heat. She truly wasn't interested in finding a husband anytime soon, and the idea that Aunt Mabel had that impression may well be how others saw her coming to live there. The train whistle screeched through the early afternoon air. Abigail clutched her handbag and closed her eyes. *Please, Lord. Don't let this be a mistake. Help me to do the things I want to do for Porterfield with books and accept whatever else You have planned for me.* Although a husband wasn't at the top of her priority list, if God happened to send one along, she wouldn't object.

The train stopped with a jolt that sent her forward with a lurch. She reached out and steadied herself then assisted Aunt Mabel with her bag and followed the older woman down the aisle. Dozens of people lined the platform waving as the train emptied itself of its load. Abigail scanned the crowd to find a familiar face, and her heart leaped with joy when she spotted Rachel.

Rachel rushed forward and grabbed Abigail when she stepped from the train car. "Oh, I'm so glad you're finally here. I didn't think the last three months would ever end." Then she turned to hug her aunt. "I'm glad you're here too. With Seth, Sarah, you, and Abigail, I won't feel at all lonesome, not that I could the way the Muldoon clan has taken us in."

"When I met them at Seth's wedding, I knew they would make all of you feel right at home. I'm anxious to talk with Mae again."

"You'll get to see her soon enough. She's having us all for dinner at the boardinghouse tonight."

Aunt Mabel stepped back and eyed Rachel. "My dear, are you in the family way?"

Heat flooded Rachel's cheeks, and she grinned. "Yes, I am, and so is..." She clapped her hand over her mouth. "Oh, I almost slipped. She wants to tell everyone herself at dinner."

Abigail ran through the list of possibilities. Kate? Erin? Sarah again? Whoever it was, the baby would be welcomed by many loving aunts, uncles, and cousins. Arms wrapped around her shoulders from the back, and she craned her neck to see who it could be.

"Daniel!" She turned and hugged her brother. "Isn't this exciting? I'm here at last. We had a delightful train trip, and I can't wait to see your new house. And where's Kate?"

"Doc Jensen and Elliot had an emergency at the infirmary, so she's there. She said she'd meet us wherever we were when she finished."

"I believe Aunt Mabel will be staying with Sarah and Donavan. At least that's what she plans on. Mrs. Sullivan said she has a room for me at the boardinghouse, so I'll stay there."

Daniel frowned and peered at her. "But Kate is hoping you'll live with us."

"Oh, Daniel. You two are newlyweds still. Besides, I'd rather be closer to town so I can take care of the library." Kate and Daniel didn't live far from town, but the boardinghouse would be less of an intrusion on their new marriage.

They headed toward the cart where the baggage had been unloaded. Aunt Mabel busied herself with telling Rachel all about the trip cross country. Abigail gazed at the town beyond the depot. Porterfield, Texas, would be her home now, and it looked just as friendly and nice as it had when she'd been here in the spring.

Daniel heaved down a trunk and headed to his surrey with it. Abigail walked along beside him. He pushed the trunk onto the floor behind the front seat. "By the way, the building Nathan and I have in mind for you is across the street from the infirmary. It's where the land offices were until the new courthouse opened. Now it's vacant and just about the size you'll need for a store and library."

"I'm sure it will be fine if you and Nathan think so." She shook her head and giggled as they headed back for more of her things. "I still can't believe he and Rachel moved away from Connecticut. I always figured that when they did, it would be to North Carolina, his home."

Another man had joined the group and helped unload Aunt Mabel's bags. She recognized him as one of Kate's older brothers she had met at the wedding. What was his name? Oh, yes, Cory, the lawman and only single male in the Muldoon family, as well as one of the most handsome Abigail had ever met.

Daniel grabbed her arm and took her over to meet him. "You remember Cory, one of Kate's brothers."

Abigail smiled and extended her hand. "I certainly do. You and your brothers were quite the pranksters at the wedding."

Red tinged Cory's well-tanned face. His eyes, more green than blue, sparkled with humor. He pushed his white Stetson back on his head, revealing sandy red curls on his forehead, much like her brothers. "Guilty as charged, but we had to make up for not doing anything at Erin's. Didn't want to play tricks on the reverend."

Getting to know the Muldoon family would be fun, but getting to know Cory might be even more so. She looked forward to the dinner with the family tonight more than ever.

Elliot finished the stitches to close the wound on the head of Cyrus Fuller. He'd tripped coming out of the bank and fell. He'd cut his head on the edge of the boardwalk and needed five stitches to close it. "There, now, Mr. Fuller. You'll be right as rain. Come back to see me in a few days and let me check on the stitches. Don't get it wet for a while."

He pushed back his rolling stool and picked up a bottle. "If you experience any pain, take a few drops of this, and it should be all right, but don't take more than a few drops. Understand?"

The elderly man nodded and grasped the bottle. "I do, and I won't take it unless I really need it." He stood and grasped the edge of the bed for support.

Kate Monroe picked up the tray with the suturing supplies and equipment. "Aunt Mae will make certain you're comfortable, Mr. Fuller. She'll take good care of you."

The man's face, including his bald head fringed in gray, turned a bright red. "I'm sure she will, but I don't want her to go to any trouble."

Kate laughed. "It won't be any trouble. You know that."

Elliot turned to put the bandages back in the cabinet to hide his smile. Everyone in town knew Cyrus Fuller was sweet on Aunt Mae, and she didn't spurn his attention either. This was one patient he wouldn't have to worry about.

He walked with Mr. Fuller to the front door of the infirmary just to make sure the man was steady on his feet. At the door Cyrus shook Elliot's hand. "Can't thank you enough, Doctor Jensen. You did a fine job, and it hardly hurts at all.

Tell your uncle I said hello." He lifted his hat to set it on his head, felt the stitches, and promptly put his hand down, still holding the hat.

Cyrus Fuller took off in the direction of the boarding-house, a few blocks down the street. Elliot continued to observe the man as he made his way home. Satisfied that he was all right, Elliot turned to walk back inside when he spotted Daniel in a buggy with a young woman beside him. Her golden brown hair peeked from beneath a black hat trimmed with yellow flowers and matched the yellow dress she wore. She turned her head toward him, and their gazes locked. Something inside Elliot clicked, and a feeling he hadn't experienced in a long time came over him.

Elliot looked away and forced the emotion back into the deep recesses of his soul. He'd never let those feelings back into his life. They hurt too much. A voice beside him caused him to blink his eyes and turn to it. Kate stood beside him. "What did you say?"

"I said that's Abigail, Daniel's sister. She's come to live here in Porterfield. Remember I told you about her coming to set up a library for the town?"

"I remember." But he didn't remember her being so pretty. He cleared his throat and hurried back into the infirmary. He needed to clean up the room where they'd just worked on Mr. Fuller, and it would help him forget the girl in yellow. Kate's voice followed him.

"If you don't have anything else for me, I'm going to run down to Aunt Mae's and meet up with Daniel and Abigail. I'll be there if you need me."

He waved her out. Kate was a good assistant. He and his

uncle had come to depend on her for so many things at the infirmary. Doc should be back shortly, that is if everything went well at the Blalocks' place. Mrs. Blalock didn't usually have trouble with her deliveries, and as this was the fifth one, none were anticipated today.

Cleaning up didn't take long, and when he'd finished, Elliot went to the desk to fill out a chart for Cyrus's medical file. The image of Abigail Monroe swam before his eyes. Porterfield was sadly lacking in young women, so Elliot had no trouble staying away from what social life existed in town. He'd left Ohio with the vow that he'd never become involved with a young woman again. Everything had been fine until today when that little spark had jumped in his chest.

"I hear Cyrus Fuller had an accident. Get him all taken care of?"

Elliot jumped and dropped his pen. He greeted his uncle. "When did you come in? Yes, Cyrus is fine. How did things go at the Blalocks?"

His uncle grinned and set his bag on the desk. "Just like it should. This little boy decided to take longer than necessary, but he's good and healthy." He removed his hat and hung it on a hook then removed his coat. "I saw Daniel Monroe with a pretty young woman down at Mae's. Must be his sister from back East."

"It is. Kate was here to help with Cyrus, and then she left to go meet them."

"She's a pretty little thing from what I could see of her. It'll be nice to have a young woman like her around here for a change. You, Cory, and Philip Dawes are about the most eligible young men in town."

"There's a lot of 'em over at the sawmill, and many more on the ranches. That's why Frank Cahoon and Allen Dawes sent off for those brides. Remember?" So many other men in town would help take Abigail's eyes off him. He'd managed to stay clear of any kind of relationship so far, and that was just the way he wanted it. Never again would he experience the pain of loss like that he'd experienced in Cleveland.